RUTHLESS

THE ALPHA BODYGUARD SERIES

SYBIL BARTEL

Books by SYBIL BARTEL

The Alpha Bodyguard Series
SCANDALOUS
MERCILESS
RECKLESS
RUTHLESS
FEARLESS

The Alpha Escort Series
THRUST
ROUGH
GRIND

The Uncompromising Series
TALON
NEIL
ANDRÉ
BENNETT
CALLAN

The Alpha Antihero Series
HARD LIMIT
HARD JUSTICE
HARD SIN

The Unchecked Series
IMPOSSIBLE PROMISE
IMPOSSIBLE CHOICE
IMPOSSIBLE END

The Rock Harder Series
NO APOLOGIES

Join Sybil Bartel's Mailing List to get the news first on her upcoming releases, giveaways and exclusive excerpts! You'll also get a FREE book for joining!

RUTHLESS

THE ALPHA BODYGUARD SERIES

Bodyguard.

Protector.

Security Detail.

I wasn't supposed to join the Marines and serve three tours. I'd been groomed to be another kind of warrior. Since I could walk, I'd been primed to take over the family business. Build the real estate empire bigger, ruthlessly fight my way to the top—make everyone richer.

Instead, I'd enlisted. Wanting to protect my country, not a bank account, I'd turned my back on the family business and given the Marines eight years. Now I was a bodyguard for the best personal security firm in the business, and life was perfectly uncomplicated... until an innocent redhead smiled at me and destroyed everything.

Now she was about to find out how ruthless a bodyguard could be.

DEDICATION

For Jeff and Kristen

CHAPTER ONE

Sawyer

"H E RAN TOWARD ME, TAIL WAGGING, BIG EARS FLAPPING, AND landed with his two giant paws on my chest, he was *that* big." She grinned. "I was lucky I didn't fall clear on my a—" She stopped herself. "I mean, I was lucky he didn't knock me over." She laughed nervously. "It was adorable. Well, if you like that sort of thing, you know, dogs. Do you like dogs?"

She was babbling.

Three in the morning, and she was still fucking talking. She hadn't stopped talking for over six hours.

I didn't say shit.

I didn't have to.

She kept going.

"I mean, what's not to like? Dogs are amazing. So yeah, I didn't mind when he gave me a big welcoming kiss." Holding her tablet and her phone precariously in one hand, she again went to lift another chair.

Again I stopped her. Taking the chair, stacking it on the others I'd already placed, I moved around the table and grabbed the last three chairs.

She inhaled deeply and let it out in a rush. "Well, I guess that's it for the rental chairs." Holding her tablet and phone against her chest, she scanned the lanai, then her gaze drifted to the bar that had been set up for her boss's party. "Thanks for your help. I really appreciate it, but you didn't have to stay for cleanup." She smiled. "I'm sure that wasn't on your list of body-guard responsibilities."

Personal protection, I mentally corrected her.

She waved her hand through the air as she spun in a half circle, and her wild red curls bounced around her face. "I'm just going to… do something about the remaining alcohol so my boss doesn't have to deal with it in the morning. Then this party will officially be over and I can find another party to plan." Her smile dropped. "And another boss, er, client." She blew a strand of hair off her face. "But she was a really good boss. Nice, you know?"

Her current boss was a client of the personal security firm I worked for. My shift had ended over an hour ago, but for some reason I was still here, staring at the red curl that had fallen over her face for the thousandth time tonight. And her ass.

Black silk hugging her curves, she waved her hand over her shoulder. "Anyhoo, you can go. I'm sure you have much better things to do than listen to me talk your ear off. And my boss seems to be safe from whatever you and the other bodyguards were protecting her from. No one told me what happened, and it would be unprofessional of me to pry, so I'm not, I swear, but I know something happened. Or, at least I think it did. Anyway, whatever it was, it seems fine now, so you can go." She corralled three bottles of booze from the bar in the arm that wasn't hold-ing her tablet and phone and brought them to her chest like she was going to lift them all at once. "I'll just take these into the kitchen where the catering company can pick them up tomor-row. Thanks again for your help."

I saw the accident waiting to happen a mile away.

Fortunately, I wasn't a mile away. I was two strides, and I

took them.

I reached her as the middle bottle slipped from her grasp, and I caught it.

She laughed. "Wow. You're like a ninja. I think that's the fifth time tonight you've saved me from dropping something."

Eleventh.

I took the other two bottles from her, and she reached for three more.

"Seriously." She swept her arm around her haul. "You don't have to help. I got this." Her phone slipped out of her grasp. "Oh!"

I caught her phone, but then I lost my patience. "Enough." I took her tablet and shoved the bottles away from her.

Her eyes went wide, and she blinked. "Oh. Oh wow."

I put my hand on her shoulder and steered her toward a stool in front of the bar. "Sit." I tossed her tablet and phone on the bar and grabbed a glass and the whiskey.

Her ass landed on the stool. "That's the first time you've spoken to me in… *hours*."

I poured a double and shoved the tumbler toward her. "Drink."

She blinked again. "But I don't drink alcohol."

"Start."

"Ohh-kay." She drew the word out, picking up the glass.

Except she didn't drink. She looked up at me like she'd been looking at me all night—with big, hazel doe eyes, and the single thought I'd been trying to avoid since I first laid eyes on her came back in spades.

Her, submitting.

Under me, over me, on her knees, I didn't care. I'd imagined a hundred ways to take her, and all of them involved the same thing. Dominating the fuck out of her nervous energy and innocence.

She swirled the glass in a move that I was sure wasn't practiced for seduction, but was merely because she didn't sit still. "Any particular reason for the drink?"

"Pick one." There were dozens.

She was a hot mess.

She never shut up.

Her hair was everywhere.

She dropped everything.

Her black dress was too tight.

She smiled too much, and she was innocent to the point of naïve. But I wanted to fuck her more than any woman I'd ever laid eyes on.

"Okay." She smiled wide. "How about to new friends?"

"I'm not your friend." Friends didn't have the thoughts I was having.

Hurt filtered across her features before she masked it. "Oh." She shifted on the stool, and her foot slipped from the footrest. "Oops." She righted herself with a shy smile. "Well, how about to scotch with a stranger?"

"It's whiskey."

She dropped her gaze and her voice. "Right." Bringing the glass to her lips, she tentatively took a sip. Her face scrunched up, and she put the glass down. "Yeah, so, that's why I don't drink. I mean, I've tried it." She half laughed. "Believe me, in my line of work, I've tried all kinds of alcohol. But nope, not for me. Not this girl. I'm just not cut out for the finer things in life I guess. Cheap date and all that." Her hand flew to her mouth as she looked up at me. "Oh! Not that I was implying this was a date or anything remotely close to it. I mean, I get

4

it. You…." Her gaze dropped to my chest, and she waved her hand. "I mean, you, you can—" She blew out a breath. "Yeah. Not a date. Not with me." She shook her head, and a sad smile touched her full lips. "Not with me," she repeated.

Christ. "What do you drink?"

Her head cocked, but her body stilled. "What?"

"Drink?"

"Oh. My favorite drink?" She blushed. "It's lemonade."

Lemonade.

I'd killed a man earlier that night in defense of her boss, and she wanted lemonade.

CHAPTER TWO

Genevieve

His hand landed on my nape, and I almost jumped out of my skin.

"Let's go." His deep voice, more quiet than baritone, was one hundred percent commanding as he pushed the glass in front of me away and ushered me off my stool—a stool he'd told me to sit on.

"Go where?" I managed, but not without a shiver.

"To eat."

"I… um…." Okay, *wow*. I did not see that coming. "It's three o'clock in the morning." I only pointed out the obvious because I couldn't go out to eat with him. I couldn't even handle having his hand on me. My whole body felt like pins and needles from a single touch.

"This is Miami," he clipped.

I knew where we were. I'd lived here most of my life. I wasn't saying there weren't places open to eat, there were lots, and they'd be busy after the clubs closed—not that I knew firsthand, but I'd driven home late plenty of times. I saw all the pretty women in their skimpy outfits with their beautiful bodies, and I wasn't that. I didn't fit in with that kind of crowd.

But Mr. Bodyguard definitely did.

Well over six feet, full of muscles, and unlike most guys you saw around Miami Beach, he had almost white-blond hair and piercing blue eyes. In fact, he looked so much like another blond-haired man I frequently saw in the local media that I'd had my suspicions about who he might be related to since I'd first met him yesterday. But I hadn't had a single free moment in the past twenty-four hours to check my hunch with an internet search. Not that it mattered who he was, because I didn't have a chance with someone like him. Staring up at his perfect jaw and the almost angry expression he'd worn since I'd met him only drove that point home.

I had no business sharing a meal with him. "I can't go out to eat with you."

He paused, and his intense stare cut to me. "Can't or won't?"

"Does it matter?" I hedged, fighting another shiver as the warmth of his touch spread from my neck to my shoulders. I stupidly wondered what it would feel like if he dropped his hand. The deep V down the back of my dress showed more skin than I normally did, but this party tonight had called for a special dress.

My client's party was at her palatial estate, and while it wasn't specifically a black-tie affair like some of the parties I'd organized for other clients, everyone had come dressed to impress. Including the blond bodyguard next to me, who was in a perfectly cut suit that fit his narrow hips and bulging biceps.

I was glad I'd found my dress on the clearance rack last week. It was just edgy and unique enough with an uneven hem and conservative cut in front, but sexy dipping V in back, that I'd bought it immediately. It'd been a little tight, and it'd cut into my funds way more than I was comfortable with, but I thought I'd pulled it off. More than half a dozen people tonight inquired about my services, so I was calling it a win.

Except right now I didn't feel like a winner with a giant, muscled ex-Marine bodyguard staring down at me like he was dissecting me. And he was an ex-Marine. That had been the only bit of personal information I'd been able to get out of him when he'd relented and answered one of the hundred questions I must've thrown at him over the past few hours.

I couldn't help it.

He made me nervous, and when I got nervous, I rambled. A lot.

"You need to eat," he stated. "You missed dinner."

"I...." I stopped. "How do you know I missed dinner?"

"You were working."

"So were you." I liked it far too much that he noticed anything about me, even if it was something small and silly like that I'd been too busy making sure the party went smoothly to help myself to any of the delicious-looking hors d'oeuvres

"I'm fine," he countered with no intonation in his voice.

"Well, so am I," I lied. I was starving. "I can stand to miss a few meals."

He scowled. "No, you can't."

I couldn't help it. I laughed.

His frown deepened. "I wasn't joking."

"I know. That's what's so funny." I was sure he didn't date women like me with full hips and non-athletic bodies.

His scowl turned up another notch, and his hand landed on the back of my neck again, but he dropped the missing meals comment. "Let's go. I'm driving."

Reaching for my phone and tablet on the bar, I hated myself for the next words that came out of my mouth. "Thanks for the offer, but its fine, really. I'm good. I'll grab something at home after I finish cleaning up here. I don't like to leave a client to deal with a mess after an event. It's unprofessional. So really, I'm good here. You can leave." I turned and reached for a few of the bottles of liquor to carry them inside and braced myself for another of his bossy comebacks.

But it didn't happen.

Nothing happened.

There was only silence.

Like total, utter, I didn't even hear the water on the intracoastal slapping against the seawall silence.

He'd left.

He had to have.

No one was that quiet.

Exhaling, not sure if I was disappointed or glad, I tucked my phone and tablet against my chest, then grabbed two more bottles. Turning, I almost dropped all five bottles in shock.

Arms crossed, not two feet in front of me, he stood staring. Hard. "Are you involved with someone?"

My heart slammed into my chest, my mouth went dry, and my phone decided to slip from between my breasts.

Before it slammed onto the travertine-tiled lanai, he grabbed it, and the back of his fingers brushed across my stomach. My mouth popped open with an involuntary gasp as heat rushed between my legs.

Holding my phone in one hand, he grasped three of the bottles by their necks in his other hand. "I asked you a question."

Involved. I swallowed past the sudden dryness in my mouth and squeaked out an answer. "No, I'm not seeing anyone."

He set the bottles on the bar and grabbed the remaining two from me only to put them down next to the others. "Then why do you object to eating a meal with me?"

"This isn't a date," I blurted, suddenly feeling naked

without my bottle armor.

He didn't hesitate with a clipped response. "If I were asking you on a date, you would know it."

My pride took a hit, and I dropped my gaze. "Of course." Jeez, how humiliating.

"Grab what you need," he stated in the same bossy, emotionless tone.

"Okay, wait." I held a hand up. I'd been on my feet over twelve hours. I hadn't eaten since lunch yesterday, and I was sure I smelled less than fresh. I didn't need any more humiliation in my life. I didn't want to sit across from him at some restaurant and inhale food, or worse, pretend I lived on salad without dressing. I wasn't going to dinner with him. I wasn't going anywhere with him, no matter how scarily hot he was. Inhaling, I steeled my resolve. "Mr. Sawyer, as I'm sure you can appreciate, I'm pretty tired. Thanks for the offer, but I am respectfully declining your invita—"

"Sawyer isn't my last name," he interrupted.

Caught off guard, for once I didn't say anything.

He kept staring at me. Then a glimmer of anger flashed across his face. "Savatier," he clipped, not pronouncing the *r*. "Sawyer is my first name."

My jaw dropped.

His name rolling off his tongue with disdain did nothing to camouflage the beauty of the exotic-sounding surname or its significance. Savatier Enterprises. Savatier Holdings. Savatier Center for the Arts.

I closed my mouth and forced myself to swallow.

Savatier Stadium.

I swallowed again.

I was a fool. All night, in my nervousness around him, I'd

pathetically name dropped, talking about former clients and the events I'd planned. I'd even stupidly asked if we knew any of the same people because one of the few questions he answered for me was to tell me he was from Miami.

"You're…." I cleared my throat. "You're Sullivan Savatier's son." The elusive, never photographed, military hero son.

A shadow fell across the sharp angles of his face and his jaw ticked. "Yes."

He looked just like him. I knew it. *I knew it.* But I couldn't believe it. The Savatiers were billionaires from real estate, *big* real estate, all over south Florida. From high-rises to the new sports complex for the professional football team, they owned any property worth owning. The Savatiers were the closest thing to American royalty.

And Sawyer Savatier had just asked me to dinner.

The Sawyer Savatier.

CHAPTER THREE

Sawyer

"Y̲ou're...." She cleared her throat. "You're Sullivan Savatier's son."

It wasn't a question, but I answered anyway. "Yes."

"But you're a *bodyguard*." She said bodyguard like it was shit. "Why would you be doing this-this"—she waved her hand around—"body guarding, party cleanup stuff when you can be doing... whatever it is your father does?"

My jaw ticked. "I am *not* my father."

"Ohh-kay." She quietly drew the word out before pointing over her shoulder. "I'm just going to... go." She abruptly spun and reached behind the bar, picking up a bright yellow purse that was half the size of a damn combat loadout.

Christ. "Genevieve."

She froze for half a second. Then she turned to me, and a big, fake smile spread across her pretty face as she hefted her bag over her shoulder. "Yes?"

"You like burgers?" A diner a few miles away was the only place I could think of that would have lemonade. But the more important question was why the hell I wasn't walking away.

She laughed, and her purse slid off her shoulder. "Who doesn't? But that's not the issue. I don't need a burger."

That was exactly the issue. "You're eating." I took her heavy purse off her arm. "Let's go." My hand landed on the small of her back, right below the dip in her dress that showed off too much of her smooth skin.

She stiffened. "Really, Mr. Savatier, you—"

"Sawyer," I corrected, hefting her bag that was twice as heavy as it looked.

"Right." In a rare moment of stillness, she clasped her hands across her tablet and phone and looked up at me for three seconds. "I can't go to dinner with you."

Jesus. This was a first. "I'm not asking you to bed, Genevieve." Not yet.

Her face flushed bright red. "Okay." She held a hand up and laughed as she dropped eye contact. "Pretty sure you already made that crystal clear. I don't need any more clarification." Her voice turned quieter. "I got it."

Fighting for patience, I exhaled. The fact that getting her lemonade was taking precedence over me hitting my bed for a solid five hours should have had me questioning my sanity. "Self-pity is indulgent. It's dinner, and I'm driving. It's not a date." I was an asshole for throwing that last part out, but she'd pissed me off when she'd turned me down after finding out who I was.

"Fine." She shook her head and the curl fell over her face again. "But I'm driving myself there."

I wanted to argue, but I didn't. Taking the win, I led her across the lanai, through the kitchen and out the front door. For the first time all night, she didn't babble as I took her to her car and opened the driver door. In fact, she didn't say a word. I handed her purse back, and her head practically disappeared inside as she dug around for her keys.

She was a fucking mess. She needed a search party to find anything, she dropped everything, and I'd never met another person who talked more than she did. She was the opposite of me in every single way. Yet here I stood, watching her dig through her purse.

When her keys rattled for the third time, I took her bag. Shoving my hand in, I palmed them on the first try and held them and her purse out to her.

"Oh." She put her cell and tablet in her purse as I held it, then she took it and her keys. "Thanks." She blew out a breath and the errant curl shifted.

I wanted to fist a handful of her hair. "Do you know where Mel's diner is?"

Her head bobbed with a yes as she said, "No."

I frowned. "No, you don't know where it is?"

"No, I can't do this." Her expression earnest, she clutched her keys and her purse to her chest. "I'm sorry."

This wasn't the military, and she wasn't my subordinate. I couldn't order her to share a meal with me. Schooling my expression, I clipped out a response. "Understood." I tipped my chin at her car. "Get in. I'll make sure you get home."

Her head was shaking and her curls were bouncing before I'd finished my sentence. "Not that either."

I studied her for a moment. Her eyes weren't blue or green or brown, but a combo of all three. Her lips were full, her features were delicate, and she really was stunning, but she looked nervous as hell, more so than she had all night. Instinct kicked in. "Where do you live?" *Who* did she live with?

She laughed uncomfortably. "Nowhere a Savatier would step foot in."

"This is about an address?" I shouldn't have told her my last name. Her reaction wasn't unique. Women usually acted one of two ways when they realized who my family was. They

14

either wanted a piece of me at any cost, or they did exactly what Genevieve was doing right now—they backed the hell off.

The latter was rare.

Which was why I was still standing here.

She made a derisive sound. "You think it isn't?"

"I don't presume." The Marines had taught me not to.

She let out a sigh. "Well, Mr. Savatier, maybe you should. Even if you do have a regular job for now, okay, not regular or even common, but still a working-class job, you're still a Savatier." She got behind the wheel of her beat-down Grand Cherokee. "Good night." She jammed the key into the ignition and turned it.

It clicked, then nothing happened.

"Damn it," she muttered, pumping her foot on the gas and trying again.

Still nothing.

"Come on." It looked like she was getting dinner after all. "I'll take you home after we eat."

Her eyebrows drew together. "You can just give me a jump. I know I need a new battery. I mean, I need lots of things, so it could be something else, but still. You're not even going to look under the hood?"

"No."

"But... you were a Marine."

I didn't reply. I took her purse off her lap.

Making no move to stop me, her frown deepened. "You carry *a gun.*"

I held my hand out.

She looked at me like I was crazy. "You're an ex-Marine billionaire bodyguard who not only comes from the wealthiest family in Florida, but you work for the best personal security firm in the business, and you can't fix cars?"

"No," I lied.

Her eyes narrowed. "I'm pretty sure you went to college."

Online degree while I was enlisted. Engineering. But I didn't tell her that. "I'll have someone take a look at it." I'd text the guy my boss André Luna brought on after one of our last jobs. Luna had him sitting at base watching security feeds twelve hours a day while he finished vetting him. He'd probably jump at the chance to get out of the office.

"Who?" Genevieve asked suspiciously, taking her keys out of the ignition.

"His name is Ty." I helped her out of her Jeep.

"Who's that?"

"Another Luna and Associates employee."

"Another bodyguard?"

Not bothering to correct her terminology, I led her to my company vehicle. "Yes."

"Is he as good-looking as the rest of you?"

My jaw ticked at her last four words. Two other Luna and Associates guys, Tyler and Collins, had been here on the assignment all night, as well as two men, Dane Marek and Jared Brandt, who we'd served with. We were all ex-Marines, and we all knew how to handle ourselves. I wasn't surprised she'd noticed the other guys, but I didn't like it. "I'm not a connoisseur of men's looks."

She smirked. "You don't look in the mirror each day?"

I opened the passenger door of the Escalade. "Your indirect compliment isn't necessary."

"I can't compliment you? Not that I was being indirect. I'm pretty sure I talk too much around you to be indirect about anything. And I'm definitely sure you look in the mirror every day."

She gave me one of her small, nervous laughs. "I don't need to tell you you're good-looking."

I'd bet my bank account she talked too much all the time. Ignoring her comments, I helped her into the SUV. "Keys." I held my hand out.

She dumped them in my hand without making contact. "For the record, I could've called for a tow myself."

"Now you don't have to."

She leaned back in her seat, and her shoulders slumped. "I don't even know why I'm letting you talk me into this."

Because she was tired and probably hungry. "Because you know I'll handle it." And this woman needed help.

Her stomach growled, and she laughed outright as her hand landed under her full breasts. "Well, that's embarrassing."

And completely unacceptable. "I'm taking you to eat." I shut her door before she could protest.

Striding to the Cherokee, I stashed her keys on the rear tire, then pulled my cell out as I walked back to the Escalade and sent a text to Ty, asking him if he knew shit about cars.

He texted back immediately.

Ty: *Fix your own damn Range Rover*

I fired off a response.

Me: *Not my vehicle. Green Grand Cherokee. It's parked in the driveway at the address of the assignment I was on tonight. Won't start. I need you to handle it. Keys are on back left tire.*

He replied as I got behind the wheel of the Escalade.

Ty: *Whose Jeep?*

Me: *Just get it fixed. Let me know what I owe you.*

Ty: *It's fucking 3 a.m. What do you expect me to do?*

I sighed.

"Problem?" Genevieve asked.

"No." I started the SUV and responded to Ty.

Me: *Probably the battery. Figure it out.*

I glanced at Genevieve. "What's your address?"

She hesitated then rattled it off.

I sent the address to Ty and told him to deliver the Cherokee to her place after he got it running. Tossing my cell onto the center console, I threw the Escalade into drive.

"So, what are the chances you'll take me directly home?" she asked quietly.

"None." I pulled out of the driveway. "I'm taking you to eat first."

CHAPTER FOUR

Genevieve

I GAVE UP PROTESTING AND STARED OUT THE WINDOW AT THE QUIET, dark streets of Bal Harbour before Sawyer drove over the bridge and off the exclusive island.

I kept my mouth shut for five whole minutes before I couldn't take his silence anymore. "Can I ask you a question?"

"Yes." His deep voice rumbled around the quiet interior of the giant SUV as his scent filled my head with thoughts I had no business thinking.

"Do you have a girlfriend?" I dared to ask.

"No," he answered immediately with no intonation.

I couldn't handle his emotionless responses to every question I'd fired at him today. I didn't know what that meant. I'd seen him frown plenty of times. I got it, I was irritating him, but then why was he so insistent on taking me out to eat at three o'clock in the morning of all times? It didn't fit. *Nothing* about him fit.

His suit was custom made, his hair was perfectly trimmed, the five o'clock shadow he sported was magazine cover model sexy, and his shoes cost more than I made in a week. He spoke with a courtesy that went beyond manners, his watch was a Vacheron Constantin, and he smelled like money and sandalwood.

Everything about him was refined.

Except it wasn't.

His muscles were bigger than any man's I'd ever seen in the elite social circles of Miami's upper crust. They were bigger than any man's I'd ever seen, period. He carried a gun in a holster under his left arm, his eyes never stopped scanning, and his clipped, emotionless responses to my questions weren't out of boredom or irritation alone, they were guarded.

His intensity, the set of his shoulders, the way he clasped his hands in front of him and stood with his feet slightly apart, all of it was guarded.

But when he actually made eye contact and looked at me?

That was all predator.

Every move he made, every word he said, it was calculated.

Inhaling, I breathed in the intoxicating scent that was all him. Then I asked another question because I literally had nothing to lose. "If you aren't asking me out on a date, then why are you taking me to dinner?"

For two whole heartbeats, silence filled the SUV.

Embarrassed, uneasy around him, I laughed. "Okay, forget I asked."

"I like your eyes," he replied quietly.

Heat flamed my cheeks, and I blinked.

Thankful for the dark interior of the Escalade, I swallowed past the sudden dryness in my mouth. "Thank you," I whispered.

"You're welcome." Pulling into the packed parking lot of the diner, he expertly eased the giant vehicle into a spot. Then he threw the gearshift into park, scanned the other parked cars, and pulled the key out of the ignition. "Wait there."

Exhaling after he got out, I whispered to myself. "Holy shit."

My door opened, and his stark blue eyes met mine. He wordlessly held his hand out.

Not a date, not a date, I silently chanted as I took his hand.

His huge fingers engulfed mine, and awareness shot up my arm, zinging through my body. Giddiness I couldn't squash fluttered in my stomach, and I smiled.

His gaze tracked the movement of my lips, but he didn't return the smile. Holding my hand with purpose, he helped me out of the SUV as his other hand landed on the small of my back.

My feet hit the ground, and I stumbled in my five-inch heels.

He pulled my arm at the same time as he stepped against me, and I fell into his chest instead of on my ass on the pavement.

"Oh God," I gasped.

"You're all right." His breath touched my skin, fluttering a strand of my hair.

A tremor went up my spine, but this time I didn't laugh away my nervousness. Leaning against him, feeling his hard body support me, having his arm around my waist—*oh God*, I didn't want to move. *Ever.*

"Thanks," I breathed, not trusting my balance enough to step away.

As if reading my thoughts, he stood perfectly still as his chest rose and fell three times. Then he shifted, and his quiet voice filled my head with wayward thoughts.

"Inside," he commanded, stepping to my side. "Let's get you dinner."

"Okay." One touch of his hand, one feel of his body against mine, and the last of my resolve to push this dominant, alpha man away disappeared into the southern Florida nighttime humidity.

Dropping my hand but keeping his palm against the small of my back, he led me across the packed parking lot and opened the door of the diner as he took me inside. Giving his first name to the hostess, ignoring the way her blatant gaze dragged over his biceps, he then corralled me in a corner and stood with his back to the other people waiting, effectively caging me in.

I would be a total liar if I said I didn't like every single second of his protective dominance. But I had to remind myself I wasn't his client and this wasn't a date.

"So…." I craned my neck to look up at him. "Have you eaten here before?"

He scanned the afterhours clubbing crowd without actually looking at any of the women in dresses and skirts that barely covered their asses before he brought his gaze to me and stared a moment. "Yes. You?"

"I'm not really the clubbing type. I don't usually go out to eat at three a.m." Or ever. Dining out alone wasn't on my short list.

He nodded once in acknowledgment, then his gaze cut to a group of drunk, rowdy guys who walked in.

He moved to his left a few inches.

The shift of his tall body was slight, but the implication was huge. In protective bodyguard mode, he blocked me from the guys.

I couldn't stop myself, I smiled.

He frowned. "What?"

The hostess came up behind him and tapped him on the

shoulder. Perfectly straight, long brown hair, model thin, a full face of makeup, she smiled flirtatiously at him. "Your table's ready."

He tipped his chin at her, and my smile dropped. No matter how many meals I skipped, I'd never be like her. My curly hair had a mind of its own. I didn't have a seductive bone in my body, and makeup wouldn't change my pale skin or fire-engine-red blush.

Oblivious to my thoughts and shortcomings, Sawyer's hand landed between my shoulder blades and he guided me a step in front of him as the hostess led us to a booth.

Looking up at Sawyer, completely ignoring me, the hostess dropped the menus on the table. "Your waitress will be right with you. Let me know if you need anything else."

When Sawyer didn't make eye contact with her and only nodded, she spun on her heels and walked off.

Wishing I had paid more attention to all the reasons why I shouldn't have come to eat with him in the first place, I started to slide into the booth.

Sawyer caught my arm, stopping me. "Other side."

"Oh, okay." I moved to the other side of the booth.

He slid in across from me after I was seated and unbuttoned his suit jacket.

"This side wasn't good enough?" I joked.

He didn't smile. "No view of the front."

Feeling stupid, I picked the menu up. "That's important?"

"Yes." His eyes on me, he didn't even glance at his menu.

The hostess walked by again, leading the group of rowdy guys past our table. One of the guys checked out my cleavage as he passed and winked at me.

Sawyer scowled.

Not a date, I reminded myself, turning my attention to the menu. "So, do you come here a lot?" I couldn't see a man like him eating in a diner like this, even as an after-clubbing stop. The booths were bright red, the tables were retro Formica, and everything else was chrome. He looked like a Michelin-star restaurant regular, not a burger joint connoisseur.

"No," he clipped as a waitress approached.

Older, a little frazzled, she smiled wearily at us. "Hi, what can I get y'all?"

Glancing at me, Sawyer took my menu. "Two deluxe cheeseburgers and two lemonades." He raised his eyebrow at me. "Is that good?"

Warmth hit my chest, my stomach fluttered, and I blushed hard. That's why he'd brought me here, for lemonade. "That's perfect," I managed, choking on the lump in my throat.

He nodded and handed the menus to the waitress.

"Be right back with your drinks." The waitress left.

Suddenly feeling naked, not knowing what to do with my idle hands, I dropped them to my lap. "Thank you."

"For?"

"The lemonade. You remembered." Oh my God, *idle hands*. No wonder I felt naked, I'd left my purse in his car. I was never without my cell phone and tablet. I even slept with them right next to me on my nightstand. Shit, how could I have forgotten them in the car? I moved to the edge of the seat.

Sawyer studied my face, then tracked my movement. "What's wrong?"

The waitress came back with our lemonades. "Your burgers will be up soon." She set the drinks down and retreated.

"I forgot my purse in the car." I grasped the edge of the table and slid one leg out of the booth as I started to push up.

"If I could just borrow your keys for a second?"

His hand landed on my wrist. "You don't need your purse. I'm buying." Warm and firm, his fingers felt like they could caress my skin as easily as they could crush my bones.

"It'll just take me a minute." I pulled out of his grasp, wondering if there were two distinct sides of him, a refined billionaire and a lethal Marine, or if he managed to meld the two very different lives together and be one person all the time. I shook my head and pushed the thought away. "I don't want to leave my purse in the SUV. It could get stolen, you know, if someone broke into the car while we were sitting here, and that would be bad. I have my cell phone and my tab—"

"Sit," he commanded sternly.

Taken aback by the stern tone to his voice, a tone exactly like what I imagined a Marine would sound like, I sat.

His chest rose with an inhale. Then he exhaled slowly, and his voice came out quieter. "You don't need your devices right now."

"My life is on those devices." I couldn't lose them.

"The car is locked. No one's going to steal them. They'll be there when we're done eating."

Torn between the rationality of what he was saying and the inexplicable feeling of being naked in front of him without my phone and tablet as a buffer, I stared at him.

His eyes weren't bright blue, but they weren't pale blue either. They were just… blue. Like the sky on a winter day. And his hair wasn't white blond, but it wasn't dirty blond either. It was wheat blond, like pictures of golden fields I'd seen in magazines, but never in real life. I hadn't noticed the true color of his eyes or hair until just now. When I'd first met him, he'd had a baseball cap with the logo of the company he worked for pulled low over his face. But now that I was truly looking at him in the bright florescent lights of the diner, there wasn't a single thing out of place about him. Not a speck of lint on his jacket, not a single strand of his close-cropped hair was out of place, even his stubble was symmetrical on both sides of his face.

Everything about him was perfect.

Right down to the fact that he could leave valuables in a car and not panic about it. He could eat a meal without checking social media or emails or a messenger app. He could sit still and not fidget, and he could get out of a car without tripping.

I took a steadying breath.

Then I did something I hadn't done since I'd first started working for myself.

I acquiesced.

"Okay, fine." I threw my empty hands up in surrender and smiled sheepishly. "I'll leave my purse in the car."

He didn't smile, but he leaned back in the booth. It seemed like his version of relaxed, or as relaxed as he could get.

My smile turned to a grin, and I pointed a finger at him. "You know, even though you don't walk around with your phone glued to your hand, I bet you have as hard a time relaxing as I do."

He didn't take the bait. He didn't even glance at my finger pointing at him. He simply held my gaze.

I took his lack of a frown as an opening. "What do you do when you want to unplug or relax? Or have fun," I boldly added.

He laced his fingers together, rested his forearms on the table and leaned forward. His eyes intently focused on mine, he asked the last thing I expected him to ask. "Have you ever dated?"

Thrown off guard, a half snort, half laugh escaped. "Is that a trick question?" Was he making fun of me?

He kept staring at me, but he didn't answer. He waited.

I'd dealt with a lot of clients over the few years I'd been working for myself. As an event planner, it was usually women clients I dealt with, and they were almost always particular. I'd learned to navigate minefields of emotions. I'd figured out ways to work around unattainable requests and temper tantrums, and I'd dealt with a whole host of different personalities.

But I'd never dealt with someone like Sawyer Savatier.

Everything about him intimidated me and excited me in a way I wasn't sure I could put into words. Not that I wanted to, because then it would make the feelings real, and nothing about this was real life. Men like him didn't ask women like me to dinner.

But that didn't mean I couldn't hold my own.

Squaring my shoulders, I gave him more than he deserved. "I'm not sure you weren't trying to insult me with that question, but I'll answer you anyway. I don't have time to date."

"I would never insult you."

He already had, several times. "Right."

The waitress showed up with our food and set our plates down. "Can I get you anything else?" she asked in a rush.

"No," Sawyer answered without taking his eyes off me.

She retreated, and I picked up the ketchup as the heavenly smell of grease and carbs wafted up from my plate.

The ketchup was plucked out of my hand as I fumbled with the sticky flip top. "Explain," Sawyer demanded.

"Explain what?" I knew what.

In direct contrast to the stern, almost angry look on his face, he shook the ketchup bottle once, flipped the top open without a problem, then squirted a liberal amount on my plate as if being conciliatory. Setting the bottle down, he picked up the wrapped straw next to my lemonade, unwrapped it and shoved it into my drink. "Why do you assume I'm lying?"

He was mercurial and brooding, and I was beginning to grasp just how alpha Sawyer was, more so than any man I'd ever met.

"I didn't say you were lying to me. You said you would never insult me, and I said *right*, sarcastically." I picked up a fry, suddenly not sure my stomach could handle it.

"Because?"

"Because," I sighed, "you already insulted me." I forced myself to eat the fry.

His eyebrows drew together. "How?"

Okay, I lied. I could eat. I dunked another fry in too much ketchup and ate it before picking up my burger. Barely swallowing the fry, practically salivating at the delicious smell, I brought the burger to my mouth.

"*Genevieve*," Sawyer reprimanded. "I asked you a question."

I took a bite.

Oh.

My God.

Hamburger, melty, drippy cheese, crisp lettuce, firm tomato—flavors exploded in my mouth, and I closed my eyes as I chewed. It was official. Burgers at three a.m. tasted better than at any other time of day.

Opening my eyes just so I could look at the burger with lust, I took another bite... and studiously ignored the angry ex-Marine slash billionaire bodyguard across from me.

I may drop my tablet on occasion, or talk a mile a minute, or be going in five different directions at any given moment.

And I may not have any experience with being one of those pretty girls who knows how to flirt with a man, but I did have another skill. I was excellent at ignoring things.

I ignored clients' temper tantrums. I ignored my mess of curls that ruled over every attempt to tame them, mocking me for the effort, and I ignored the funny noises my car had been making for six months. I even ignored the fact that I still hadn't changed my locks since....

I shook my head, ignoring the thought.

And I ignored Sawyer.

I took another bite.

Hard blue eyes stared me down, then he exhaled. "Impressive shutout." He finally picked up his hamburger.

Maintaining my ignoring streak, I dunked a fry and brought the ketchup bite to my mouth as a model-thin blonde in a barely there silver dress stopped at our table.

"As I live and breathe." Her sultry bedroom voice dripped disdain. "*Sawyer Savatier.*"

CHAPTER FIVE

Sawyer

I BARELY GLANCED UP BEFORE FOCUSING BACK ON THE MUCH MORE enticing woman in front of me. "What do you want, Talia?"

"I didn't know you were home." Her hand landed on my shoulder and squeezed. "You didn't tell me."

Genevieve choked on the bite she was chewing.

Picking up her lemonade, bringing the straw toward her mouth, I didn't make eye contact with Talia. She didn't warrant the courtesy. "I don't know why you think I'd tell you anything, Talia." I dropped my voice for Genevieve. "Drink."

Genevieve's eyes watered as her full lips wrapped around the straw. Her hand covered mine, and she did exactly as I told her.

"How charming." Talia smirked. "Fattening burgers and a child's beverage."

Three carbon-copy, too-thin blondes walked up behind Talia. One of them opened her idiotic mouth. "Oh my God, Talia! Isn't this your ex?"

Talia ignored her as she glanced at Genevieve with a sneer. "Apparently he likes them thick and unrefined now."

My nostrils flared. "*Apparently* you're still ignorant and classless." I forced myself to look at her. "Leave. Before I have you removed."

Talia laughed. "I see you're still throwing your weight

around. I guess running around with play guns in the desert did nothing except encourage your savage ways." Her lips pursed in fake sympathy. "How sad."

Genevieve turned bright red. *"Play guns?"*

I put my hand over hers because I didn't need a woman to defend me, but before I could stop her, she did what Genevieve does best. She started talking.

"Talia, is it? Well, I'm sure I don't need to explain to you that freedom isn't free, but since you seem to not grasp that, standing here spouting ignorance, I'll explain it to you. When you encounter someone who has served in our military, your appropriate greeting is, and always should be, *thank you for your service*. That way, you acknowledge that you both understand and appreciate that the ground you are standing on did not come without a price, and that price is the sacrifice of the service member standing, or sitting, right in front of you. So, as far as I'm concerned, the only *unrefined* person here is you."

Talia opened her mouth to respond.

"Go ahead." Genevieve marched on with her verbal lashing. "By all means, give us your best retort. I'm sure anything you say will only improve upon Mr. Savatier's good opinion of you."

Crossing my arms, I leaned back in the booth.

Genevieve glanced at me. "Do you have anything to add?"

"I think you covered it." In spades.

Pasting on a demure smile, ignoring one of the blonde carbon copies who'd pulled her phone out and who was either recording or snapping pictures, Genevieve looked back at Talia. "You may leave now."

Talia snorted. "How pathetic, Sawyer, letting this… *woman* speak for you." Turning in her too-high heels, she strutted off with the carbon copies rushing to keep on her six.

I opened my mouth to tell Genevieve that while I appreciated her efforts, I didn't need her to defend my honor, but she held her hand up.

"Keep it." She dropped her gaze, but not before I saw her expression falter. "I'm ready to leave now." She made to get up.

I grabbed her hand. "Don't let someone else dictate whether or not you finish your food." The Marines had taught me to appreciate every damn meal. You never knew when you might eat your last.

Her chest rose and fell with an inhale, and she practically snapped at me, "I'm not."

"After that speech, you're ready to leave?" I challenged. I was being an asshole. If she wanted to leave, I should've accommodated her. But I wasn't about to let her tuck tail and duck out. "The woman who told Talia off isn't a runner."

Her head whipped up as anger contorted her features. "Is that what you think? That I was just telling off your ex?"

"She isn't my ex." Sex didn't make a relationship.

Genevieve blinked. Then she pulled her hand away and averted her gaze. "Whatever. I want to leave."

"Finish your burger."

For three seconds, she didn't respond. She didn't even move. Then she looked at me and her face said it all. She was pissed. "Are you telling me what to do?"

I didn't hesitate. "Yes."

Staring at me, she picked her cheeseburger up and took a giant bite. Barely chewing it, she took another bite, then another. Grabbing her drink, sucking hard on the straw, she gulped, washing down her stubbornness. Sixty seconds later, the burger was gone.

"Done." She wiped her hands, then in direct contrast to the way she'd eaten the burger, she dabbed the napkin to the corners of her mouth. "Let's go."

For the first time in as long as I could remember, I fought the urge to smile. Catching the waitress's eye, I nodded at her as I pulled out my wallet.

The waitress came over. "Anything else?"

"Just the check." I grabbed a few twenties.

The waitress fished the handwritten bill out of her apron. "Here you go."

I handed over five twenties. "Keep the change." Buttoning my jacket, I stood.

The waitress looked down at the money and blinked. "Not to look a gift horse in the mouth, but—"

"We're all set, thank you." I held my hand out to Genevieve. "Shall we?"

Ignoring me, she got out of the booth and gave the waitress a small smile. "Thank you."

Fighting a smirk, I angled Genevieve to my left side, then caught the small of her back.

She stiffened, but she didn't push me away.

The scent of her hair filled my head as the errant curl fell over her eye again. Shoving down all thoughts of getting her naked, I led her out of the diner.

Two strides into the parking lot, she let loose. "You tipped her more than the cost of the meal." It wasn't a statement, it was an accusation.

I palmed the key in my pocket and scanned the parking lot out of habit before unlocking the Escalade. "She needs the money more than I do."

Genevieve stopped dead in her tracks and threw out a

single word like a condemnation. *"Needs?"*

Something moved in my peripheral vision, and I frowned. "Excuse me?" I unbuttoned the jacket of my suit and scanned the parking lot again.

Genevieve tracked my movement. "You heard me. Why do you think the waitress needs the money more than you? Because she works in a diner?" Her voice took on an edge. "Because she isn't rich like you, so that makes her inferior?"

Instinct, years of training, a sixth sense for trouble—I palmed the 9mm in my shoulder holster under my jacket. "We'll discuss this in the car. Let's go." My left hand landed on her back again, and I cursed myself for parking at the back of the lot where the security lights didn't reach.

"That's an elitist attitude," she protested, but her feet moved.

"It isn't elitist to tip well, and I never implied she was inferior." I opened the passenger door. "Get in."

"No, what's *elitist* is thinking you can order me to—oh!" Her high heel slipped on the running board and she started to fall.

The second I caught her in my arms, I felt the distinctive shape of cold metal hit the back of my skull.

"Arms up, motherfucker!"

CHAPTER SIX

Genevieve

"**A**RMS UP, *MOTHERFUCKER!*"

Every muscle in Sawyer's body tensed as his grip around me tightened. His eyes on me, he spoke to the masked man behind him who was holding a gun to his head in a lethally quiet tone. "If I raise my arms, I drop her."

Sheer panic stole my breath.

"I'll drop both of you with a single bullet, asshole. Keys, *now!*" the masked man demanded.

Slow, like he had all the time in the world, Sawyer's hold on me shifted as he pushed me upright and grasped my chin. "You're okay," he quietly enunciated.

The masked man shoved the gun harder against Sawyer's head. "Hurry the fuck up!"

Sawyer released my chin and slowly raised one hand. "Calm down. I'm reaching for my keys."

"You calm the fuck down, *motherfucker.* Hand over the keys! This is a carjack—"

Sawyer spun.

The arm that he already had raised slammed elbow first into the man's masked face, connecting with his nose. Grabbing the hand holding the gun, Sawyer twisted the robber's wrist so hard, a sickening pop sounded a split second before he screamed and dropped to his knees.

Still holding on to the man's broken wrist, Sawyer grabbed the robber's gun and jammed the barrel to his forehead. "Move and you die." His eyes on the man on his knees, Sawyer nodded at me. "Get in the SUV, Genevieve."

Oh my God, oh my God.

Shaking, freaking out, I reached for the handle just inside the door to hoist myself up and into the passenger seat, but a click sounded the second I stepped onto the running board.

"She moves another inch, she's dead," a new male voice ground out.

Fear coating my every breath, expecting another robber, I turned.

Except it wasn't just one more.

It was three.

All standing behind Sawyer, all with guns. Two in ski masks aimed at Sawyer, and one with a hood pulled low over his face aimed at me.

My heart threatening to stop, I stepped off the running board. "Sawyer?" *Oh dear God,* we were dead.

Sawyer didn't hesitate. "Get in the car, Genevieve," he commanded, as if three men weren't pointing guns at us.

"You not hear me, pendejo?" The man pointing the gun at me kept his gaze solidly on Sawyer. "You want your bitch to die?"

I shook. Hard.

Ignoring the man, Sawyer kept his gun wedged against the forehead of the man still on his knees. "It's armored, Genevieve. Get in and lock the door." He tossed the key fob into the front passenger seat.

"Are you fucking deaf, motherfucker?" the man yelled.

Panic like nothing I'd ever felt before rushed through me,

but I didn't move. I kept my eyes on Sawyer. "I'm not leaving you." I couldn't get in the SUV. I just couldn't. I wasn't faster than a bullet, and he wasn't invincible.

"*Genevieve*," Sawyer's angry bark of my name barely had time to cut through the heat-stiff night air before everything went to hell.

The man on the ground grabbed the hem of my dress with one hand and yanked.

My bare knees slammed into the pavement, and Sawyer moved.

Faster than I could blink, he'd reached in his coat, came away with his own gun, and aimed dead center at the man in the hood's chest. Sawyer's movements were almost a blur as the momentum of my fall pitched me forward. My hands flew out, and the rough parking lot tore through the flesh of my palms and knees. A split second later, the man who'd yanked my dress wrapped an arm around my neck and wrenched me back up. Taller than me, his grip too strong, my back to his heaving chest, I had to go on tiptoe so I wasn't strangled.

"Sawyer!" I cried out before the robber's forearm crushed my throat too hard to speak.

Sawyer's nostrils flared. "Let. Her. *Go*."

The man strangling me didn't even flinch as I clawed uselessly at his arm.

The hooded man spit words at Sawyer. "You're outnumbered."

"Try me," Sawyer taunted. With both arms out, he had one gun aimed at the man holding me, and one aimed at the hooded man speaking.

Tears sprang, my vision started to tunnel, and I fought for air. Panicked, I kicked out as my arms reached over my head to his face.

"LET HER GO," Sawyer bellowed.

My hand grasped a handful of sticky, wet material, and I didn't think twice. I yanked.

Then everything happened at once.

My hand came away with the mask.

A gunshot rang out, piercing the night air with a deafening blast.

One of the masked men ran to the SUV's driver door.

The arm left my neck.

My body pitched forward.

Sawyer yelled my name.

Choking for air, I turned to protect my face from smashing into the pavement.

The back of my head slammed into the ground.

Pain exploded.

The de-masked man lunged, his bloody face swimming into view as his hand latched around my throat. "I'm gonna kill you!"

Sawyer kicked the side of his head.

The bloody-faced man's neck snapped sideways, and his hand left my throat as his body fell.

Sawyer dropped to his knees.

The hooded man yanked the back door of the Escalade open, dragging the bloody-faced man inside with him.

Wet coated the back of my neck, the SUV started up, and the last masked man jumped in the front passenger seat.

My head spun.

Shots rang out.

Everything went black.

CHAPTER SEVEN

Sawyer

ONE SECOND. *ONE GODDAMN SECOND* I TOOK MY EYES OFF THE TWO assholes behind me to kick the prick with his hands on Genevieve, and I got fucking pistol whipped.

The blow momentarily stunned me as I fell to my knees, but the carjackers made a crucial mistake.

Same as their warning shot, they didn't use deadly force.

They should've killed me.

Enraged, I risked unloading three rounds as the last asshole jumped into the Escalade, yanking the door shut. My shots ricocheted off the armored siding as the tires spun and they took off.

Holstering my 9mm and shoving the other gun into my back waistband, I whipped my cell out as I rolled and moved toward Genevieve.

Ty answered dryly on the first ring. "How's your date?"

Fuck. *Fuck.* Blood pooled under her head. "SUV was carjacked. Client down." I checked her pulse. "I need an ambulance and backup STAT." I rattled off our location.

Ty's tone sobered. "On my way. Four minutes out. She alive?"

"Affirmative." He could get here faster than an ambulance, but I wasn't moving her with a head injury. "Start tracking my SUV." I wanted those assholes.

"Copy that. Calling for an ambulance now." Ty hung up.

"Genevieve," I clipped uselessly, but she was unconscious. *"Goddamn it."*

"Oh my God, what happened?" Heels clicked across the parking lot as Talia appeared beside me. "Are you okay? I saw that man hit you before you shot at him." Ignoring Genevieve, she put her hand on the back of my neck.

I jerked away from her. "Step back."

"But, Sawyer, *you're injured.*"

I lost it. Shooting to my feet, I got in her face. "I said, step back. That means step the fuck back. Don't touch me, don't pretend I ever meant more than an open wallet to you, and do not kid yourself that I give a single damn about you. Ignoring an unconscious woman on the ground in front of you tells me everything I ever needed to know about you. *Leave.*" Ignoring her shocked expression and her carbon-copy friends as they stood a few yards back, I squatted next to Genevieve and checked her pulse as another company SUV pulled up next to us.

Ty got out and sized up Talia in half a second flat before taking in Genevieve. "Ambulance is on its way. Perimeter?"

I nodded once as sirens sounded in the distance.

Ty stepped in front of Talia and barked an order. "Return to your vehicle or the diner."

"You can't tell me what to do," Talia huffed. "I'm a witness. I saw what happened, and I know Sawyer."

Ty glanced over his shoulder at me.

I shook my head. I didn't need any witnesses. I saw the gang ink on the asshole's wrist. I knew they were gangbangers.

Ty crowded Talia. "He says you don't know him. Leave. *Now.*"

Talia didn't move.

40

"Come on, Talia," one of the carbon copies coaxed. "I have it on video anyway. We should go."

"Hey," Ty snapped at the carbon copy. "Blondie. Come here."

"Me?" she asked nervously.

"Yeah." One hand on his piece, he made a come here gesture with his other hand. "Show me that video."

"It's... not that great." She hesitated nervously. "It's dark out, and we were in the diner when everything happened, so I don't know if I actually got anything."

"Evidence," Ty stated, sounding like a cop. "I need to see that."

She didn't move.

"Right now," Ty barked.

The carbon copy flinched, then walked toward Ty. Sweeping her finger across the screen, she held the phone up to show him.

Ty snatched it out of her hand.

"Hey, that's mine! You can't take my phone!"

"Relax, I'm not taking it." Ty's thumbs flew across the screen a few times, then he handed her phone back.

The carbon copy grabbed her phone and scrolled. "Oh my God, you deleted the video," she accused.

The ambulance pulled into the lot.

"Get the fuck outta here. All of you," Ty snapped at Talia and her groupies before gesturing to the ambulance.

The ambulance pulled up in front of us, forcing Talia and her entourage to get the hell out of the way.

The first paramedic approached, dropping next to Genevieve with his medical kit. "What happened?"

"We were carjacked, and she was shoved down. Her head

hit the pavement."

The paramedic looked up from Genevieve and did a quick scan of the parking lot before leveling me with a look. "Hey, man, the police need to clear the scene before we get here. Did you call them?"

I pulled out a business card. "I work for Luna and Associates, personal protection, and I'm former military, Special Forces. You're in no danger. The assailants are long gone. Please, attend to her."

Nodding, the paramedic pocketed my card and spoke to his partner. "Go get a full C-spine."

The second paramedic grabbed a backboard, neck collar and two blocks.

The first paramedic grasped Genevieve on either side of her head. "Ma'am, can you hear me?"

Genevieve didn't respond.

Ty stepped up next to me and lowered his voice. "We got a problem."

No fucking shit. My eyes on Genevieve, I tipped my chin.

The first paramedic held Genevieve's head and checked her breathing while the second laid the backboard down next to her.

"One, two, three, roll," the first paramedic commanded.

The second paramedic rolled Genevieve to her side and slid the backboard under her while the first held her head steady.

Ty checked his phone before shoving it back in his pocket. "Two problems if you count the trust-fund bitch."

"Ma'am, can you open your eyes for me?" the first paramedic asked Genevieve as he checked out the wound on the back of her head. When she didn't reply, he glanced at the second paramedic. "Let's get a dressing under here."

The second paramedic went back to the ambulance.

I didn't ask Ty how he knew Talia lived off her trust fund. I was quickly realizing he had a sixth sense. "Out with it."

"Luna's on his way. Your SUV was traced to the middle of gang territory in Northwest Miami before the tracker went dead. Luna sent Preston to the last known location, but he won't find shit. You know what it's like over there." Ty nodded toward Talia and her friends. "Second problem. I deleted the video of the carjacking, but the Barbie bitch is already filming again. I'm guessing you don't want your face plastered all over social media." Ty raised an eyebrow. "You want me to handle that bullshit?"

So far, I'd been lucky working for Luna and Associates. I'd kept my head down and my last name out of everything. Since I'd been out of the tabloids for over eight years, I'd been lucky enough to fly under the radar. Minus the color of my hair, I looked a hell of a lot different than I did when I left town at eighteen and enlisted in the Marines. But Talia seeing me tonight could change all that.

"Yeah, take care of it." I didn't need any media attention.

"Who's the trust-fund bitch to you?" Ty asked.

"No one." The two times I'd come home on leave during the first couple years of my service, Talia had been at the house. When I figured out my mother had invited her to be part of the welcome home parties, I'd stopped coming home.

Ty nodded, paused a beat, then he casually said, "Saw the video."

Pissed that I'd let Genevieve get hurt, pissed that I didn't take her home when she'd first asked, and pissed that I let those fucks get away, I didn't comment. Guilt eating at me, I watched the paramedics put a neck brace on Genevieve, then put blocks on either side of her head.

"You had one down, there were only three of them," Ty continued.

I knew where he was going.

His cell vibrated. "You could've taken them." He pulled his phone out, glanced at it, then shoved it back in his pocket. "Double tap, two more shots, they all would've been down," he said offhandedly, like killing four men was sport.

I leveled him with a look. "We're not downrange."

Unfazed, he lifted his chin. "Your point?"

The paramedics strapped Genevieve to the backboard, then lifted her onto a stretcher.

"You can't shoot people. This isn't a warzone," I reminded him.

"Isn't it?"

I leveled him with a look. "Lock that trigger finger down or you're going to have a problem."

"Four dead gangbangers is a problem?" he challenged.

When your last name was Savatier, one dead body was a problem, let alone four, but I wasn't going to waste my breath explaining that. "I'm riding with her to the hospital. Follow me after you get rid of any more video that blonde took."

Ty nodded. "Copy."

As the paramedics loaded Genevieve into the ambulance, two police cruisers with their lights on pulled into the parking lot.

Ty smirked. "Here comes some bullshit."

Goddamn it. "I don't have time to deal with them." And Ty was the last person you wanted talking to the cops. "Luna on his way?"

Ty glanced across the lot. "Is he ever not on his way?"

I followed Ty's gaze and saw Luna approaching on foot. "I didn't see him pull in."

Ty eyed Talia and her friends with a sneer, then he scanned the length of the video chick's body. "I told him to park across the street to avoid the shitshow."

I couldn't tell if he wanted to shoot Talia's friend or fuck her. "Catch Luna up to speed, let him talk to the cops, then meet me at the hospital." I grabbed the carjacker's gun from my back waistband. "Take this and have Luna run the serial number. It belonged to one of the assholes."

Ty took the gun. "He won't find shit."

No kidding. "Worth a shot just in case."

Ty chuckled. "Pun intended?"

I scowled.

He smirked and nodded toward the ambulance. "You really took Pollyanna on a date?"

"Fuck you."

A sinister smile hit his face. "Rumor has it you don't swear. The guys full of shit or am I just special?"

I ignored his bullshit. "Did you take care of her car?"

Ty cocked an eyebrow. "Is that gonna determine whether or not I'm your special bitch?"

"No." It was going to determine whether or not I fucking hit him.

Ty smirked. "Car's handled." He pulled her keys out of his pocket and handed them to me. "Battery's replaced, and it's parked at her place. You're fucking welcome."

Taking the keys, I didn't thank him. Instead, I stopped one of the paramedics from closing the door. "I'm riding with her."

"You can meet us at the hospital," the paramedic deferred.

I played hardball. "You have an unconscious woman with

no ID. I'm not letting her ride without me."

The paramedic nodded, and I got in the ambulance.

Taking a seat, I looked down at Genevieve's pale complexion and still body as the paramedic put an oxygen mask over her face.

I felt like a selfish prick.

CHAPTER EIGHT

Genevieve

REATH HITCHED IN MY LUNGS, AND I SUCKED IN AIR IN A PANIC.
Choking, I tried to sit up, but my head exploded into a
nauseous sea of pain.

"Easy." A hand landed on my arm. "You're okay."

Okay? I wasn't okay. I couldn't breathe, my neck felt
crushed, air wouldn't fill my lungs, and my head was pounding.
I wanted to sit up, but I couldn't move. Something covering my
face, *I couldn't move.* I sucked in a panicked breath, then another.

"Ma'am—"

"Genevieve, open your eyes," a vaguely familiar male voice
commanded.

How did I know that voice?

I blinked, but bright lights blinded me.

A hand grasped mine. "Look at me, Genevieve. *Right now.*"

I opened my eyes.

Stark blue eyes, almost white-blond hair, sharp angular
face, five o'clock shadow…

Sawyer Savatier.

"What…." I tried to shake my head, but I couldn't move.

"You're okay." He squeezed my hand. "You're in an
ambulance."

What? I panicked. "I-I can't move!"

His face swimming above me, his expression stern, he put a

hand on my chest. "Breathe. You're okay. You can move. You're just strapped in. You hit your head. Take a breath."

I didn't take a breath. I took five. Short and panicked, I sucked in air like an addict.

"Slower," he demanded.

Oh God. "Ambulance?"

He nodded once, succinct and efficient, like he practiced the gesture in the mirror to convey maximum acknowledgment with minimum movement. "You hit your head."

"Did I fall?" *Again?*

He stared at me a moment. "No."

I waited.

"You were pushed," he admitted.

"Why was I pushed?" Did he push me? My head was killing me. I tried to lift my arm and couldn't. "I can't move."

He glanced at the paramedic.

"Grade two concussion," the paramedic explained, as if that answered anything. "You're in an ambulance, strapped to a backboard on your way to the hospital. You'll be able to move once we get you off the stretcher."

Ambulance? Hospital? "My head hurts." Bad. "Why was I pushed?"

Sawyer's nostrils flared as he inhaled. "We were carjacked."

Alarm spread. "My car is gone?" Oh my God, I needed my car. I couldn't run my business without it.

"No, mine was."

If I hadn't been strapped down, I would've stepped back. "Why was I in your car?" I wasn't in his car. I was at a client's party. I had to break down the tables and clean up the outside bar, and…. "Oh God. I can't remember. Why can't I remember?"

His stark, blue-eyed gaze, intense and serious, didn't waver.

"You hit your head."

"I hit my head?" What was going on?

"Calm down. It's going to be okay."

Calm down? "I'm not going to calm down. I'm in an ambulance, and you won't tell me what happened, and—"

The ambulance jerked to a stop, and the paramedic started to get up.

"Wait!" I screeched, panicked, trying to hold the hand that was holding mine. "Wait, wait, wait, you need to call him!"

Sawyer frowned. "Call who?"

"Brian," I blurted.

The ambulance doors opened, and my body lurched forward as the paramedic pulled the gurney out.

"Who's Brian?" Sawyer demanded, stepping out with me.

"My husband."

CHAPTER NINE

Sawyer

HUSBAND?

She was married?

The paramedic practically shoved me out of the way. "You'll have to step aside, sir."

Her face twisted with anxiety, Genevieve looked pleadingly at me. "Please, *please*, call him," she begged. "He'll know what to do."

Every ounce of self-control I'd learned in the Marines came in to play. My expression locked down, my voice calm, I fucking asked for his number as if she just hadn't insulted the hell out of me after making me the fool. "What's his number?"

She rattled it off. Easily.

She couldn't be bothered to tell me she was married, but she could recite ten numbers from heart like it was nothing.

Unbelievable.

The paramedic pushed her gurney toward the hospital entrance. Pulling my cell out, I followed as I dialed the number she'd given me.

After four rings, a man answered, his voice groggy. "Hello?"

"Brian?" I snapped.

"Um, yeah. Who's this?"

"Genevieve Jenkins was in an accident." I couldn't bring myself to say his wife. "She's stable, but she's in the hospital."

"Jesus. And she asked for me?"

What the fuck? "Yes, she asked for you." Who was this asshole?

"And you are?" he asked indignantly, picking up on my tone.

"I'm with Luna and Associates. We were hired to do security for one of her clients' events," I evaded.

He paused. "And she's okay?"

"She's concussed."

"And she asked for me?"

My irritation hit a new level. "Yes. I'm out of time. If you—"

"What hospital?" he asked on a sigh.

I told him.

"I'm on my way." He hung up.

The paramedic wheeled her into one of the emergency exam rooms as the second paramedic walked in. They lifted her onto the hospital bed and a nurse came in, helping them slide the backboard out from under Genevieve.

Genevieve looked nervously at me as the nurse turned to speak with the paramedics. "Did you call him?"

I couldn't believe she'd lied to me, and not about something insignificant. "He's on his way."

She exhaled, and her gaze drifted to the ceiling. "Thank you."

"Welcome," I ground out.

"I hit my head?" she asked again.

"Yes." Where the fuck was Ty?

"Where?"

I couldn't figure out if I was more pissed that she was married or that she'd lied to me about it. "What?"

"Where did I hit my head?"

I fought for patience. "The back side." I'd stupidly thought she was different. I never pegged her as one of the conniving women in my parents' social circles who'd do anything to get my attention. Women like Talia. I hated those women. Always had.

Genevieve rolled her eyes at me. "I know where I hit my head. It hurts really stinking bad, but I'm asking where I was geographically when I hit my head."

I tried to think of a single other woman who'd ever rolled her eyes at me. I couldn't. "The parking lot of Mel's diner."

She frowned. "I went to Mel's diner?"

Even though it wasn't her fault, the fact that she couldn't remember made me even more pissed off. "Yes."

"Why?"

I glanced at my watch. "I invited you." I needed her husband to get the fuck over here so I could walk the hell away from her.

"And I said yes? To *you*?" Looking at me like I had two heads, she said *you* like it was a four-letter word.

"Yes." Fuck this. I needed to find the Escalade. I pulled my phone out and shot off a text to Luna asking him if Preston had found anything in northwest Miami, then I texted Ty and asked if he was here.

"Wow," she mouthed, glancing at my phone.

Yeah, fucking wow.

Ty texted back that he was two minutes out, and Luna said they had nothing yet.

The nurse turned toward Genevieve. "Hi, Mrs. Jenkins. I'm Mandy. We're going to get a CT scan of your head. Then we'll take it from there, okay? Your husband can wait while the technician takes you for the scan. Any questions?"

A tall, lanky, brown-haired fuck stepped up to me.

Genevieve smiled with relief. "You came."

The nurse looked from me to the guy. "And you are?"

"My husband," Genevieve said the same time the prick said, "Brian."

A young guy in scrubs came into the already crowded room and spoke to the nurse. "They're all ready for her."

The nurse glanced between me and the computer-geek-looking fuck. "She'll be back soon. One of you can stay here. The other can wait in the waiting room."

Brain nodded at the nurse. "Of course." He glanced at Genevieve as the technician put the rails up on her bed. "They'll take good care of you."

"Okay," she said softly, sounding like a child.

"Here we go." The technician smiled at Genevieve. "I'm going to take you for a ride." He wheeled her out as the nurse told us she'd be back when Genevieve returned.

Brian watched Genevieve go, then looked at me. "You're the one who called?"

Trying to gage his lack of reaction to seeing her injured, I tipped my chin.

"Well," he sighed. "Sounds like you got it from here." He turned to go.

My anger ramped up to a new level. "You're leaving?"

The prick paused. "What else am I supposed to do? I'm not a doctor."

I stared at him, incredulous. "Be her husband."

He snorted out a fake laugh. "I haven't been that in a long time. In fact, I'm not sure I ever was."

What the actual fuck? "You're either married to her or

you're not." Fucking blue button-down prick.

He rubbed the back of his neck. "It's legal." He looked up at me. "But that's all it is."

"Explain," I demanded, having no right to ask.

Shoving his hands in his pockets, he frowned. "So, who are you again?"

"Sawyer," I clipped, offering nothing more.

"Yeah, and"—his gaze cut to my suit before he looked at me again—"you were with her when she...." He took his hands out of his pockets and held them out. "What exactly happened?"

"She fell."

This time he laughed for real. "Why am I not surprised?" Smiling ironically, he crossed his arms.

I wanted to pound his face in. "Nothing to laugh about."

He had the sense to school his expression. "Yes, sorry. True."

"Your marriage?" I demanded, reminding him I'd asked the question.

"Yeah, that." His gaze darted around the emergency room, then came back to me. "We're only still married because she won't sign the divorce papers." He had the decency to look almost sheepish. "Now you know more than I probably should've told you. Good luck. Hope she gets better soon." He pivoted.

"She asked for you."

He looked over his shoulder. "She shouldn't have. She knows why."

I put two and two together. "Because you're not together."

It wasn't a question, but he answered it anyway. "Not in the slightest."

He wasn't only an asshole, he was an idiot. She was out of his league. He should've done what he could to hold on to her.

Ty burst through the doors from the waiting area. Scanning the beds and staff, he took in the prick Brian before his eyes landed on me. His hand went to his gun, and he tipped his chin back toward the waiting area.

I barked out an order at her asshole husband. "Wait here until she gets back." I strode toward Ty. "What's up?"

"Some dick in the waiting room is saying he's her husband." He looked over my shoulder. "Who the fuck is that?"

I glanced at Brian. "Her actual husband." No one would make up an apathetic story like his.

Ty gave me a look. "You sure?"

"Yeah, she confirmed it."

"Then the dick in the waiting room—"

"Is one of them," I finished for him as my hand went to my gun. "Let's go."

CHAPTER TEN

Sawyer

"TWO O'CLOCK, BROWN HAIR, JEANS," TY CLIPPED UNDER HIS breath.

I strode toward the guy arguing with the security guard at the front desk.

"I'm telling you," he protested, "I'm Genevieve Jenkins's husband. I got a call and rushed out before I could grab my wallet. I don't have my ID. *I need to see my wife.*"

"I'm sorry, sir, but without ID, we can't let you in to see anyone. I suggest you go home and get your identification," the security guard said with a bored expression.

Ty flanked me as I stepped up behind the asshole. "Mr. Jenkins." I pressed the barrel of my gun against his kidney so he would know I meant business. "We need to speak to you about Mrs. Jenkins's accident."

The prick went ramrod straight as the color drained from his face. "Ye-ah, okay."

The guard behind the desk took in my suit and Ty's Luna and Associates uniform of a black polo and black cargo pants. "I wasn't notified there was an issue with this patient."

Ty answered him before I could. "The detective can't discuss an ongoing investigation," he lied before glaring at the asshole impersonating Genevieve's husband. "Take a walk with us, Mr. Jenkins."

I didn't give the prick a chance to say no. Still holding my gun against his kidney, I put my hand on his shoulder and walked him out of the sliding front doors of the ER just as Luna pulled up in a company SUV.

Hopping out of the Escalade, André Luna didn't even blink at the situation as he walked around the front of the SUV.

Ty smirked. "Impressive timing."

"Seconds matter." Luna opened the rear passenger door for me.

I shoved the prick inside, and he panicked. "I'm not going anywhere with you!"

Getting in after him, no longer concerned about the reach of the hospital's security cameras, I aimed my gun at his head. "You don't have a choice." Without taking my eyes off him, I issued Ty an order. "Go back inside and stay with her. Make sure no one else gets near her."

Ty chuckled. "Including her actual husband?"

"Husband?" Luna asked.

"Why would I want to go inside and miss all the fun?" Standing in the open passenger door, Ty pulled his gun out and casually checked the magazine. "I've got at least half a dozen bullets I can waste on this fuck."

"Okay, okay, I lied!" The prick impersonating Genevieve's husband threw his hands up and vomited words. "I'm not her husband. I don't even know her. They told me to do this. I've never even met her. You can let me go. I won't say anything. I promise. *I promise!*"

Ty holstered his gun. "Fucking pussy."

Luna swore in Spanish, then told Ty to get his ass back inside the hospital.

I ignored them both. Putting the barrel of my gun against

the prick's forehead, I dropped my voice to a lethal warning. "You have two choices. Tell me who put you up to this, or you die."

The asshole shook. "I-I swear. I don't know!"

"Start talking," I demanded.

"For real, I don't know. I'm just a barback. I was leaving work and these guys approached me. They showed me a picture of a redhead and offered me five hundred bucks to walk into the emergency room, say I was this chick's husband, and ask to see her."

My jaw ticked. "And then what?"

Looking guilty as fuck, his voice got quiet. "I was supposed to tell her not to talk to the cops." He swallowed and shrugged. "But you know."

"No, I don't know."

"Well… like, follow it up with an *or else*."

My nostrils flared. "That's it?"

He raised his hands higher. "Yeah, yeah, I swear."

Luna's hand landed on my shoulder. "What'd they look like?"

"I don't know, man. I really don't. It was dark behind the club where I work, and they were wearing sweatshirts with the hoods up." He glanced at Luna. "I swear I don't know who they were. They gave me the money and followed me to the hospital. They said they would know if I did what I was supposed to, and I better not burn them and chicken out because they knew where I worked. After they watched me walk in and go to the front desk, they slowly pulled away. That was the last I saw of them."

"What make and model vehicle?" Luna asked.

"I don't know," the prick whined. "A big black SUV, one

that looked like this one."

Luna's hand squeezed my shoulder, wordlessly telling me to stand down.

I didn't. I was thinking.

The asshole kept talking. "Five hundred bucks is a lot, man. I have to work a week to make that."

Luna muttered *grow a pair* in Spanish before dropping his hand from my shoulder and using the key fob to unlock the Escalade's doors. "Get the fuck out of here."

The guy scrambled for the door and shoved it open, practically falling out. Once on his feet, he slammed the door shut and took off.

Luna crossed his arms as he watched the prick run toward the parking lot. "I don't fucking like that they knew which hospital and that they've got a picture of her."

No shit. I holstered my gun and got out of the SUV. "She pulled the mask off one of the carjackers, and her purse was in the SUV. They've got her ID."

"*Madre de Dios.*" Luna sighed as he scanned the hospital parking lot. "If they figure out who you are, we'll have an even bigger problem." He looked at me. "They won't just try to kill her, they'll come after her for a K and R first just because she was seen with you. Then they'll kill her."

"She's married, and her husband sure as hell doesn't have a flush bank account." He looked like he barely had a pot to piss in.

Luna's expression shifted in a nanosecond. "Ty wasn't bullshitting?"

"No. Didn't find that in your background check?" Luna had run her background for the job we were on last night with her client.

Luna frowned. "Actually, no, not that I recall."

Fucking great. "Anything pertinent you want to share with me about her before I go back inside?"

Luna studied me a beat, then he nodded slowly, as if everything suddenly made sense. "She didn't tell you she was hitched."

"Nope."

"Damn." He drew the word out. "Well, as far as her background, she's an event planner. We're not talking high-profile clients, but we're not talking kids' birthday parties either. Art openings like the one last night, fundraisers, an occasional wedding, personal milestone parties, shit like that. There was nothing else in her profile that stood out except that she was a foster kid, came up in the system, and never got adopted. She aged out at eighteen."

She didn't have a family? "Jesus." Despite her lying to me, I felt like even more of an asshole for taking her out and letting her get fucking injured.

"Yeah, rough life. All right, walk me through what happened at Mel's."

"It started out as a single carjacker with a triangle tattoo on his inner wrist."

"Fucking Tres Angulos gang." Luna muttered a curse in Spanish. "This isn't their usual MO."

No, it wasn't. "I'm surprised they didn't just shoot us and take the SUV."

"There was a lot of foot traffic in that parking lot when I got there, and even more witnesses in the diner. It was dark, but there was a clear sight line from the booths at the window to where you'd parked. Maybe the Tres Angulos have graduated to smart crime." His gaze drifting across the parking lot,

Luna watched two hospital employees walk toward their cars. "At any rate, I'll ask around. I have a few connections in that world. Tell me the rest of it."

"I took down the original carjacker and three more showed up. Before I could get her safely inside the vehicle, the original perp made a play and threw her down. I took my eyes off the perp at my back for half a second as she went down, and he used the in. Pistol whipped me." *I should've shot them all.*

Luna frowned. "You okay?"

"Fine," I clipped.

"Gracias a Dios."

I didn't say shit. I'd left faith behind a long time ago. Tonight only reaffirmed that decision.

As if sensing my mood, Luna clapped me on the shoulder. "Four armed unpredictable gangbangers at close range isn't good odds, amigo. You kept yourself and the chica from getting shot. You did good."

Bullshit. "No, I didn't." *I could've taken them all.*

Marine to Marine, he read my thoughts. "I know what you're thinking, and maybe you could've gotten four kill shots off before one hit her. But I also know you're smart as fuck and those odds were never in your favor. There's valor in protecting a life, not your ego."

I rubbed a hand over the back of my neck where that asshole had hit me. I knew he was right, but it didn't change the fact that she was in a hospital bed. "I'm going back inside. Ty has a gun I got off one of them. Maybe the serial number will turn up something."

"I'll run it, but don't hold your breath."

"Copy. Any update on the recovery of the vehicle?" I was

kicking myself even more now for not letting her retrieve her purse.

"Not yet. I sent the new hire, Preston, to northwest Miami, to the area we last tracked it. Which, now that I know the Tres Angulos are behind this, the location makes sense. Preston will canvas the area, see what he can find out. But if their last known location was actually here at the hospital, they could be anywhere by now."

"How did they disable the tracking device on the Escalade? I thought you hid them."

Luna shrugged. "I do, but apparently they figured out where it was. Hell, maybe they simply burned the vehicle by now."

"You don't burn an armored Escalade. You sell it." In parts if you had to.

"Never said criminals were smart."

"They're smarter than us right now if we can't find them." I turned to go.

"You asked her out," Luna mused.

Pausing, I glanced over my shoulder at him. "Your point?" I'd been off the clock, and the job had been over. I didn't break any company rules.

"How long you worked for me?"

It was a rhetorical question. Luna knew every detail about every single one of his employees by heart. He retained information like no one I'd ever met. I didn't bother answering.

"Been a while, amigo." He paused. "Never seen you ask a woman out before."

"I don't broadcast my personal life."

Luna chuckled. "No, you sure don't." His expression sobered. "According to your paycheck you work sixty-hour weeks, but we both know it's more than that. Not much room for a personal life in all that."

I didn't deny it.

He nodded once. "She must be special."

She was a walking train wreck. She talked too much, she overshared, and she dropped everything. She didn't listen to instructions, and her hazel-eyed gaze more often than not looked at me with childlike curiosity instead of womanly seduction. She drove me insane.

Nothing about her was anything I'd ever wanted or needed, but all I could think about was having her thick hair wrapped around my hand as I made her submit.

Except she'd lied to me.

She had a goddamn husband, and that was a line I'd sworn to myself I would never, ever cross. I wasn't going to be like my asshole father. I swore to myself in high school when I first caught him cheating on my mother that I wasn't going to ever pull that shit. And I sure as hell wasn't going to wreck another marriage by taking another man's wife. My mother put up with my father, and she was still with him, but that didn't change the fact that I hated him.

"She's married," I reminded Luna before shutting down the conversation. "I'm going back inside. I need to get her out of here before the carjackers send someone else after her."

Luna nodded. "Take her to one of the client apartments. She can stay there until we resolve this bullshit."

Luna and Associates had a few apartments on the floors above the offices for this exact reason. It was a secure building, and we could control who got in or out. Normally, I wouldn't have a problem dropping a client in one of them, except she was injured. "She has a grade two concussion."

Luna read between the lines. "So stay with her."

I scowled. Staying with her at a company apartment under the microscope of every ex-Marine who worked for Luna was out of the question.

Luna chuckled. "I didn't say fuck her, amigo. I said stay with her." He got behind the wheel of the Escalade.

I resisted the urge to flip him off.

He grinned. "I heard that."

"I didn't say anything." Like a fucking fool, I was already contemplating taking her to my place.

"You didn't have to. Despite you never saying shit, I can read you like a book." Luna gave me a knowing look then switched gears. "After Preston does his recon, I'll have him check her apartment and pick up a few of her things while he's there. He'll notice if anyone's sitting on the place."

I wasn't sure Preston would notice a damn thing, the guy was seriously off, but I was out of choices for now. Reaching in my pocket and grabbing her keys, I handed them to Luna. Then I sealed my fate. "Have him bring her stuff to my place."

"Copy that." Luna didn't comment on the change in location, but his expression sobered. "For real, you got this? They already found her once, you want more backup? Ty's been on all night. He'll get you two home, but then Preston can sit on your place after he gets her stuff."

I didn't think anyone would come back tonight. Then again, I wasn't expecting them to show up at the hospital either. I didn't trust Preston as far as I could throw him, the guy was cagey as hell, but Luna had hired him, so for now, I was letting it go. "Fine on Preston." Even though I knew they were long gone, I scanned the parking lot, looking for any of those carjacking assholes. "You know if they wanted her dead, they

64

would've sent one of their own, and they sure as hell wouldn't have sent a warning."

"Not many places are harder to get a clean shot at someone than a hospital. There's security cameras and witnesses everywhere. The warning could've been a precursor." He cranked the engine and threw the SUV into gear. "But that still doesn't change the fact they found her once already, and that's too close for my comfort."

"Agree." Which was why I wasn't going to let her go back to her place until we found these assholes. "I need one more favor." I grabbed my wallet. "Can you get her a new phone and tablet? Set the phone up with her number?" I held out a credit card.

"Done, but put that shit away."

"Take it out of my pay then." I didn't need monetary favors.

"All the overtime I don't pay you?" Luna scoffed, but then he winked. "Least I can do is hook up your woman."

I leveled him with a look. "She's not mine."

"Maybe not yet." He grinned. "I give it twenty-four hours at your place."

I changed the subject before I unleashed my self-hatred on him. "What did the police say?"

Luna sobered. "What could they say? I grew up with the beat officers who showed up. They know who I am. I told them I'd take care of my own business and find my vehicle long before they would."

Christ. "Is there anyone you don't know in this town?"

He faked being offended. "You calling my city a town?"

I wasn't impressed. I grew up hearing my father tell us he owned Miami every time he brokered a new real estate deal.

"It's fifty-six-point-six square miles of backfilled swamp land." I knew the exact size because my father also told us with every other breath—when he wasn't cheating on my mother—how much of that square footage he owned. "Call it what you want." In truth, south Florida didn't belong to anyone. "It's one good hurricane away from being swamp land again."

"Cold-hearted, Savatier." Smiling, Luna shook his head. "Cold-hearted."

"The truth hurts." I wasn't talking about Miami.

Luna's smile dropped. "Amen."

I walked back into the hospital.

CHAPTER ELEVEN

Genevieve

THE NURSE PUT ANOTHER STAPLE IN AND I FLINCHED EVEN THOUGH I couldn't feel anything after she'd given me the shot of Novocain.

"Almost done," she murmured.

Brian stood by with his hands in his pockets, looking disapproving, and I couldn't remember why I'd told Sawyer to call him. "Brian, you can leave."

The scary-looking, impossibly tall bodyguard in all black with a Luna and Associates logo on his shirt smirked. "No, he can't."

Brian glanced at him with a frown.

"Following orders," the bodyguard clipped, looking smug.

"You're not in the military anymore," Brian shot back. "You can relax with the whole *orders* thing."

"What makes you think I was in the military?" the bodyguard asked.

The nurse put in another staple.

"Wild guess," Brian answered dryly.

"You're right." The bodyguard leaned toward Brian and lowered his voice. "Know what that means?"

The nurse wiped the back of my neck with something cold and wet.

"Enlighten me," Brian stated with zero interest, which was

exactly how he spoke to me for most of our marriage.

The bodyguard smiled a smile that was more sneer. "I've got good aim."

Sawyer burst through the doors of the emergency room. With his light blond hair, stark blue eyes and perfectly handsome face, he could've been an angel of mercy. But the anger contorting his features eclipsed his beauty, making me shiver.

The nurse's hand landed on my shoulder. "You're okay. I'm all done."

Brian sighed as if put out.

Sawyer glanced at the bodyguard and tipped his chin toward the exit. A silent communication passed between them, and the bodyguard walked out.

Brian pulled his hands out of his pockets and crossed his arms. "Your watchdog made me stay. She's all stitched up. I have to be at work in a few hours, can I go now?" he asked, not without a little sarcasm.

His eyes on me, Sawyer issued a single word to Brian. "Leave."

Wasting no time, Brian spared me half a glance, shook his head, then walked out.

Striding to the side of my bed, Sawyer addressed the nurse across from him. "What's her status?"

The nurse flushed under his scrutiny. "Well, she has a grade two concussion, and I just finished stapling her wound. We're waiting on the doctor for the CT scan results."

Sawyer leveled the nurse with a look. "Her safety is in danger. She's a witness to a gang-related crime, and I need to get her to a more secure location. I need to speak with the doctor immediately."

The color drained from the nurse's face, but she nodded.

"I'll speak to him right away." She hustled out of the little curtained-off area surrounding my bed.

My mouth dry and my heart suddenly in my throat, I looked up at the man who was too handsome to be standing in a hospital over my bed. "Danger?"

His gaze cut across the emergency room, then landed on me. "You saw the carjacker."

"I…." Oh God. The memory of the carjacking flashed through my head. "I pulled his mask off," I blurted.

"Would you recognize him?"

"He's coming after me?"

"Yes."

I didn't hesitate. "I don't know what he looked like."

The muscle in his jaw jumped, then he bit out a warning. "Lying won't change the situation."

Bits and pieces of the evening rained down on my memory like parade confetti. It took a moment, but then my brain slowly started piecing things together.

Oh God… *oh God.*

"You're not talking about the carjacker." He was mad that I didn't tell him about Brian.

"I'm expressly speaking about that."

"You're lying." He had to be. Why would he be mad if I said I didn't remember what the carjacker looked like? That kept me safe.

"I don't lie," he snapped.

My mouth opened, and words vomited out. "Brian is divorcing me. We're separated."

"That's of no concern to me," he clipped, sounding like he meant the exact opposite of what he was saying.

"You asked me out." I remembered it now. But truth be

told, I was being generous in my description. He'd told me I was going to dinner with him.

"Do you remember the carjacker's face?" he ground out, as if fighting for patience.

I honestly didn't know if I could pick him out of a lineup. I didn't trust my memory, my head was pounding in a way that made concentrating difficult, and all I wanted to do was sleep, but none of that mattered. I wasn't going to risk my life to identify anyone. I'd seen those movies on cable. It never ended well.

"This is nuts," I muttered.

He didn't respond. He just stared at me like he was waiting for me to rattle off the carjacker's height, weight and astrological sign. None of which I knew. But there was one thing I was absolutely certain of, and I didn't think it was enough to put me in danger, so I told him.

"He had a tattoo," I stated. "A triangle on his inner wrist."

Sawyer frowned, but he also did something else I hadn't seen him do. He nodded in approval. "That's the mark of a Tres Angulos gang member. They all have that tattoo."

I felt like a kid showing her parents a straight-A report card. Except I'd never been that kid, with either the A's or the parents. The closest I'd ever had to anyone who'd ever noticed my grades was a book-nerd kid with a superiority complex—and I'd stupidly married him. Then I put him through college with minimum wage jobs I hated while I worked on my own dream. When he became a financial planner, I quit all three of my jobs and started my own business. Everything in the marriage had gone downhill from there.

Shoving away old memories, I gripped the railing on the side of the bed and made to pull myself up. "If you think those jerks are going to come here, which I don't know why you would think that when I didn't even get a good look at his face, but whatever, we should go." I didn't want to make it easy for any carjacker or gang member to find me.

His hand landed on my shoulder, and without being forceful, but not at all gentle, he pushed me back down. "We're waiting for the doctor to release you."

As if on cue, the nurse drew the curtain aside and stepped in with an ice pack. "Here." She gently placed it under my head. "This will help with the swelling." She glanced at Sawyer. "The doctor is on his way, right after he finishes with his current patient."

"Thank you," he quietly replied, giving her a note of civility he hadn't extended to me.

I was ashamed to admit, I hated her for it. But the pain in my head outweighing my want of having her gone, I asked for relief. "Can I take something for the headache? Advil? Tylenol?"

She smiled sympathetically at me. "The doctor will give you a prescription for when you're released."

The curtain pulled back again and an older doctor stepped in. "Mrs. Jenkins, I'm Dr. Michaels. How are you feeling?" He moved to the side of my bed and gently turned my head to look at the wound.

"Well, my head hurts," I admitted.

"I'm giving you a prescription for a mild painkiller for that. An ice pack a few times a day will also help with the swelling." The doctor stepped back to the end of the bed. "Your CT scan looked good. We didn't see any bleeding on the brain or anything else to be concerned about, so I'm going to release you. Your staples will stay in for five to seven days. You can shower after twenty-four hours, but be careful of the wound. Do you have any questions?"

I started to shake my head, but even that hurt. "No, thank you."

The doctor looked at Sawyer. "Monitor her for any decreases in her mental state, or seizures, or a secondary loss of consciousness. With a grade two concussion, you can expect some repetitive questioning, mild confusion, or lapse in memory surrounding the event that caused the injury. It should dissipate quickly. If it doesn't, or if any of the other symptoms occur, bring her back to the emergency room immediately."

Sawyer nodded. "Understood. Can you release her now?"

"Yes, the nurse will handle the paperwork and she has her prescription. Considering the situation, I'm sending her home with a couple pain pills until you have time to fill the prescription." He held his hand out to Sawyer, then to me. "Take care of yourself, Mrs. Jenkins."

"Thank you," I said, wondering how I was going to watch myself for the things the doctor mentioned as he walked out.

"Okay." The nurse smiled. "Here is the pain medication. As the doctor explained, it's just a couple pills to hold you over until you can get your prescription filled, which I'll give you with your paperwork." She handed me a small bottle.

Without a word, Sawyer took the pills and pocketed them.

The nurse watched the interaction, then cleared her throat. "Okay, I got most of your information earlier before I put your staples in, but I just have some paperwork left to take care of, then we can get you out of here. Do you have your license and insurance information?"

It hit me all at once.

Oh my God.

Oh my God.

I looked up at Sawyer in a sheer panic. "My purse, my

tablet, *my wallet*, they were all in the SUV when it was stolen." I tried to swallow down the anxiety threatening to come up. "They stole everything." I choked on a sob.

Sawyer already had his wallet out. Handing a credit card to the nurse, he kept his eyes on me, but spoke to her. "I need to get her out of here, *now.*"

CHAPTER TWELVE

Sawyer

THE NURSE WALKED OUT, AND GENEVIEVE STARTED TO hyperventilate.

Careful not to touch the back of her head, I took her face in my hands. "Genevieve, look at me."

She did, but she wasn't seeing me. "My life, my whole life, everything was in my purse. My wallet, my cell phone—*oh my God,*" she cried. "That's my entire business. Everything is on that tablet."

Goddamn it. "Do you back up regularly?"

Her breath hitched, but her eyes focused. "Back up?"

"Your tablet, your cell, do you use the cloud, something else?" She seemed more disorganized than anyone I'd ever met, but the party she'd organized had run smoothly. I was hoping that was an indication of some level of organization.

"Okay, okay." She nodded. "I do that."

She looked so damn vulnerable, for a beat I forgot how pissed I was at her. Swiping at the tears on her soft cheek with my thumb, I stupidly made her a promise. "We'll get it sorted."

She looked up at me with childlike trust. "Okay."

The nurse walked back in, and I dropped my hand, mentally reminding myself this woman was off-limits.

Handing me a clipboard with my credit card and paperwork, she pointed. "Just sign here and here. And I have a wheelchair all set so we can get you out of here."

An orderly pushed the curtain all the way back and brought a wheelchair to the end of the bed.

I signed the credit card receipt, pocketed the paperwork and my credit card, then I helped Genevieve sit up.

She sucked in a sharp breath.

I went on alert. "You okay?"

"Are you dizzy?" the nurse asked.

Her head down, her voice tentative, she swiped at her face, then tugged at the hem of her dress. "I'm fine."

I noticed the abrasions on her knees from when she'd hit the pavement, but I was a fucking asshole for also noticing the smooth ivory skin of her thighs. "Can you stand?"

"I, um…." She stared at her legs as they hung over the side of the bed. "I don't have any shoes."

"Oh, let me get you some socks." The nurse took off.

Fuck. *Fuck.* With everything that'd happened, I hadn't even realized she'd lost her shoes.

Without a word, I scooped her up.

She gasped like she was in pain.

"Arms around my neck," I ordered, hating the fact that she was injured.

Her body shaking slightly, she complied. "You can't lift me. I'm too heavy."

"I already did." I walked her to the end of the bed. "And you're not." She was perfect. Too goddamn perfect.

I set her in the wheelchair, and the nurse came back and handed her a pair of hospital socks.

"They're not shoes, but at least you won't be barefoot." Smiling at Genevieve, the nurse patted her shoulder. "Take care." She nodded at the orderly. "They're all set."

The orderly turned her wheelchair around, but I stopped him.

"Hold on." I pulled my cell out and dialed Ty.

He answered on the first ring. "What's up?"

"We're coming out. Status?"

"All clear out here."

"You know what vehicle you're looking out for?"

"Copy. Luna told me what the pussy barback said. Bold move on those fucks' part driving our SUV around, if you ask me. If I see them, I'm gonna shoot—"

"I didn't ask. Pull up in the loading zone."

"Ten-four. Twenty seconds." He hung up.

I nodded at the orderly. It'd take us that long to walk out of here.

Stepping in front of the wheelchair, I led us out of the emergency area and through the waiting room. I scanned everyone as we left, but the only people in the reception area looked like people waiting to be seen.

As we exited the front doors, Ty pulled up and got out. His hand on his holster, he scanned the parking lot and loading zone as he walked around the vehicle and opened the rear passenger door.

I nodded at the orderly. "I got it from here." Before she could protest, I picked Genevieve up.

Her eyes darted around, following Ty's gaze, then she grasped at my neck in a death grip.

"You're good. We're clear," I reassured as I set her in the SUV and held the seat belt out for her.

She didn't move.

Staring straight ahead, gripping her socks to her chest with both hands, dried blood down the back of her neck and on her dress, she was the most beautiful woman I'd ever laid eyes on. She was also married and scared as hell, and it was my fault.

I brushed the errant curl off her face. "Look at me."

Pain etched across her features, she turned toward me.

"We need to move," Ty warned.

Ignoring him, I pulled the seat belt across her lap. "I'm going to make you a promise."

She didn't respond.

"If I tell you you're safe, then you're safe in that moment." I buckled her in. "I promise."

"What about the next moment?" she asked, her voice small.

I gave her the truth. "If the situation changes, I won't lie."

Staring at me for a moment, she finally nodded. "Okay."

I tipped my chin and shut the door.

Ty smirked. "Who knew? The billionaire does have a vice. His downfall?" He grinned and waited a beat like I was going to answer his bullshit question. *"Redheads."* Slapping me on the shoulder, he walked toward the driver door. "Should've told me that was all it took. We could've gotten your uptight ass laid awhile ago. I know plenty of strippers with red—"

"Just drive," I ground out, reciting my address before opening the front passenger door and getting in the SUV.

Ty got behind the wheel, but the smile had dropped from his face as he glanced at me. "You know what you're bringing to your doorstep?" he asked under his breath.

As much as I didn't trust Ty, knowing who he'd worked for before Luna, knowing his propensity for pulling the trigger first and asking questions later, I knew he was smart. Before he worked for Luna, he'd been the inside man on one of our ops, and he'd played it smart. Using American Sign Language to communicate, keeping his cover, evading authorities after the bust, leaving no trace he'd ever been in his last boss's employ—he had skills. And he knew enough about my background to try and warn me off bringing a married woman with a gang after her to my penthouse.

I had respect for his question, but zero patience for it.

"Drive," I ordered.

Without another word from any of us, Ty drove to my building and pulled into the underground parking.

"This isn't where I live," Genevieve said nervously.

"It's where I live." I glanced over my shoulder at her. "For now, it's not safe for you to go home."

Her lip trembled before she bit it. "Can't I just go to a hotel?"

Angry at myself, at the situation I'd gotten her into, at the fact she'd lied to me, I fought to temper my voice. "This is a secure building with a good security system, and another Luna and Associates employee will be stationed out front."

"Why can't he be stationed out front of a hotel?"

"I can't secure an entire hotel." And until those carjackers were caught, I didn't want her out of my sight. Her useless husband sure as hell wasn't going to protect her.

She looked between me and Ty. "Am I really in that much danger?"

I reminded myself of my promise to her. "Yes."

Tears welled, but she blinked them back and nodded. "For how long?"

"For as long as it takes for us to find who took the vehicle."

"And that is?" she asked, her voice stronger.

I shouldn't be noticing she had a backbone, or anything

else about her, but fuck I was noticing. "Hours or days. I don't know."

"Then what happens when you find them?"

Ty smirked. "Don't ask questions you don't want the answer to, sweetheart." He turned in his seat to face her. "You'll be safe with Sawyer."

As much as I wanted to hit him for calling her sweetheart, I didn't say anything. Hearing from someone else that she'd be safe with me might ease her anxiety, and I wasn't going to deny her that.

Her gaze dropped to her lap, and after a beat, she nodded. "Okay." She inhaled and looked up at me with determination. "I'll go with you."

I didn't hesitate. I got out and opened her door.

But before I could pick her up again, her hand shot up. "No, I'm walking. No argument."

For the second time since I'd met her, and despite everything that'd happened, I wanted to smile. Except this time, I didn't fight it.

I offered her my hand and let the corner of my mouth tip up.

CHAPTER THIRTEEN

Genevieve

H E SMILED.

Not a real smile, more one side of his mouth moving in a northerly direction, but it was no less life-altering, and it made my already faltering heart fracture with a new round of erratic beats that threatened to do me in.

Sawyer Savatier, smiling.

Yesterday I was worrying about what shoes to wear to a client's event that would say I had everything under control, but also wouldn't kill my feet after standing for twelve hours.

Now I had no shoes.

And no purse, no wallet, no cell phone and no tablet.

But I had staples.

I didn't know if I should laugh or cry. My head hurt so bad, I'd been leaning toward the latter, but then he'd smiled. Sawyer Savatier, amused by the girl with blood all over her dress and no shoes.

And now he was offering his hand to me like a gentleman.

Hesitant, I stared at his outstretched palm. I wasn't wearing heels anymore, and I'd put on the grippy socks from the hospital, but still. If I took his hand, it felt like I was crossing the threshold from independent to needy, and I didn't want to be someone's burden. I didn't want to be what was written all over Brian's expression at the hospital. But right now, the man in front of me wasn't looking at me like I was a burden.

So I took his hand.

And immediately wished I hadn't.

Large, firm, strong, calloused.

He was everything Brian wasn't. He was everything *every* man I'd ever been around wasn't.

Awareness shot up my arm and almost made me forget about the incessant pounding in my head. Almost. But then my feet hit the cold concrete garage floor and vertigo hit me.

I swayed as I reached behind my neck to gingerly feel my wound. I wanted to know how many staples the nurse had put in, but I also wanted to distract myself from the fact that not only was I in a garage that had a cleaner floor than my apartment, but that I was in a zip code that outranked my salary by multiples of a thousand. Not to mention a man more austere than anyone I'd ever met was holding my hand.

"Leave your staples alone." His large hand squeezed mine. "We'll clean you up when we get upstairs."

I practically choked. *"We?"* I wasn't sure I could handle much more we.

As if he brought home girls with bloody dresses and staples holding them together every night, he didn't hesitate. "Yes."

"I don't think I can handle a we," I blurted.

He didn't comment. He glanced at the driver. "As soon Preston shows up, you're clear."

"Copy that." The driver smiled at me. "Take it easy, sweetheart."

Sawyer's eyebrows drew together as he shut the door, then the Escalade disappeared up the ramp and into the night.

Leading us to one of two elevators that didn't have a call button, but had a keypad, Sawyer entered a code and the doors immediately slid open.

I glanced up at him. "Private elevator?"

"Penthouse," he clipped, ushering me inside and briefly holding his wallet against a small black pad. A ding sounded and the light for thirty lit up as the doors slid shut.

Thirtieth floor.

Penthouse.

The elevator shot up as the last of my confidence plummeted. Staring straight ahead, my dress stuck to my back with blood, my feet in hospital socks, I didn't feel like I should be next to a man who lived in the sky.

I felt like a woman with no dignity left.

The elevator doors opened to a small vestibule with a round table in the middle with mail on it, and straight ahead were two large, heavy-looking doors. Sawyer walked to the right and pressed his thumb against a small screen on a keypad and a click sounded.

He pushed one of the doors open, then looked expectantly at me.

No turning back now, I stepped across the threshold.

Taking in the opulence in front of me, I immediately wished I'd done every single thing differently tonight. I wished I hadn't peppered him with questions at the party. I wished I'd never gone to dinner with him, I wished I'd never seen the woman he used to date, and I wished like hell I wasn't standing next to him in a ruined dress with staples in the back of my head.

I wasn't completely ignorant of wealth. I'd had famous clients and rich clients. Hell, my last client lived in practically a palace on the intracoastal. I'd seen all kinds of wealth.

But this?

Shiny, white, polished stone floors, a restaurant-quality kitchen gleaming with stainless steel and high-gloss cabinets, two-story-tall windows looking out on the ocean, leather furniture that looked butter soft....

He was a Savatier, all right.

And I was... a foster kid. "I, um, *wow*."

His hand landed on the small of my back. "Let's get you cleaned up, then you can sleep."

I didn't want to sleep. My head was spinning, and I wanted to run away from every perfectly placed piece of furniture and lack of clutter as much as I wanted to crawl on his couch and stare out at the stars that looked close enough to touch until the sun came up. Every single thing about his home was different than mine.

There were no throw pillows on the furniture, no blankets, no discarded sweater or shoes or coffee mugs left out. No nail polish spilled on the carpet, no interesting fabric hung on the wall as art because it was pretty. No, he had real paintings and lamps without scarves over the shades and floors so clean you could eat off them.

I didn't belong here.

I didn't belong anywhere even remotely close to here.

But I didn't have time to tell him that. He'd already led me past the stunningly perfect living room and kitchen and formal dining room with seating for ten. His touch on my back generating waves of heated awareness that spread over my entire body, he led me down a corridor with half a dozen doors before ushering me into a room that I knew was his before he'd turned on a single light.

The smell of sandalwood and musk and shoe polish and fresh laundry hit me so strongly, my conscience betrayed me and completely gave up on the notion that I didn't belong here. My senses on overload, my body aching for comfort, I wanted to breathe in this scent for the rest of my life. More, I wanted to lose myself in the very man attached to that scent who was leading me to the edge of a giant bathtub with jets.

"Sit," he commanded.

God help me, I fell victim to his commanding presence. Like an addict, I wanted to forget every single thing about my life and get drunk off his bossy orders, because I was quickly realizing that every time he told me to do something, I didn't have to think.

Oh God, I didn't have to think.

There were no decisions to be made about what kind of wine went best with what food, or what color invitation conveyed understated excitement. I didn't have to figure out how to seat warring divorced parents of the groom next to each other.

Except it wasn't just work that slipped my mind as I did exactly what he'd told me to do.

My ass landed on the edge of the tub, and I was already awaiting further instruction. I wasn't mired in worry about my next car payment, or rent, or wondering where the next client would come from. I wasn't even freaking out about my stolen purse and everything in it anymore.

Because when he spoke to me like that, when he gave me his intense stare and issued a command, I felt like I was the only person in his universe.

And I'd never been someone's world.

Not Brian's, not my birth mom's, not any of my foster parents', not anyone's.

I was alone.

I always had been. Even when I was married, and it had

taken me to this very second to fully understand that, because not one thing Sawyer was doing for me would have ever been anything Brian would have done for me.

Not that I would, or could, ever compare the two men, because they were night and day, but Brian would've been yelling at me about my missing wallet before he would've helped me get cleaned up.

And that right there, the thought of my old reality, it was enough to kick some sense back into me. "I'm going to need to borrow your phone to cancel my credit card and close my bank account card."

A billionaire bodyguard in a custom-made suit bent over me and gently pulled my blood-stuck hair off my shoulders after turning on the faucet to fill the giant bathtub. "We'll take care of it after we get you cleaned up," he reassured, fingering the zipper on the back of my dress.

I jerked away. "I, um…." *Oh God.* "I can do that." Suddenly ashamed at myself for my wayward thoughts of letting him order me around and take care of me as if I were helpless, I had to remind myself that I wasn't helpless. I'd taken care of myself my whole life.

His hand landed on my shoulder. "Relax. I'm only unzipping it for you. It needs to come off."

My emotions in whiplash overload, a shiver went up my spine. "I can do it myself."

"Stand," he ordered, reaching for a towel and ignoring me.

No resolve behind my previous declaration to do it for myself, I did exactly as he said. I stood, but apparently my submission was only relegated to my body, because words spilled out of my mouth. "Are you always like this?"

"Like what?" He handed me the towel as the bathroom

filled up with steam.

I didn't hold back. "Disregardful of what people say to you. Hearing only what you want to hear."

"I am neither ignoring you nor being disrespectful." Holding my gaze, he put his arms around me.

I sucked in a sharp breath. "What are you doing?"

"Helping you." My zipper slid down my back. He dropped his hands and turned around, giving me the illusion of privacy. "Take the dress off, wrap the towel around yourself and sit back down on the edge of the tub. I'll wash the blood out of your hair."

"I...." I was going to say I could do it myself, but I couldn't, not really, not without getting my head wet, and the doctor had said not to get the wound wet for twenty-four hours. And if I was being honest with myself, I didn't even want to attempt to do this myself. I didn't want to touch it anymore. It was throbbing and sore and felt hot, and I just wanted the pain to go away.

"Fine," I relented, shoving the straps of my dress off my shoulders. "But you can't get the stitches wet." I wrapped the towel around me.

"I know." He slid his jacket off, tossed it on the counter, and turned back around. His holster with the very large gun looked even more imposing than when I'd first gotten a glance of it when he was helping me stack chairs.

Tired, uncomfortable with his gun hanging out, and at my limit, I snapped at him. "What if I hadn't had the towel around me?"

He removed his cuff links, tossed them on the counter and rolled his sleeves up. "I heard your dress hit the floor." His hands landed on my bare shoulders, and he gently shoved me down to the edge of the tub. "And it wouldn't have been anything I haven't seen before."

"You haven't seen me," I protested, feeling both insolent and jarringly jealous at his rude statement.

His eyes on me, intense and unreadable, he dropped to a squat. "You're right."

I pressed my legs together, and my voice came out a whisper. "What are you doing?"

"Taking care of you." He pulled my hospital socks off, and thoughts bled out of my mouth.

"I'm uncomfortable." More uncomfortable than I'd ever been. But I was also fighting an urge to fall into his arms. An urge so strong, it eclipsed every feeling I'd ever had for Brian, even if you shoved them all together and bundled them up like a messy armful of yanked weeds.

"I can sympathize," he stated quietly.

That took me off guard. "When have you ever been uncomfortable?" He was gorgeous, rich and commanding.

He stood and grabbed a washcloth and the handheld faucet. "When I had staples."

My mouth opened but no words came out. I was an idiot. He'd served our country, and no part of being deployed sounded comfortable. "I'm sorry."

He wet the washcloth. "Not as sorry as the man who pushed his wife, strapped with explosives, in front of our convoy."

Oh God. "Were you injured?"

He wiped the warm washcloth across the back of my neck. "Yes." Rinsing it, he did it again.

"What happened?" I dared to ask.

"I got lucky." He wiped the back of my neck one more time before setting the bloodstained washcloth on the edge of the tub. "Hold on to my waist and lean back." One of his hands gathered up my hair while the other held the showerhead.

I stared at the washcloth with my blood on it as we skirted the subject of his bloodshed. The irony wasn't lost on me as I avoided his holstered gun and tentatively grasped his lean, hard waist before leaning back only a couple of inches. The movement made the throbbing intensify at the same time as my hands on him made me wish I was touching him for any other reason.

More than all that, I wanted to ask what had happened to him, but I was afraid. Part of me didn't want to know the gruesome details, but another, selfish part of me was concerned he wouldn't tell me if I did ask. And I didn't want to be that to him—another person who gawked at him for his injuries, only to exploit the bad parts of his service then give platitudes about bravery and valor.

So I didn't ask.

I just held on to him.

CHAPTER FOURTEEN

Sawyer

A KNOCK SOUNDED ON THE FRONT DOOR AS I WAS ABOUT TO TELL her about Afghanistan.

I squeezed the water out of her hair and grasped her arm to pull her upright. "Stay here."

Weariness, more so than in the hospital, crept into her tone, and she dropped her hands from my waist. "Expecting someone?"

Having her hands on me was fucking with my head, but I still knew what she was asking. "Yes, Preston. He works with me."

"Is that who was at the hospital and who drove us here?"

"No, that was Ty." She looked so damn small and fragile sitting on my tub with my oversized towel wrapped around her. "I'll be right back." I strode to the front door and opened it.

Preston waltzed in with a scowl and a flower-print suitcase. His gaze cut across the living room. "You fucking owe me." He dumped the suitcase next to the entry table as his restless energy bled out around him. "Actually, you more than owe me. How the hell do you step foot in her place? There's shit everywhere."

Alarm spread. "It was tossed?"

"If by tossed, you mean someone hung scarves on lamps

and tacked hippy shit to the walls and left a week's worth of dishes in the sink, then yeah." He shook his head. "It was tossed." Agitated, looking like he wanted to crawl out of his own skin, he scanned my place again.

"Anyone waiting outside her place?"

Distracted by whatever the hell he was looking at, a beat passed before he shook his head.

I barely refrained from snapping my fingers in his face. "You sure?"

He looked down the hall, then glanced toward the kitchen. "Yeah."

Goddamn it. "*Focus*, Preston." What the fuck was he on?

His gaze cut to the floor, and he tapped his foot twice, then twice again. "I am fucking focused."

I lost it. "How the hell do you know someone wasn't at her place if you can't stand still for five seconds?"

His head whipped up, his steel-eyed gaze cut to me, and he went still dead still. "No security cameras once you get outside the elevator, fourteen four-by-six windows, four columns, eighteen recessed lights, seven paces from the front door to the wall safe behind the landscape picture, six doors in the hall, wolf range, subzero fridge, six barstools and one penthouse pecker asshole. I fucking pay attention. You wanna know about her place now?"

I blinked, then somehow managed to tip my chin.

"Five coffee mugs in the sink, twenty-seven pairs of underwear, no security cameras anywhere on the property, sixteen units, twenty-four parking spots and zero fucking bad guys unless you count the old man in two-B who stole the paper from the doorstep of four-A seventeen seconds after it was delivered."

Jesus Christ. "You counted her underwear?"

"You didn't?"

I held his incredulous stare and gave it back. "How do you know it's a wall safe?"

His eye contact didn't waver. "Picture's skewed. Eighth of an inch. Nothing about you is crooked. There's a wall safe."

I didn't confirm or deny it, but now I wondered if the guys called him Trace behind his back because tracked shit or because he never left a trail. Either way, I wanted him out of my place, stat. "Thanks for getting her stuff."

One of his eyes narrowed in challenge. "You owe me."

I didn't say shit. I wasn't going to commit to owing him a damn thing.

"That's what I thought." He nodded once then his expression went blank. "By the way, you and Luna are overthinking this."

I bit. "How so?"

He reached out and straightened the picture covering my wall safe, then he spun in a circle. "Ever been in a gang?"

He knew who I was. "No."

"Ever been friends with someone who has?"

"No."

He nodded slowly. "Not surprising."

The fucking point? "I don't hide where I come from."

"Me either."

"Where's that?" He'd enlisted after me and deployed after I was already back stateside. I didn't know shit about him except that Luna had recently hired him and he seemed like a loose cannon.

"Here and there." He looked up and made eye contact with me for the second time since I'd known him. "Mostly the streets."

"I'm sorry to hear that."

"I'm not." He fingered the edge of the kitchen island, then rested his hand on his piece. "Sorry, that is."

Fucking great. "I need to get back to what I was doing."

"What or who?"

My jaw ticked. "Watch it."

Unfazed by my warning, he switched subjects. "I'm not sorry about where I came from because it taught me to appreciate certain things."

I didn't respond. This was the most he'd ever spoken to me, and I wasn't sure that Luna hadn't lost his fucking mind hiring him.

"Lots of thing you take for granted until you don't have them anymore," he continued. "Roof over your head, closing your eyes without fear of being stabbed, hot meal, running water, a name you can call out at four fifty-seven a.m."

His back was to the clock in the kitchen. But mine wasn't.

I saw the glowing numbers.

Four fifty-seven.

My arm brushed against my holster and the weight of my own gun. "Your point?"

He took a step backward. "Kids off the street don't join a gang because they got options."

No shit. "Never thought they did."

He ignored my comment. "They join because they don't wanna get stabbed in their sleep or shot for the shit rations their food stamps get them. They pick up a gun and choose a color because it's security." He took another step backward, moving around a table that was behind him and not in his line of vision.

I needed him to get to his point and get the fuck out, but I also wanted to know what he was getting at. "Is that why you joined the Marines? Security?"

"No." He stepped another pace backward. "I joined because the ammo was free."

Fucking psycho. "Great. Why are we overthinking this current situation?"

Reaching behind him, his hand unerringly landed on the doorknob. "That kid who had his ski mask pulled off? Jail isn't security to him. Getting caught's a death sentence. The cops will try to make him roll on his friends, then lock him up when he doesn't. Once he's in lockup, he'll get shanked for the simple fact he chose a color to give him security. He has no choice now. In his eyes, it's kill or be killed."

My jaw ticked. "I'm not going to let anything happen to her." I'd kill any of those Tres Angulos pricks if they came after her.

Looking at me like he was seeing me for the first time, he studied me a moment. "Good. That's good. Keep that thought." He paused. "And remember, the guy she pulled the mask off has something you don't have."

Fucking prick. "What's that?"

"Time." He opened the door. "And lots of it."

"Meaning?"

Trace shrugged. "You can't stay up here forever. He can wait you out."

"Luna will find him." I wasn't staying holed up indefinitely.

"Maybe."

"Not maybe," I argued.

"And that's where you're overthinking this. He'll find her."

"No, he won't," I ground out.

He shrugged again like this wasn't a life-or-death matter.

"Maybe you'll get lucky doing it your way, but hiding her away is less efficient than dangling her as a carrot. Either way, you know where I'll be." He walked out.

I wanted to hate him, but he had a point.

With a sense of dread, I walked back into the bathroom.

CHAPTER FIFTEEN

Genevieve

GRIPPED THE SIDE OF THE TUB WHILE A HERO IN A DRESS SHIRT STOOD next to me and washed the bottom half of my hair. Warm water, large, competent hands, his stoic presence—for once in my life, I felt still.

Until he started talking.

"I was deployed to Afghanistan, Helmand province. Our assignment was to clear a road leading into one of the districts because the local government was boxed in and losing territories to the Taliban. The insurgents had gotten a stronghold, so we were there to clear them out. Second day out in our convoy, a man approached the side of the road dragging his wife."

My heart sped up as dread filled my stomach.

Setting the handheld showerhead down, he grabbed shampoo and squirted some on his hand. "I was in the second vehicle. The first vehicle was forced to stop when the husband shoved his wife in front of it." He lathered the bottom half of my hair, carefully keeping my wound and the top half of my hair dry. "I was in the front passenger seat, and I had a perfect sight line. I could've taken the man out, but he looked panicked and his wife had blood on her clothing around her swollen midsection. They looked desperate." He paused, and I felt his stomach under my hands rise and fall with three breaths before he continued.

"We weren't supposed to get out of the vehicles, but I wanted her to get off the road before she got shot. We weren't authorized to offer medical assistance, and I could've faced a court martial for trying to assist, but she looked pregnant and like she was bleeding. So I opened my door and had one leg out when a concealed bomb that was strapped to her stomach exploded."

Oh my God. "Sawyer, I'm so sorry."

"I took shrapnel in my thigh. Thankfully the front vehicle had armor plating to protect the Marines inside." He rinsed my hair. "I know what staples feel like." He replaced the handheld faucet and helped me back upright before grabbing another towel. "They aren't comfortable." He gently dried my hair.

"Thank you for telling me." I glanced at him.

He tipped his chin, but he didn't look at me.

"I didn't mean that kind of uncomfortable," I confessed.

He tossed the towel on the marble floor. "I know."

"Was anyone else injured?"

His expression turned to stone as he looked me right in the eye. "Besides her husband after he used her as a human bomb?"

I didn't have to ask what happened to the man. I nodded.

"Not that day." He stood. "I'll get you something to sleep in." He walked out of the bathroom and returned a moment later with a T-shirt and a pair of sweatpants, handing them to me. "Change and I'll show you where you can sleep." He walked out again, but this time he closed the door behind him.

Releasing a breath I didn't know I'd been holding on to, I stood and used the towel around me to get my hair a little drier.

Then I made the mistake of looking in the mirror.

"Oh God," I whispered.

Makeup ran down my face, my hair was an absolute mess,

and traces of blood were smeared on my shoulder.

I turned the water on in the sink and bent to wash my face, but when my head went horizontal, a wave of nausea and vertigo hit me so bad, I thought I'd lose it. Grasping the edge of the counter with one hand, I breathed short and shallow through my nose as I frantically wet my face with the other. When I stood back upright, the vertigo eased somewhat, and I took deeper breaths until the nausea passed.

Okay, I could do this.

I wasn't the first person to get a few staples. I didn't need to look like a horror queen reimagined. Picking up the washcloth he'd already soiled, I rinsed it out and put soap on it. Then I washed my face and my shoulder. Rinsing the washcloth, I was wiping one more time when a knock sounded on the door.

"Need anything?"

I slipped his T-shirt over my head. "No, I'm good. Be right out." I stepped into his sweatpants while trying not to bend over again, and rolled them a few times at the waist. Not feeling brave enough to attempt to brush or comb my hair yet, I resigned myself to crappy-looking hair and opened the bathroom door.

My heart caught in my throat.

He'd changed into gym shorts and a T-shirt. I didn't think Sawyer Savatier could get any more handsome, but I was wrong. So very wrong.

"You, ah, look nice." Awkwardly stumbling over my words, I blatantly stared at every one of his ridiculously formed muscles, from his giant biceps to his mouthwatering thighs.

Being the gentleman he was, he didn't comment on my pathetic compliment. "I have a guest room all set up for you."

"Great." Fantastic.

He stared at me a beat. "What's wrong?"

I hadn't known there was a male on the planet who could reduce me to feeling like a needy, dependent child at the same time as making me acutely aware of every curve on my body. But there was, and he was blond and tall and smelled unbelievably good, and he was so out of my league it wasn't even funny.

"Nothing." I exhaled. "I'm just tired."

Studying me a moment longer, he finally nodded once and turned. "This way."

He led me back down the hall and opened a door to a smaller, but equally impressive bedroom facing the ocean.

Reaching for the prescription from the doctor that was already sitting on the nightstand, he opened the bottle, shook out a pill and handed it to me, along with a bottle of water. "Here."

I didn't even question his dominant, bossy routine anymore. I took the pill and drank the water, and suddenly, I was so tired, I couldn't stand another second. "Thanks," I muttered, crawling onto the bed.

He watched me arrange the pillows with a frown on his face that was so severe, I rolled over and gave him my back. When I was under the covers and settled on my side, he turned out the light.

"If you need anything, I'm down the hall."

"I know where your bedroom is. I was just there, remember?" It was a shitty thing to say, but I was feeling extra ornery after the look on his face.

"What's wrong?"

"Nothing."

"Genevieve—"

I cut him off. "Goodnight. Thank you for everything."

Silence.

I counted down from ten, telling myself if I got to one and he was still standing there, I'd apologize.

I got to four.

"Goodnight." His deep voice, smooth and refined, brushed over me like a winter chill.

A moment later the door closed.

I lay there.

And lay there.

But sleep didn't come.

As I curled up in the softest bed I'd ever been in, in a bedroom that was nicer than the nicest hotel I'd ever stayed at, every bad part of the night started replaying on a loop in my head, and I couldn't shut it off.

Throwing the thick comforter off, I padded down the hall. Everything was so quiet, so still, yet there was an energy here I could only equate to him, a man who moved in his own orbit. And now I was moving in that same orbit, walking past the kitchen and stopping in front of the wall of windows.

I looked out at the beginning shades of the sunrise.

Staring at the ocean, I couldn't remember the last time I'd seen a sunrise... Or the last time a man had washed my hair, or given me his clothes to sleep in, or handed me medicine and a bottle of water.

I couldn't remember because none of it had ever happened.

The first rays of a promise of a new day broke past the ocean's border and a kaleidoscope of orange, yellow, red and pink burst from the horizon.

I didn't realize I'd dropped to the floor and pulled my legs up, hugging them to my chest.

I didn't know I was falling apart as the sky exploded with beauty.

Tears dripped down my cheeks as two large, bare feet appeared a second before a billionaire bodyguard sat down next to me.

"It's beautiful," I whisper-cried.

His arms resting on his knees, his head turned toward me, he stared into my eyes like he knew every fear and regret that was eating me alive.

I wanted to lean into him. I wanted to run away. I wanted his arms around me, and I wanted to forget I'd ever laid eyes on him.

But when he spoke...

"You're beautiful."

I wanted my heart back.

CHAPTER SIXTEEN

Sawyer

T HE SUNRISE LIT UP HER HAIR AND FACE. LOOKING LOST AND vulnerable, she all at once crushed me and took my breath away.

It was the only excuse I had for dropping my guard and telling her she was beautiful.

But I couldn't let it go any further.

Forcing myself to look away from her tears and the raw need in her eyes, I stared at the ocean. "Are you in pain?"

"No."

"Why are you sitting on the floor?" I'd never sat on the floor in the penthouse just to sit. Push-ups, sit-ups—yes. Sitting like this? No.

"I was trying to feel grounded."

Her voice, quiet and sad, made me glance back at her.

She turned away. "Your compliment just ruined that."

I wouldn't apologize. "I'm not going to lie to you."

"Aren't you?" she accused, bringing her gorgeous eyes back to me. "I'm here. Isn't that lie enough?"

"How is protecting you a lie?"

She turned back to the sunrise again. "I don't belong here."

"You're right." I kept my word. I didn't lie to her.

Her gaze snapped to mine.

"But not for the reasons you think," I explained.

"And what reasons do you think I'm thinking?" she challenged.

"I know you grew up in the foster system, and I'm a Savatier. That makes you uncomfortable." I'd seen her expression when she first walked into my penthouse.

She let out a half laugh, half snort. "Don't mince words, say what you mean, why don't you?"

"You don't belong here because you're married." I waited a beat, but she didn't comment or look at me. I laid out the rest of it. "And what I'm feeling, I shouldn't be feeling for a married woman. It has nothing to do with where you came from." I didn't give a shit what her last name was or that she grew up without privilege. I'd watched my father cheat on my mother every chance he got over the years, and I'd sworn to myself I would never end up like him.

She didn't say a word.

Tired, guilt-ridden, frustrated, I stood. "Get some sleep, Genevieve." God knew the painkiller I gave her should've knocked her out by now. I turned toward my bedroom.

Her voice, small and vulnerable, hit me square in my chest. "I can't sleep." She sucked in a sharp breath. "Every time I close my eyes, I see them, their guns...." She trailed off.

I told myself not to.

I told myself to walk away.

But I hadn't made one smart decision since I'd poured her a whiskey.

I walked back and scooped her up. Folded like a child, her knees fell over my arm and her hands entwined around my neck. I took the first full breath since I'd stepped into my penthouse. Carrying her to my bedroom, laying her on my bed, I told myself this didn't make me a shit person like my father.

When I crawled in behind her, gently slid my arm under her head and brought her back to my chest, I told myself it was for her comfort.

When she let out a long breath, I justified my actions as the right decision.

"Go to sleep, Genevieve." It took everything I had not to touch my lips to her skin. "I'm not going to let anything happen to you." Including myself.

"You already did," she whispered.

She was right, and I knew it, but it still cut like a knife. "I'm sorry."

"The carjacking wasn't your fault," she said, even quieter.

The entire night was my fault. "Close your eyes," I ordered, putting just enough force into my tone.

"Okay," she breathed, submitting to my command.

Ignoring the desire pounding through my veins, I catalogued the feel of my arm around her waist, the swell of her hips covered in my bedding, and the rise and fall of her breathing as I watched the clock on the nightstand.

Then I allowed myself five minutes just to feel.

She was beyond anything I'd ever expected. She smelled like hospital, antiseptic and my T-shirt, but she also smelled like woman. Not cloying perfume, but purity. Sunrises, red hair, green eyes, ivory skin, she smelled like she belonged to someone else, and nothing I'd ever wanted. She smelled like everything a Savatier wasn't, and I wanted to sink inside her.

But she'd lied to me.

My five minutes up, I forced myself to close my eyes.

As if she knew the exact moment I did, she whispered into the dark, "Goodnight, Sawyer."

I inhaled everything that was her. "Goodnight, Genevieve."

CHAPTER SEVENTEEN

Genevieve

MY MUSCLES STIFF, MY BODY SORE, MY SKIN TOO HOT, I OPENED MY eyes.

Groggy, as if a haze had descended over me, I fought to focus my eyes, but when I did...

Holy shit.

My head on his shoulder, my arm across his six... oh God, *eight*-pack, and my leg embarrassingly thrown across his thigh. Late afternoon light filtered in from where the curtains didn't meet all the way and highlighted every hard angle and ripped muscle on his body.

"I'm sorry," I squeaked, jerking back.

"Don't be." His arm under me, his hand around my waist, he tightened his grip. "Stay."

Oh God, oh God, oh God.

I tried not to look, I did, but I couldn't help myself. His impossibly long, impossibly huge hard length, barely concealed in his workout shorts, rested mere inches from my leg over his thigh.

One hand under his head, his biceps bulging out of his T-shirt, his eyes closed, a five o'clock shadow dusting his face— he wasn't handsome. He was a god. A gorgeous, blond-haired, blue-eyed, so out of my league god.

His hand coasted over my hip. "How did you sleep?"

Like the dead. "Good."

He opened his eyes and looked at me. "Your head?"

Not pounding nearly as much as my heart. "It's okay."

His stare as intense as it always was, but somehow differ-ent, he rolled to face me. Lifting his free hand, he brushed my hair off my shoulder, then ghosted a finger across the back of my neck. "May I?"

May he what? Touch me? My neck? My staples? My hair? My body? I didn't know. I didn't care. I bit my lip and nodded.

"Roll over," he commanded, using a tone that made my insides liquefy and my mind go blank.

Closing my eyes, not knowing if I was more afraid or turned on, I did exactly as he told me.

His gentle touch swept across my back as he pushed my hair out of the way. Then a single finger barely coasted over where my skin felt pinched. "How bad does it hurt?"

Not nearly as bad as the ache between my legs or the crush-ing feeling in my chest. "I'm okay."

"That's not what I asked."

"It doesn't feel good," I admitted.

He let out an exhale. "After I feed you, I'll give you another pain pill."

I didn't want another pain pill. They made me feel sad and out of sorts and groggy in a way that didn't make me feel safe— not while I was around him. Because despite what my traitor-ous body was saying, that I needed to climb on top of him and force myself on him until he kissed me senseless, he was right about one very important fact—I was still married, and Sawyer Savatier was better than that. He didn't deserve a woman too pathetic to cut ties with an almost ex-husband who'd never wanted her. He didn't deserve a woman who couldn't make it on her own, emotionally or financially.

Sawyer Savatier wasn't only the heir to a multibillion-dollar real estate empire, he was a war hero. He deserved more than someone like me.

Regretfully, I moved away from his touch. "It's okay. I don't need one."

As if knowing my emotions were spiraling, his hand landed on my arm. "What's wrong?"

I didn't look at him. I couldn't and still say what I had to say. "I need to go. If I can't go home, I'll find an out-of-the-way hotel." And hide. Forever.

His thumb that had been caressing my arm stilled. "Why?"

"You were right," I admitted. "I shouldn't be here."

He dropped his hand and his voice turned instantly formal. "My apologies."

Regret swelled, and I fought stupid tears of frustration. "Don't. Don't be nice to me, not like that." I swung my legs over the edge of the softest bed I'd ever slept on and stood. Vertigo hit, and I squeezed my eyes shut. "I don't need your guilt or your sympathy." My hand waved pathetically around his bedroom. "This... this is all you. Not me." I sucked in a breath. "And that's okay. I don't expect anything from you."

"Genevieve." He dropped his voice to the one he'd used last night. "Turn around and look at me."

Don't do it, I told myself. Just walk away. One foot in front of the other. Spare bedroom. Get your stuff, get dressed, and walk out. He couldn't force me to stay here. That's all I had to do. Walk out.

"*Genevieve.*" Lower, darker, he said my name like a warning.

And this time, I couldn't ignore it.

I turned.

And then I saw it.

Blood. Smeared and dried, on his pillow, some on his sheets, all of it staining his perfectly perfect snowy-white bedding.

"Oh God," I choked out, my hand going to my mouth before frantically reaching for the pillow and sheet. "I'll wash these. I'm so sorry. I didn't know I still had blood on my neck, or that my cut was still bleeding. I never would've laid down on your pillows if I did. I didn't mean for it to get all over. *Oh God.*" I grasped the pillow.

Sitting on the edge of the bed, he moved. Quick, sure, his hand shot out and he gripped my wrist and pulled.

Gasping, I stumbled.

But I didn't fall.

Because his movements, unlike mine, were perfectly coordinated.

Pulling me onto his lap, bringing my hand around his neck, he cupped my face. His nostrils flared, and the control he so diligently held on to crashed around us. "Stop," he bit out angrily. "I don't give a shit about the sheets, you hear me?" He stared into my eyes. *"They're just sheets."*

I kissed him.

Awkward and fumbling, I pressed my lips to his and did what I'd wanted to do since I'd first laid eyes on him.

But that's as far as I got.

The second my lips touched his, he took over.

Except he didn't kiss me.

Holding my face, angling me into his touch, he took my mouth, slid his tongue in, and he claimed me.

Oh God, *he claimed me.*

A growl ripped from his chest and vibrated his throat.

Then he surged like he'd been starving and I was his last

meal. Gentle, dominant, hot, forceful, he swept through my mouth and explored every inch like he was kissing me to remember me. Like he was kissing me because he couldn't get enough of me. Like he was kissing me as if he'd been waiting his whole life for me. Everything that had been missing in every kiss I'd ever had, I felt in his.

Sawyer Savatier didn't just kiss me.

He ruined me.

Gripping my face, dominantly holding me where he wanted me, he pulled back only to stroke once more through my mouth, tasting me like I wanted him to taste me everywhere.

My hand settled in his short, soft hair, and I leaned into him, needing more. I wanted every touch, every stroke, every thrust and every grind that his kiss promised.

But I didn't get it.

I didn't get any of it.

His hand on my face slid to my jaw, and he pushed me off his mouth until his hard eyes met mine.

My heart dropped.

Gone was the man who'd brought me to bed last night.

Back in his place was the man who caught my tablet from falling out of my arms and told me to take up drinking.

Unwavering and unforgiving, his stare cut into me. "That's only going to happen once, understand?"

Rejection and shame crawled up my neck and exploded across my cheeks. "I'm sorry," I whispered, mortified and fighting tears.

"You're staying here where I can protect you. You're not going to a hotel, and you're not going home, and you will *continue* to stay here until we find out who was behind the carjacking. You will rest, you will stay safe, and you will concentrate on healing. That's it. Questions?"

Sucking my swollen lower lip into my mouth, his taste on my tongue, I shook my head.

Grasping me by the waist and setting me on my feet, he stood. Then he took my chin and angled my face up to his. "Do not apologize to me again. Understood?"

My heart thumped against my ribs in complete denial that his touch was anything but alpha, but I nodded.

"Words," he demanded.

"I will not apologize to you again," I recited like a lost schoolgirl.

"You're staying here," he reiterated.

I didn't say anything. I couldn't. Despite wanting to run away from him and my own embarrassment, I was trapped. I didn't have any close girl friends I could crash with, and I wasn't about to show up at Brian and his new girlfriend's doorstep. And as much as I wanted to leave, he was right. A hotel wouldn't be as secure as his palace in the sky, and going home while some gang member had my purse and wallet and address was probably not a good plan for longevity.

"Words," he repeated, gripping my chin tighter.

"I'm staying here," I whispered, giving in, hoping for the softer Sawyer to come back.

But he didn't. The cold Sawyer nodded once and dropped his hand. "Go shower. I'll make dinner."

CHAPTER EIGHTEEN

Sawyer

TURNED ON THE OVEN, THEN YANKED SHIT OUT OF THE FRIDGE AS I called Luna.

He answered on the first ring. "Still no updates. We haven't found the SUV, the serial number on the gun you gave me was scrubbed, and none of my contacts know anything."

Shit. "Did you try her cell phone?"

"Yeah, nada. Goes straight to voice mail, and I can't track it."

Damn it. "We still don't know how they disabled the tracking on the Escalade?" I threw two potatoes in the oven.

"Anyone with half a brain can disable the system that comes with the vehicle, but my secondary system? I still don't know how they managed it. They would've had to look hard for it. So they either destroyed the vehicle, or maybe…." Luna trailed off.

André Luna never trailed off. "Or maybe what?"

"They're using a signal jammer."

"Those are illegal."

"I know. Which doesn't make me happy thinking someone has one and is using it. That makes my job a hell of a lot harder."

Maybe that was the point. "The Escalade could've been the target. What better way to test out a signal jammer than to try it on one of your company vehicles?" The gangs all knew who Luna was. Hell, he'd grown up with half of the members. They usually steered clear of us, as we did them, but they all knew our vehicles.

I heard him pound away on his computer keys. "GPS is still offline. Same with her cell phone. So yeah, those fuckers could be messing with me."

"What's the range on one of those things?"

"Depends on the signal strength."

"Create a larger perimeter around the last known location in northwest Miami and let's do another search." They had to return to their home turf eventually.

"We already did that twice. I did a third run myself. At this point, even if we did find the vehicle, do you know how many gang members are in that area? Toss a coin, you'll hit a hundred of them."

"I don't need a hundred. I just need one."

Luna scoffed. "You think the threat will stop if you take out the one pendejo whose mask she ripped off?"

He was starting to sound like Preston, and I didn't like it. "It'll be a start."

"And then what? We both know how this goes."

"She didn't witness a murder."

"You think in their eyes that matters?"

So I take out all fucking four of them. "I'll handle it," I ground out.

"No," Luna clipped. "You won't. I will."

My nostrils flared with an inhale. "I'm not letting this drag on."

"What are you gonna do, Savatier?" he asked, purposely using my last name. "Go on a killing spree?"

"If I have to."

Luna sighed. And when he spoke again, his tone wasn't the tone of my boss. "All right, look. We had this conversation when I hired you. We both know what comes with your last name. I'm fucking lucky, hell, I'm *honored* to have you at my six, but we agreed. If the day ever came where the tables were reversed and I needed to protect your interests, there wasn't gonna be any question. I make the hard decisions. You have more to protect. We both know no matter how much you dislike your padre, one day it's gonna be your name behind that empire. As much as you think you want to play bodyguard forever and walk away from that, as your friend and your brother, I'm not gonna let that happen. And I'm sure as hell not gonna let some gangbangers destroy a good man's name. You hear me?"

My back teeth ground. "I'm not going to run his company." My sister could have it.

"If you think he's gonna leave it all to your sister, you're dead wrong, amigo."

I didn't give a shit what my father did. "Are you done?"

"No." He took a deep breath and let it out slow. "I'm making you a promise that I'll handle this. You're not getting your hands dirty. Period. That said, in the bigger scheme of things, I've got thirty-seven active jobs running right now. I'm on this, I want my vehicle back too, and I want those pendejos to know they can't fuck with me. I will make an example out of who did this, but I'm doing it my way. Hang tight. Take care of the chica. I got it on this end."

"How long?"

Luna chuckled. "You're on paid leave with a beautiful lady, amigo. Fucking *relax*."

"I'm not on paid leave." I wasn't taking his money for doing nothing.

"Yes, you are. Medical leave. I saw the size of the welt on the back of your neck. Can't feel good."

"I'm not injured. I'm fine," I ground out.

"Glad to hear it, but enjoy your time off anyway. And FYI, Ty is outside while Preston handles something for me tonight."

"Preston is a loose cannon. You shouldn't have hired him."

"I do a lot of things I shouldn't."

"What's his deal? I don't want him around Genevieve."

"He has a particular skill set I need."

"Which is what? Besides cataloguing shit like a professional criminal?"

Luna hesitated, then evaded. "He served with Ty. Ty vouches for him."

I was pissed off enough not to filter my response. "Ty's trigger happy with zero loyalty."

Luna chuckled. "He's loyal to his bank account, and that I can trust."

"Ever wonder what he needs money for?" I was being a dick. Luna vetted all his employees.

"Every one of my men needs money except you. That's why they work, amigo."

"Fine. Point taken."

Luna exhaled. "All right, bro, listen. I know you're used to being in the driver's seat, it's why I hired you. But trust me, I got your back. Take the time, stop with the fucking guilt, and take care of the chica. I'll be in touch."

"Copy."

"Later." He hung up.

I tossed my phone on the counter.

"You're injured?"

I spun to see the look of alarm spread across her features. "No." Goddamn it, how long had she been standing there?

Her eyebrows drew together. "Did you get hurt bad last night?"

Her hair wet, still wearing my clothes, she was beautiful. And married, I reminded myself.

"I said I'm fine." I turned back to the stove and put the heat on under the grill section.

"Who were you talking to?"

"Luna."

"Did he find the SUV?"

I hated the hope in her voice. "No."

"Oh." She blew out a breath.

"He will." He better.

"And my purse?"

"I don't know." I opened the fridge and scoured the fruit drawer. I grabbed two lemons.

"Oh shoot, I need to cancel my credit card and bank card. I can't believe I didn't do that last night."

"You had a lot on your plate." I picked up my phone and slid it across the counter toward her. "Call them now."

She took my phone and looked at it for a moment. "Are these your friends from the Marines?"

I'd forgotten about the picture on my lock screen. "Yes." They were more than my friends. They were my brothers.

She walked over to me, holding the phone out. "Who are they?"

I looked at the picture, and my chest tightened like it always did. "Left to right, André Luna, Jared Brandt, Alex Vega, me, Matt Folsom, Reggie Parker and the guy looking over his shoulder is Talon Talerco."

A shy smile touched her lips. "He looks like he's laughing."

"He usually is."

She pointed at Luna. "And that's who you work for?"

"Yes."

She smiled shyly again. "Tell me about the others."

Her innocence was disarming, and I was about to crush it. "Folsom and Parker didn't make it home. Brandt was medically discharged, and him, Vega and Talerco live in Florida."

"Oh." Sorrow etched across her face. "I'm so sorry for your loss."

I was sorry Parker left behind a wife and a newborn, and Folsom an aging parent who needed him. I tipped my chin at the phone. "Make your calls."

She took my phone and started toward the living room, but then paused. "You, um, have a text." She handed my phone back.

Savina: *Where the hell are you? I've been texting you for days.*

I fired off a response to my sister.

Me: *Working*

She replied almost instantly.

Savina: *That's such bullshit. You have the time to call me back.*

I didn't respond, but she texted again before I could hand my phone back to Genevieve.

Savina: *I have papers for you to sign. Don't make me come over there.*

She always had shit for me to sign. Since I was on the board of my father's company, she needed my signature every time they made legal changes, but I was over it. I didn't need the money. The quarterly payments I'd been receiving for over a decade that were sitting in a bank account I hadn't touched yet would more than carry me if I never worked again. I didn't give a shit about my father's company and I'd never wanted anything to do with it. Savina knew this.

I texted her back.

Me: *Simple solution. Take me off the board.*

Savina: *Don't be an ass. Come sign the shit and take me to lunch.*

I wasn't going to lunch with her. She was a mini version of my father. She'd harangue me for an hour about my life choices before telling me to grow up. Then she'd remind me I had an office at Savatier headquarters waiting for my ass to sit down behind a desk and rot for the next forty years.

That was never going to happening.

I texted her back.

Me: *Not happening. Courier the papers. I'm tied up for the next couple of weeks.*

"Everything okay?" Genevieve asked.

Savina: *You're a pain in the ass. I'll wait two weeks, but only because you're my brother. We'll have lunch and you can sign the paperwork then. Call Mom, she misses you.*

"Yeah, just my sister," I answered Genevieve as I fired off one more text to Savina.

Me: *No on lunch. Courier the papers. Mom knows my number.*

My sister being the person she was, didn't take the hint.

Savina: *See you in two weeks.*

I deleted the texts and handed my phone to Genevieve. "Make your calls. You can ignore any more texts that come in."

She looked at me for a beat. "Are you okay?"

I frowned. "I'm fine."

"Oh, I'm sorry. You were frowning, and I just thought...." She trailed off.

It hit me like a freight train. No woman had ever asked me

if I was okay. Not even my own mother. But this woman, who had no family of her own, who had staples in her head and a gang after her, was standing in my kitchen asking if *I* was okay.

My head spun, shit hit my chest, and I had to stop myself from reaching for her.

"My sister's agenda is not mine," I admitted.

Her head dipped as she studied the floor. "Oh."

I realized my mistake too late. "I'm not ungrateful I have a sister, we're just two very different people." If we weren't related, we'd never be friends. "Everything's fine. Make your calls."

"Okay." She made her way into the living room.

I cut a lemon, squeezed it into a glass, fished out a couple seeds, then added honey because I didn't have any sugar. Some water and ice later, I stirred it and left it on the island.

I was grilling peppers when she came back.

"Well, I got lucky." She set my phone on the counter. "No charges appeared on the bank card, and the credit card only had one charge at a gas station but the credit card company reversed the charges."

I glanced at her. "What gas station?"

"They said it was some station downtown on Third Street." Her eyes went wide. "Oh! Do you think that will help find them?"

"Not sure." I picked up my phone and texted Luna the information. "Luna will follow it up." I tipped my chin at the glass. "That's for you. Dinner will be ready shortly." I went back to grilling.

She didn't say anything.

I turned the peppers, then glanced at her.

She was staring at the lemonade.

"What's wrong?"

She didn't look up. "There's a cut lemon on the counter."

I didn't deny it.

She looked up at me with innocence and trust. "You made me lemonade."

She'd said it was her favorite. "Let me know if it's sweet enough."

"It's perfect," she whispered, her eyes welling.

CHAPTER NINETEEN

Genevieve

H E MADE ME LEMONADE.

Honey and a cut lemon on the counter, the evidence was right there.

He made my favorite drink. *From scratch.*

Except he'd pushed me away and said we'd never kiss again, but when my lips had touched his, he'd *groaned.* I know he did. I'd heard it all the way to my soul. But now that kiss was dead and I was sitting here staring at homemade lemonade.

I was so confused and so out of my element, my eyes welled with emotions I didn't know what to do with.

As if he were my saving grace, I looked up at him.

Just like when he was texting his sister, he frowned. "It's just lemonade."

It wasn't *just* anything. "Okay." It was kindness and thoughtfulness, and no one had ever done anything like that for me.

"Drink," he commanded, using the same tone of voice he'd used when he'd put the whiskey in front of me.

And just like then, I took a sip.

Tart, perfect amount of sweetness, and ice cold—I wanted to sob in my lemonade. How come I couldn't have met someone like him before I'd foolishly married Brian? Who was I kidding? What did I have to offer someone like him? Clumsiness that made me pull a ski mask off a gang member who was robbing us?

His frown deepened. "Not sweet enough?"

"Why am I really here?" That was a better question.

He turned back to his fancy stovetop that had a grill in the middle of six burners, and he flipped the red peppers he was cooking. "You shouldn't be alone when you have a grade two concussion."

"That's what I thought." Miserable, I pushed the lemonade away as a knock sounded on the door.

Sawyer set the tongs down and issued a command I wasn't even sure he was conscious of saying, he was so accustomed to protecting people. "Wait here."

I watched the muscles in his thighs carry him toward his front entry as his wide shoulders stretched the fabric of his T-shirt.

He opened the door. "Hey."

A man said something in Spanish I couldn't decipher.

"Yeah," Sawyer answered him in English. "We're in the kitchen."

Sawyer came back, followed by a dark-haired, dark-eyed man who was a couple inches shorter than Sawyer, but every bit as muscular. But unlike Sawyer, a smile spread across his face when he saw me.

"Miss Jenkins, at last we meet." The man held his hand out. "André Luna."

I scooted off the stool and shook his hand. "Mr. Luna, I'm so sorry about your Escalade."

He brushed it off. "Cars are replaceable, chica. People are not. No worries. I'm just glad you're okay. And call me André." He nodded at the stool I'd just vacated. "Have a seat."

I sat back down.

Sawyer went to the stove. "You hungry?"

"No, gracias." Luna sat next to me and set a tablet and the latest model of a new cell phone down, pushing them toward me. "Your number's programmed into the phone for you, chica, but I'm afraid you're on your own as far as contacts. Do you have a backup anywhere? I can program it in for you if you do."

I stared. "Those are for me?"

André tipped his chin in a movement that wasn't unlike Sawyer—quick and precise. "Yes, to replace the ones you lost. If you have a backup for your files for your tablet, I can update that too."

I looked between him and Sawyer, but Sawyer still had his back to me. "I, um, *thank you*." Sawyer must have put André up to this. As someone who owned her own business, I knew this wasn't just an incredibly nice gesture, it was time and effort that took away from what I was sure was André's very busy day. "I can update them." I could figure it out.

He picked up the cell phone. "This is a slightly newer version of your old phone. It has face recognition. You'll have to set it up." He swept his finger across the screen a few times and handed me the phone. "Just follow the prompts."

I took the phone. "How did you know what model cell phone I had?"

He chuckled. "I know lots of things, chica." He winked. "Set up the face ID."

Wow. He was devastatingly handsome. He wasn't Sawyer, but his smile alone I was sure stopped women in their tracks. Looking away from him, I did as he said. When I was done, I set the phone down.

André's expression turned deadly serious. "You willing to talk about last night?"

My stomach knotted. "Okay, but I don't remember

much," I lied.

"Can you tell me anything about the carjacker that you remember? Any identifying marks, description, anything?"

"It was dark," I said too quickly, adding, "and it happened really fast." I glanced at Sawyer, who'd turned to face us. "Maybe Sawyer remembers what the man looks like?"

Sawyer shook his head. "I didn't see his face. He was already heading for the SUV. All I saw was his back after his mask came off."

"And the tattoo on his wrist," André added, before looking back at me. "The men who took the SUV are part of the Tres Angulos gang, and unfortunately, they now have your personal information. As I'm sure Sawyer explained to you, it's in your best interest to lie low until we find the guys behind this. In the meantime, you'll be safe here." He stood to leave. "We have a man out front, and you're in good hands with Sawyer. I'll be in touch when we know more."

"How long will it take?" I blurted. "I mean, how long before you think you'll find them? Or my purse?" Or before I could go home?

"Unfortunately, chica, I would count your belongings as a loss. If we're lucky, we could wrap this up in a few hours. If not?" He shrugged one shoulder. "Hard to say, but we're working on it. We don't want this to drag out any more than you do. We know you have a life to get back to." He glanced at Sawyer and said something in Spanish.

Sawyer nodded once.

"I'll see myself out. Enjoy your evening." With a smile that was more natural than practiced, André left.

But his words replayed in my head like a cruel joke.

We know you have a life to get back to.

CHAPTER TWENTY

Sawyer

S HE PUSHED BITES OF CUT MEAT AROUND ON HER PLATE.

"You don't like steak?"

"No, I love it." She'd barely touched her food.

"Then what's wrong?"

She glanced toward the entryway. "When did my suitcase arrive?"

"Early this morning."

"Mm-hmm." She nodded. "Before or after you gave me your clothes?"

"Before," I answered truthfully.

"Then why did you give me your clothes to wear?"

Because I couldn't fuck her, but I wanted my mark on her anyway. "Mine were closer."

"It is a big apartment," she mused.

Penthouse, I silently corrected. "Eat some more."

She stabbed a bite of meat and slowly chewed before swallowing. "Why are you a bodyguard?"

"I don't want to work in an office." It was mostly the truth.

"Doesn't it upset your family?"

Like she wouldn't believe. My father most of all, which was why I did it. "They would prefer I did something else." My father had even tried to bribe me into coming to work for him by giving me the penthouse and the Range Rover when I didn't reenlist with the Marines.

"Who's they?"

"Pardon?"

"Your family?" she asked. "I mean, besides your sister."

"Just my parents and my sister." Which I was acutely aware was more than she'd ever had.

"How old is your sister?"

"Thirty-three. She's two years older than me. She runs the day-to-day operations of my father's company."

"Wow. She must be… good at what she does."

She was ruthless. "My father's been grooming her since she was a teen." Since the day I'd caught him cheating on my mother and told him he was dead to me, he'd flipped his attention to her like the callous tyrant he was.

"Mm." Genevieve took another bite of steak.

I changed the subject. "How did you wind up in foster care?"

"Teenage mother. She tried to raise me. Kept me until I was six, then she couldn't make ends meet anymore." She shrugged like it was no big deal, but her hand tightened around her fork.

"I'm sorry."

She shrugged again.

"Do you remember her?" As much as I hated my father, I couldn't imagine not having a mother. I didn't talk to her often. I steered clear of most interactions with my family because my father turned everything into a clusterfuck anytime I showed up at the house or called my mother. So I avoided it altogether, but I did check in with my mother once a week with a text.

"I remember her red hair." Unconsciously, Genevieve pushed a red pepper around on her plate.

"Did she ever try to contact you, or vice versa?" I couldn't imagine what she'd been through.

"Nope." She got up and cleared her plate. "Should I load my plate in the dishwasher, or do you have a maid?"

I stood and cleared my plate, purposely brushing past her as I opened the dishwasher. "I don't have a maid, and I neither earned nor paid for this penthouse."

She stiffened. "This isn't your place?"

"It's mine." I rinsed my plate and put it in the dishwasher.

"But you didn't buy it?"

I took her plate from her. "No, my father did and gifted it to me."

"Is that why you hate him? Because he gave you a condo?"

"I never said I hated him." For my mother's sake, I didn't speak ill of him out loud.

"You said you weren't anything like him."

"I'm not." I tossed the few utensils I used to cook dinner with in the dishwasher.

She watched me a moment. "So, he doesn't want you to go into the family business?"

"He does." I couldn't remember the last time a woman had asked me questions about myself, let alone grilled me.

"But you aren't going to?"

"Not if I can help it. My sister has it handled." I shut the dishwasher. "My turn. Why haven't you signed your divorce papers?"

Her face turned bright red. "Brian told you that?"

Leaning against the counter, I crossed my arms. "Yes."

Her head dipped, and she folded her arms across herself as if for protection. "He shouldn't have told you that."

"Why?" I demanded.

She looked up at me defiantly. "Because it's none of your business."

"Isn't it?" I played hardball. "You kissed me. I don't get to know why a married woman lies to me then gives me something only her husband should have?"

Anger, fast and hot, spread across her features. "He's not my—"

"Watch it," I warned.

Her arms dropped to her sides, and her hands fisted. "Watch *what?*"

"What you say to me next." I leaned toward her. "Do not lie to me again."

"I did not—" She stopped herself.

Then she stepped around me, went for her suitcase and yanked on the handle. The flowered bag fell over.

Jesus. "Need help?"

She growled, but she didn't say shit. Jerking her bag upright, she dragged it down the hall as one broken wheel shimmied it back and forth behind her.

A second later, the door to the guest room slammed shut.

I started the dishwasher and strode to my bedroom. Throwing on a long-sleeved moisture-wicking shirt and sneakers, I grabbed a baseball cap and walked back to the guest room. Feeling generous, I knocked.

"Go away," she said through the door.

"Open up."

"No."

"Now," I ordered.

Five seconds later, she yanked the handle to open the door an inch.

I pushed it open. "I'm going to the gym. It's downstairs in

the building. Don't open the front door for anyone."

Her back to me, staring out at the ocean, she didn't reply.

"Genevieve." Goddamn it. I wasn't going to apologize for asking the question earlier. "Turn around."

She spun and let loose. "I don't have to do what you say just because you say it."

I studied her a moment. Anger flaring, her hair tangled, her suitcase on its side in the middle of the floor, she was a mess. But I'd meant what I'd said to her last night. She was beautiful. Beautiful in a way that was raw and broken, but she wasn't defeated. Far from it.

"Do we need to talk about it?"

"Talk about what?" she snapped.

"The kiss." Or the way her body melted every time I put the slightest bit of dominance in my tone. Or why she hadn't fucking divorced that prick from the hospital.

She spun back around. "Go to the gym, Sawyer."

I walked out, and my cell vibrated with a new text.

Sullivan: *Stop putting off your sister. Get your priorities straight and sign the quarterly paperwork.*

I deleted the text from my father and went to the gym.

CHAPTER TWENTY-ONE

Genevieve

THE STAPLES ITCHED UNBEARABLY. I REACHED UP TO SCRATCH THEM, but his hand shot out, grasping me around the wrist.

Instant awareness raced through my body, making my nerves sing like a full-blown orchestral crescendo.

"Leave it," he practically barked.

I fought for patience. I was the one who was injured and who had to cancel all my appointments for the week while he went to work out every day, and he was the one with a crappy attitude? Five days of complete and total crappy attitude, mind you, even while he was cooking dinner, something he claimed he enjoyed doing. *Whatever.* "You know, you volunteered."

"What?" he snapped absently, putting a cup of tea down in front of me on the coffee table. The kind of tea I casually said I'd liked on day two that had shown up later that evening in a grocery delivery by a really scary-looking guy wearing a Luna and Associates uniform.

I sucked in a breath and told myself this was just like dealing with any of the ornery clients I'd dealt with over the years. But it wasn't. He was nothing like anyone I'd ever met. He was completely self-contained. He didn't initiate conversation. He didn't even talk, not unless I asked a question, and then he would state a one- or two-word answer like he was put out by having to speak to me.

Fine.

He could be cranky all he wanted.

But I didn't have to listen to it anymore. I was tired of watching him don a stupidly sexy baseball cap and go work out for two hours every day, then come back all sweaty and ripped muscles with no better of an attitude. I was tired of his perfect gourmet dinners he cooked every night like he was some five-star chef on a day off from his restaurant's kitchen. I was tired of his perfect-smelling self after his showers and his stupid silence as he spent hours on his laptop not talking to me, let alone looking at me. I was tired of his curt daily good mornings and good nights.

I was tired of all of it.

I stood. "I'm going home. Thanks for your... hospitality." I blew out a breath, glancing around at everything that was so perfectly put in its place that not even a pillow dared to topple over. I couldn't say I'd miss it—not a single perfectly placed glass or plate or picture or made bed.

I wouldn't miss any of it.

But I was going to inexplicably miss him. And his scent. And his stupid staring contests that I always lost. Speaking of which....

He studied my face. "What's wrong?"

What was right?

I didn't answer. I stepped around the coffee table. Carefully. Because I didn't need any more staples.

My eyes on my feet, it was too late to move out of his trajectory when I saw his boots come into view.

Craning my neck, I forced myself to look up at his too handsome face. Then I lost my battle to keep my mouth shut. "You know, you would be more handsome if you smiled once in a while. I'm not saying you're *not* handsome. I'm just saying, well, a smile, it goes a long way, and you could use one. A good one like this." I smiled like a crazy person.

He stared.

Dropping the pretense, I swallowed past the sudden dryness in my throat and soldiered on. "Fine, whatever, but just so you know, smiles tell someone you don't resent them. Or that you care, or that everything is okay, or that you made them smile, or a whole host of other things, all of them good. So yeah, smiles. They're great, but forget I mentioned it." I shook my head. "Anyway. I'll get out of your hair." I moved one step to the side.

"Turn around."

Quiet, commanding, and not at all like he usually spoke to me, his voice barely touched the silence in his penthouse palace, but it cut through the air like nothing I'd ever experienced. Carving a block of submission around me as if I were made of nothing more than air and need, his command swirled through my head, then touched every inch of my body.

I didn't understand it. I wasn't sure I wanted to. All I knew was that for my own sanity, I couldn't trust it. But that didn't stop me from looking up into his stark gaze and asking the simplest of questions. "Why?"

"Turn around, Genevieve," he directed, his voice suddenly smooth and effortless.

Curious, nervous, scared, flushed—I never had a choice.

I turned.

His huge hand brushed across my back, sweeping my hair to the side, and his finger gently touched my staples. "I can have these removed for you."

"The doctor said five to seven days. It's only been five."

"The sutures closed the wound, and it's healed enough. If you're careful, it'll be fine. Taking them out will also make the wound site itch less."

I didn't care about the stupid staples anymore. "Why did you offer to have me here if you didn't want me around?"

His hand stilled. "I never said I didn't want you here."

"No, you just act like it, in your mannerisms, your tone. I get it, I'm not an easy person to be around. I don't even like my own company sometimes. I know I'm…. I know I talk a lot." I'd talked at him for what had seemed like a month.

His hand dropped, and then he did what he'd been doing all along. He didn't respond.

I couldn't even be disappointed anymore, or hurt. I'd had days of this kind of behavior, and frankly, it wasn't like I ever experienced anything different from Brian. Half the time he'd acted like I was a child.

"Whatever." I stepped away from him. "You don't have to answer that. In fact, don't answer it." I didn't want to hear how I was a charity case or he was appeasing his guilt. I didn't need a man to validate me or my existence. I made my own living, and I was pretty damn good at what I did.

"Are you still in love with him? Is that why you didn't sign the divorce papers?"

Caught off guard, I froze. For five days we hadn't mentioned the kiss, my impending divorce, or his family. "I don't see how that's any of your business." He would never understand.

"Turn around," he demanded.

I spun. "I'm not a dog. You don't get to constantly bark out orders at me. Sit down, turn around, drink this, eat this, do that, do this—when is it ever good enough for you?" I laid every ounce of frustration and transference on him.

He didn't so much as blink. "He's moved on."

Angry, hurt tears instantly welled, and I threw my arms up. "No kidding!"

"Then why hang on to someone who doesn't want to be married to you?"

I lost it. "It's none of your business!" I yelled, spinning around and storming off toward his spare bedroom.

I didn't hear him follow me, but when I went to slam the door, he was right there.

His expression hard, his jaw locked, he glared at me. "He doesn't deserve you."

My hand on the door, I froze. Of all the things I expected him to say, that wasn't even on my radar. Brian was... together. He wasn't a billionaire's son, but he had his life planned. He didn't drop things or lose his keys or wake up at two a.m. and have to write stuff down. His clothes were always pressed, and he never forgot a dentist appointment. He was a financial planner, for God's sake. He planned everything.

If anyone didn't deserve anyone, it was me who didn't deserve him. But that didn't change a damn thing. "It's between me and Brian."

Sawyer's eyes narrowed. "What are the terms of the divorce?"

Shit. "None of your business."

"He wants your business," he stated, as if he'd suddenly figured it out.

I snorted. "He wants nothing to do with it."

"Then why not sign?"

"Because I can't!" I made to slam the door, but an ex-Marine's infuriating reflexes were no match for my frustration and anger.

Sawyer's hand shot out, and he gripped the door in one hand at the same time as he grasped the side of my face. "And I can't have a married woman in my penthouse," he growled.

My heart slammed into my ribs, my stomach dropped and my mouth went dry. "I...." *Oh my God.* "Then I'll leave."

"I don't want you to leave!"

Speechless, I stared at him.

His intense gaze burning into mine, his nostrils flared. "Why aren't you *signing?*"

I blinked. Then I whispered the shameful truth. "He wants his name back."

"Jenkins." His chest rose with an inhale. "It's his last name... and your business name."

Trying not to cry, I bit my bottom lip and nodded. "Jenkins Events."

His thumb stroked my cheek. "I know an attorney."

I was sure he knew several. "I can't fight him."

"Yes, you can."

"I don't want to," I clarified. It was more than him just wanting his name back. It was me losing the only family I'd ever belonged to. Not that Brian's parents or siblings were overly supportive or even warm, but they were a family, and for the first time in my life, I'd belonged somewhere. Or I thought I had.

Sawyer frowned. "But you don't want to change your business name."

I shook my head as much as I could in his grasp, and I admitted the truth. "I would lose business. His family name, while nothing like yours, holds weight in Miami." Brian's mother was involved with so many charity groups, I continually had business through her referrals.

Sawyer pointed out the obvious. "You can rename."

"I know. And I will. But I wanted to be in a position financially where losing some accounts tied to his family's connections wouldn't sink me, and I'm not there yet. I asked him to wait, but he...." I waved my hand. "Never mind. He wants his name back, and I wasn't ready. End of story."

"Why does he want you to give up his last name?"

I pulled out of his hold. "Because he wants to give it to someone else." And irony was a four-letter word. A man with a name much more powerful, much more influential said I was beautiful, but I wasn't a fool. He'd have a million more reasons to protect his name from the likes of me. Who was I? I was no one.

"It's not an uncommon name."

I toed the soft carpet that was so thick, it was like walking on a cloud. "Yeah, well, try telling him that."

Sawyer caught my chin and brought my head back up. "You asked for him after the carjacking."

I averted my gaze. "I was confused." Brian had always been my person. He was who I'd always called. But I didn't realize until too late that I'd relied on him too much. "I made a mistake relying on him."

"Your husband should have been there for you."

"No." I stepped back from Sawyer. I had to. I was doing the same thing I'd done with Brian, and I swore to myself I wasn't going to ever be that kind of girl again. "You don't understand. *I* relied on *him*."

"You're supposed to rely on your spouse."

"No, not like that. Not for everything. Not when someone has their own life and their own job and their own responsibilities," I parroted, giving him the same speech Brian had given me.

Sawyer's voice dropped to a tone I didn't recognize. "Is that what he said to you?"

"I'm done talking now."

Sawyer stared at me a moment. Then he threw me another curveball and said the last thing I was expecting. "If you were my wife, I would've made damn sure you understood that you could rely on me for everything, *always*." Walking out of the room, he quietly shut the door behind him.

I stared at the space he'd occupied that now felt incredibly empty, until the sun dipped below the horizon and a muted orange hue took over the room. Every minute that ticked by, I cared less and less about the reasons I'd not signed the divorce papers from Brian and more and more about how pathetic I felt.

I didn't drink, but if I was being honest, I wanted a drink. And I wanted more than a closed door separating me from a Savatier.

I didn't belong here.

And admitting to him the pathetic reason I'd held on to Brian only made that more clear.

The last of the sunset bled into night, and I made a decision.

I pulled my suitcase out from the closet, the one that'd magically appeared after the hospital, and I started tossing the clothes I had lying around in it. I didn't have any cash or my wallet, but I had the new cell phone André Luna had gotten me, and I had my emergency credit card number that I had memorized that wasn't in my wallet when it'd gotten stolen with the Escalade.

I could set up a new account for a car service.

Which was exactly what I was doing when a knock sounded

on the bedroom door a half a second before it flew open and a blond man, all swagger, smiled wide.

"What's up, darlin'?" Not as tall and not quite as muscular as Sawyer, but one hundred percent player, the green-eyed man waltzed into my room. "I heard you needed a house call." He set a black medical kit on the dresser and grinned as his gaze traveled the length of me.

"Um...."

Sawyer strode in after him, looking pissed as hell. Then his gaze cut to my suitcase and his expression turned nuclear. "I told you to wait in the living room, Talerco."

Talon Talerco, the man from the picture on Sawyer's phone.

Talon chuckled, his gaze briefly taking in my suitcase. "What's the fun in that?"

Looking like it was the last thing he wanted to do, Sawyer introduced us. "Genevieve, this is Talon Talerco. He was a hospital corpsman assigned to my unit in the Marines. Talon, Mrs. Jenkins."

Talon's grin amped up. "Oh, she's missus now?" He tipped his chin at Sawyer, but winked at me. "How tellin'."

"Talerco," Sawyer warned.

Talon slapped Sawyer on the back. "Nothin' doin', nothin' doin'." He glanced at me before opening his kit. "I hear I'm takin' staples out."

My neck tingled and the wound itched. "I, um, that's okay. I can take care of it later." Much later. With a real doctor.

Without looking up, Talon rummaged around in his kit. "Sounds like she doesn't trust me, Playboy."

Sawyer's jaw ticked.

"Playboy?" I asked, not sure I wanted to know.

Half of Talon's mouth tipped up in pure mischievousness. "You don't think he's a playboy?" He glanced at Sawyer. "Looks like one." He laughed.

Heat flamed my cheeks. "I, ah, wouldn't know."

Talon dropped his smile. "Course you wouldn't, darlin'." He took what looked like a pair of pliers out of his black bag. "Have a seat for me right here."

Before I could make an escape, Talon was between me and the door, urging me into the reading chair by the window.

I panicked.

"No, no, no." I stepped back, and my legs hit the bed. "I'm good. I don't need you to touch anything. I'm good with my staples." My head started to pound. "Really, no thank you, I'm good. I don't, um, I don't need—" I stumbled and my ass hit the bed.

"Genevieve," Sawyer warned.

Talon spared Sawyer a brief glance before squatting next to me. His eyes on me, he spoke to Sawyer. "Playboy, give us a minute."

"No," Sawyer immediately responded.

Still squatting, Talon threw Sawyer a look. "Not a request, Marine."

His gaze on me, Sawyer's chest rose and fell. Then he abruptly turned and walked out.

Talon looked back at me and smiled casually. "You okay?"

His scent, like coconuts and beach, drifted around me. "I'm fine."

His expression sobered. "You don't look fine."

I smoothed a lock of my hair, bringing it over my shoulder and twisting it. "I mean, I, um, I've had better days. But it was only a little bump on the head and I'm okay."

"A grade two concussion and six staples ain't a little bump, darlin', and that's not what I'm talkin' 'bout. You okay bein' here with Playboy, or do you need me to get you out of here? Because I'm lookin' at a packed bag, a scared woman, and a pissed-off Marine, and I'm feelin' tension that's thicker 'an mud."

Everything hit me all at once.

The carjacking, my head getting split open, being in the penthouse of Sawyer Savatier, my purse gone, gang members knowing where I lived, my business in the toilet, another muscled, dominant ex-military alpha in front of me, Sawyer telling me he couldn't have a married woman in his home, divorce papers I should've signed a year ago, embarrassment, guilt, loneliness—all of it heaped into an impossible mountain of insurmountable despair, and I couldn't breathe.

I wanted out.

Far away, out.

"I need to leave," I whispered, both hating myself for saying it and feeling relieved.

Talon, a man I'd met mere seconds ago, didn't hesitate. "Say no more." Grasping my arm, rising to his full height, he tossed his plier-looking things into his kit. Nodding at my suitcase, he asked, "You got everythin' you need?"

Tears welled. "Mm-hmm."

Sparing me a glance, he dipped his head toward me and lowered his voice. "I'm not expectin' Savatier to cause a problem, but just the same, I'm gonna grab my kit and your bag, and we're gonna head straight for the door. Keep your head down and let me worry 'bout Playboy, okay?"

A tear slipped loose. I nodded.

In the exact same gesture as Sawyer had done, Talon

swiped my cheek with his thumb. "Hold those tears 'til we're outta here. Then you can let loose, darlin'. You with me?"

Biting my lip, I nodded.

"Good girl," Talon murmured without any affection before slamming my suitcase shut and shouldering his black bag. Zipping my suitcase, then picking it up, his free hand landed on the small of my back. "Here we go."

Oozing frenetic energy like he was itching for a fight, Talon led me out of the bedroom and down the hall, aiming us toward the front door.

Standing in the living room, looking out at the night sky, Sawyer turned.

Anger hit his face so fast that I had to drop my gaze.

"Talerco," Sawyer barked. "What the hell are you doing?"

"Keep walkin'," Talon whispered to me before raising his voice. "Respectin' the lady's wishes, Savatier." Dropping his hand from my back, he stepped in front of me and opened the front door. "Elevator, darlin'."

"*Talerco*." Sawyer came at us.

"Elevator," Talon repeated, gently pushing me forward as he stepped between me and Sawyer. "Done deal," he warned Sawyer.

"Genevieve!" Sawyer yelled.

My heart crushing in on itself as if I were walking away from a lover, I frantically hit the elevator call button as tears slid down my face.

"Stand down." Talon's hand landed on Sawyer's chest. "You and I both know I'll take you. Don't make me do it, Playboy."

Sawyer looked at me, and for a split second the closely guarded expression of stone he always wore slipped. Disbelief and something close to pain or hurt flashed for a second before it was gone and anger twisted his features. He glared at Talon. "She has the Tres Angulos after her," he ground out. "You walk her out of here, you *risk her life.*"

"Nothin' I haven't dealt with before," Talon clipped.

The elevator dinged and the doors slid open.

Talon threw me a command over his shoulder. "Get in the elevator, darlin'." He dropped his hand from Sawyer's chest and backed up a foot. "I'll call you."

Sawyer's nostrils flared and his jaw locked. "You're risking her life," he bit out, punctuating every word.

"I'm savin' her dignity." Talon walked backward toward the elevator.

"Talerco," Sawyer warned one last time.

Talon stepped inside the elevator and hit the button for the garage. "I'll keep her alive."

The doors slid shut.

CHAPTER TWENTY-TWO

Sawyer

Fury, raw and aimed at Talerco, consumed me.

I pulled out my cell and dialed.

Luna answered on the first ring. "Luna."

"Talerco took her," I bit out.

"Hold." Shuffling sounded, then I heard a door open and close before Luna came back on the line. "Repeat," he demanded.

Fuck, fuck, FUCK. "She wanted her staples out. I called Talerco. He shows up, and two seconds alone with her and he's leading her out of my place, telling me to stand the fuck down."

"Jesucristo," Luna muttered. "What'd you do to her?"

"I didn't do a goddamn thing!" I yelled, snatching my keys.

"All right, all right, amigo, calm down. Where's Talerco taking her?"

"I don't fucking know." And that was the problem. "Who's on shift? They need to follow Talerco."

"Ty. I'm texting him now. Talerco aware of the situation?"

Goddamn it. Trigger happy and remorseless Ty. I headed out the door. "I told Talerco, but he brushed it off, saying it was nothing he hadn't dealt with before."

"It's not," Luna reassured.

I jammed my fist against the elevator call button. "I don't need an endorsement of his fucking skills, Luna. He *took* her."

Luna exhaled. "Okay, listen up, brother, because I'm only gonna say this once."

I ground my teeth and refrained from telling him to fuck off.

Luna took my silence for consent. "Talerco's a lot of things, but overreactive isn't one of them. He also isn't baselessly impulsive when it comes to something like this." He paused, then he dumped the rest of his bullshit speech. "He wouldn't have removed her from the situation unless she asked for it. Brother to brother, you know I'm right."

I slammed my fist into the wall.

"Sawyer," Luna snapped.

"What?" I ground out.

"Do what you gotta do to calm the fuck down, then head to the office. I'm calling Talerco, and I'll have him bring her here. You, me, and Talerco will hash it out in a conference room once she's secure in one of the client apartments. Comprende?"

I didn't say shit. I hung up and got on the elevator.

I drove my Range Rover like it was a Maserati all the way to the office, scanning every fucking intersection as I went, looking for them. I pulled into the garage at Luna and Associates twelve minutes later.

Talerco's black Challenger was nowhere in sight.

Anger-fueled adrenaline pounding in my veins, I skipped the elevator and took the stairs up to the third floor where the conference rooms were. I knew something was wrong the second I looked through the glass wall of the largest conference room and saw Preston, Tank, Collins and Tyler all standing around Luna and his laptop.

I shoved through the door, my glare on Luna. "What the fuck are they doing here?"

Tyler, the prick, smiled. *"Damn, he swore."* He looked around at the rest of the guys with an expression of fake shock. "Was that just me, or did you all hear that?" His smile amped up. "Does this mean it's love?"

"Women." Collins shook his head. "Fucking trouble is what that is."

Crossing his arms, Tank threw Collins a look. "Shut the fuck up." Tank nodded toward Luna. "You need to see what he has."

Luna spun his laptop to face me and hit play on a security image feed. "They caught them coming out of your garage."

I watched Talerco's Challenger pull out of the garage, and before the black company Escalade parked across the street could fall in behind them, a tinted-out gray van gunned it out of a construction lot across the street, cut off the SUV and got on Talerco's six. The Challenger shot forward, obviously seeing the tail, and in the last second of the video, I saw Talon take a corner, turning in the opposite direction of Luna and Associates.

I surpassed anger. "Where the hell is he going?" I asked Luna. "Get him on the phone, *now*."

Luna didn't answer. He typed on his laptop and another image appeared. This time the familiar software program of the tracking system he used to monitor all the company vehicles came up. "This was from a couple minutes ago."

I watched the red blip of Ty's SUV parked on my street. Then the red dot shot down the street in front of my condo, took the same corner as Talerco's Challenger, then nothing. It disappeared from the screen.

I looked from the screen to Luna. "What the hell just happened?"

Luna held my gaze. "We lost GPS monitoring, and both Talon's and Ty's cell phones are going straight to voice mail."

What the fuck? "What does that mean?" I asked, but I already knew.

"Signal jammer," Luna confirmed. Turning back to his laptop, he pulled up a map of the city. "The question is, where would Talon head to?"

"No," I bit out, my anger ramping up to a new level. "The question is why the hell didn't he come here?" He knew there was security here around the clock. At any given time, there were at least three Luna and Associates men on duty. We were all ex-military, and we were all trained.

Breaking his silence, Preston pushed off the wall. "You're both wrong. The real question is what gangbangers are doing with a jammer. They typically don't mess with anything like that. The cartel doesn't even use them." His gaze shifted around the room, never landing on any one of us, before he stared at the carpet. "You sure it was just a carjacking?"

I spun on him and did something I never fucking did with the guys. I lost my temper. "What's that supposed to mean?"

"Exactly what I asked." His hands on his hips, never looking at me, Preston shrugged. "What do we really know about this chick?"

Tyler smirked. "You do know who his dad is, right? If anyone's a target, it's Playboy."

I glared at Tyler. "They don't know who I am. They were going for the vehicle, period."

"How many cars were in the lot that night?" Tank asked offhandedly.

"Too many," Collins answered. "It was Mel's after the clubs closed. They would've had their pick. The place is packed after hours."

"But they chose Sawyer's SUV," Tyler added skeptically.

"Enough," Luna cut in. "It's a company SUV, and speculation isn't gonna help us find Talerco and the chica right now." Spinning his laptop to face all of us, he stood. "We need to split up and find them. We don't know how many are in that van, and while I'd bet on Talerco any day of the week, numbers are numbers. He and Ty could be grossly outnumbered and outgunned." Pointing to the screen, he assigned grids. "Since we're all gonna be subject to the jammer, we're traveling in teams. Tank and Preston, take the south end of the city. Collins and Tyler, take the northern quadrant. Sawyer and I will head west."

"West doesn't make sense," I argued. "The city grid dwindles, and there'll be too many opportunities for the van to shoot at them. Talerco would be an idiot to go west."

"Disagree," Luna clipped. "West will be less populated, which means less collateral damage. It's what I'd do. Talerco isn't stupid, and he isn't gonna fire warning shots." He eyed me. "He's gonna shoot to kill."

"So will Ty," Preston added.

Ignoring Preston, Luna glanced at his watch. "Gear up with the assumption you'll be on your own. Take enough ammo to hold off a small army. You all know the gangs travel in packs." He looked up, glancing at each of us. "Stay on comms, do your grid searches, call in your locations to base every ten minutes. Report any potential sightings ASAP so we can track via traffic cams if we lose you, assuming those don't get jammed too. Meet back here by oh-one-hundred." He paused. "If you lose comms, cell and GPS, use your best judgment. I don't want to put our families in danger or suspend client activity to fight a gang war, but we will if we have to. Your best defense is to stay invisible until you need to be seen. Remember that. Any questions?"

"Yeah." Preston crossed his arms. "Is one chick worth a gang war? Because that's where this is heading."

My nostrils flared.

His eyes on Preston, Luna's hand shot out and landed on my chest. "I'm gonna humor that question only once, and only because you're new, so listen up." He dropped his hand from my chest and held up one finger. "One. We protect our own. This isn't a client. This is personal to one of our brothers. Even if it wasn't, we'd still be heading out, doing exactly what we're gonna do." He held up a second finger. "Two. This isn't about a single chica. We've got two of our brothers out there. We're going after them because we don't fucking leave anyone behind. Ever. You want out? Fine. No judgment. But stand down now so we can get on with it."

"Throw me under the bus for being the new guy here all you want." Preston shrugged as if not offended. "But if you think gangbangers will let it go, your head's in the sand."

Luna's voice dropped to a lethal warning. "Underestimate me again, and it'll be your last move as my employee."

Preston didn't back down. "If stating the truth gets me walking papers, so be it."

Silence fell over the room as the tension ramped up, and for a split second I thought I was going to witness a bloodbath.

Then Tank stepped up to Preston. "Shut the fuck up and grab your gear. I don't have time for this shit. Let's go." He shoved past Preston, throwing the door to the conference room open.

For a heartbeat, Preston didn't follow. He stood staring at the fucking carpet.

Then Tank bellowed from the hall. *"Now, Preston!"*

He walked out.

Tyler smirked. "Crazy *and* an attitude." Shaking his head, he glanced at Luna as he walked toward the door. "Good fucking luck with that one."

Collins eyed Luna. "New guy's right." He glanced at me before walking out.

I looked at Luna.

"Jesu-fucking-cristo," he muttered on an exhale.

I glanced after Preston. "He's going to be a problem."

Luna looked at me. "What do you mean, *going to be?*" Unholstering his 9mm, he dropped the magazine, checked the clip, then slammed it back into place. "He already is."

"You shouldn't have hired him."

"You think the streets of Miami are safer with him roaming loose?"

I didn't say shit.

"Right fucking answer," Luna clipped. "Let's go."

CHAPTER TWENTY-THREE

Genevieve

O NE HAND HOLDING HIS CELL PHONE, HIS EYES DARTING BETWEEN
the rearview mirror and the road, Talon took a corner
going double the speed limit before glancing at his phone
again. "Goddamn it."

My heart in my throat, one hand gripping the handle-
bar above my window, the other holding on to my seat belt, I
forced a response out. "What?"

Talon frowned as he glanced at the side mirror. "No
signal."

Oh God. "But we're in the middle of downtown."

He didn't respond. Straddling the lane marker, he gunned
it as he wove between two cars.

Dread threatened to choke me. "How is that possible?"
Downtown Miami was not a cell phone dead spot.

Talon tipped his chin at the GPS display on the dashboard. The map, not moving, was static. "No GPS either."

I swallowed past the brick in my throat. "How is that
possible?"

"Signal jammer." Cutting across two lanes, he took a turn
at the last moment.

I dared a glance behind us. "What's that?"

"Nothin' legal."

The same gray van that had been following us ever since

it had screeched out of a parking lot across the street from Sawyer's condo made the same turn. Right after the van, a black Escalade also made the turn. "They're still there."

"On it." He took another last-minute turn. "We're gonna have a little fun. You ready?"

I didn't have time to respond.

Talon gunned his Challenger, and the engine roared as he turned down a one-way street going the wrong direction.

A delivery truck slammed on his brakes and veered.

"Watch out!" I screamed.

Horns blared and tires screeched as Talon expertly whipped the car around the truck and gunned it down the breakdown lane, barely avoiding more cars behind the truck. "Nothin' doin', nothin' doin'," he murmured cutting across two lanes when there was a break in oncoming cars.

My heart slamming into my ribs, I fought for a breath. "That wasn't nothing," I accused.

Half his mouth tipped up. "If the stakes ain't high, you ain't livin'." Jumping a curb, he spun the Challenger and braked at the same time. The car slid to a stop on the side of the road, and Talon turned in his seat, looking behind us.

My hand went to my chest. "I think I prefer no stakes." My life included.

His half smile amped up into a grin. "Lost 'em." He spun the car around and got back on the surface streets, thankfully going the right direction in the right lane.

I looked in the side mirror. No van, but no SUV either. "The Luna and Associates guy is gone too."

"Cost of doin' business." Talon glanced at his cell phone. "One bar of signal. Let's see if this works." He dialed and held the phone to his ear as he glanced in the rearview mirror.

"Hey, you home?" he asked whoever answered. "Good, 'cause I'm dragging strays and I need somewhere to land...." He pulled the phone away from his ear. "*Shit.*" He spun the wheel hard and did a U-turn as he floored it, tossing the phone onto the center console. "Here we go again, darlin'. Hold on."

I looked behind us as the gray van came barreling around a corner and then gunned it. To my horror, they gained on us and pulled up almost alongside the Challenger on my side. "Talon...," I drew out, my voice wavering.

"I see 'em, I see 'em." Except he didn't speed up. Talon's foot came off the pedal.

"What are you doing?" Panicked, I pushed on his thigh that was solid muscle. "Go, go, go!"

His glare fixated out my window, he didn't budge.

The car slowed marginally, but my panic amped up considerably as they came up level with us. "Talon!"

"Hold on, darlin'," he answered absently, his eyes narrowing. "Testin' a theory."

I dared to look at the van, but the windows were tinted completely out and I couldn't see a thing.

Then the van did the last thing I expected.

It slowed down and fell in behind us.

"Gotta admit, darlin'...," Talon glanced in the rearview mirror. "That I was not expectin'."

Which part? Them not ramming into us like in the movies, or the window not going down and a man with a giant gun firing at us? Both? I didn't know, and I didn't ask. It didn't matter. Bad guys were still after us, which I should've thought about before I left Sawyer's, because not only had Sawyer warned me, his friend André Luna had warned me. Not to mention there was a guard outside Sawyer's condo around the clock, they still hadn't found the stolen Escalade, and André had said until they did, I wouldn't be out of danger.

I cursed myself again for pulling that carjacker's face mask off. "I'm sorry."

"For what?" Talon asked absently, taking another corner too fast and cutting west. "You chasin' our tail?"

I should've been terrified. And I was. But in the cocoon of Sawyer's friend's car, with the scent of beach and coconuts surrounding us and the van falling back, it was hard to feel like any of this was real. "They'd really kill me just for pulling off some guy's ski mask?"

Adjusting the gun he'd taken from his back waistband and shoved between his thighs the second the van had pulled up behind us, Talon spared me a glance. "Darlin', they'd kill for a lot less."

I held the Oh Jesus handle, but I leaned my head back. "I didn't even see him." Not really.

Talon frowned, turning toward one of the county roads that led us even farther away from Miami proper. "You sure 'bout that?"

No. "Yes." I glanced behind us. The van was holding steady, and the black Escalade had found us again, because it was behind the van. "Can't you drive any faster?"

Talon chuckled. "My kinda girl." He winked then he sobered. "I can, but I'm not aimin' to outrun them anymore."

Alarm spread. "You aren't?"

"Nope," he said almost cheerfully, checking his rearview mirror. "I got 'em right where I want 'em."

Oh God. Did I want to know? "Where's that?"

Speeding down the county road faster than he should, but not as fast as he had been, the night settled around us as Talon

Talerco took his eyes off the road.

For one whole heartbeat, he held my gaze. Then he spoke with lethal intent. "Within my sights."

CHAPTER TWENTY-FOUR

Sawyer

IALING TALERCO FOR THE TENTH TIME, LUNA SPED WEST ON ONE of the county roads leading out to the middle of fucking nowhere.

"They're not out here," I clipped, scanning every side road we passed.

The call, on speakerphone, went straight to voice mail as Talerco's drawl filled the car. "Leave a message, or don't."

Luna hung up. "We're not far enough out."

"We get any farther, we'll be in the Glades."

"Just about," Luna answered absently, scanning the countryside.

"Where are you going?" He was up to something.

"Following a hunch."

"Which is?"

Luna checked the rearview mirrors. "If it plays out, I'll tell you."

"Tell me now." He knew he could trust me. "I don't run my mouth."

"No, you don't," he agreed.

This was pissing me off. Everything was pissing me off. "Then lay it out."

"Not my information to share."

"What the fuck does that mean?"

"Exactly what I said."

I put two and two together. "Whose place are we going to?"

Luna glanced at me, but he didn't answer the question. "Why'd she want to leave your penthouse?"

Goddamn it. I looked out the window. "I don't know."

"I find that hard to believe."

"She's married," I reminded him.

"*Dios mio*," he muttered like he was talking to a fucking twelve-year-old. "This again? How married? Because there're shades of marriage, amigo. Many shades."

No there weren't. There was only one kind of marriage as far as I was concerned. "Legally married."

"Then where the fuck is her pendejo of a husband? Because he sure as hell isn't here right now protecting her."

"He walked into the hospital, patronized her, then left as soon as possible." My jaw clenched just thinking about it.

Luna frowned. "So they're separated."

I didn't know her exact living situation. "I didn't see her place. You know Preston grabbed her shit." Which I was still pissed about.

"Did he say her husband was there?"

"No." My back teeth ground together thinking of that prick as her husband.

"Preston wouldn't have missed noticing if she was shacked up with someone."

I didn't comment.

Luna was quiet a moment, then, "Separated isn't exactly married. Intent is obvious at that point."

"Not signing divorce papers and leaving my place is also obvious. I'm done with this conversation."

"Okay, but did she tell you why she didn't sign the divorce papers?"

I turned and unleashed a temper I hadn't known I had until a hot mess of a redhead literally stumbled into my life. "She fucking *lied to me*. I asked her if she was seeing anyone, and she looked me right in the eye and outright told me she was unattached." *She'd lied.* Like every other goddamn female I'd ever fucking encountered.

Luna inhaled. "Bro—"

"I don't fucking do married, and I sure as hell don't fuck with liars." Or women who ran out on me. "*Period.*"

Luna opened his mouth to speak.

"Don't," I warned. "Do not defend her or her situation. I know what I signed up for, and I'll get her out of this bullshit because I got her into it, but don't try to placate me with shit about gray areas and intent. None of that matters."

"If it doesn't matter, then why are you so pissed off?"

Because I was. "We're done talking about it. Where are we going?"

Luna let it go, but he didn't budge on where we were going. "Not my place to say whose property it is."

"I could just reverse search the address."

"You could, but you wouldn't find anything."

I put two and two together. "Then it's either Neil Christensen or Dane Marek. And since Christensen lets us use his properties when we need a safe house, I'm going with Marek. Doubly so since Christensen wouldn't hide his whereabouts. He'd welcome someone trying to fuck with him just so he could teach them a lesson."

Neither confirming nor denying it, Luna tried Talerco again. When his voice mail picked up, Luna hung up, but then his cell rang. Glancing at the display, he swiped to answer and held the phone to his ear to take the call instead of using the Bluetooth. "Hey, thanks for calling back. Did you get my text? Have you heard from Talerco?" Luna frowned. "How long ago?" He glanced at the clock on the dash. "I'm on my way with Sawyer. A new employee I have is trailing behind Talerco, or he should be. He'll be in a company vehicle. Comms, GPS and cell phones are down because we suspect they have a jammer. When they get close, you'll be affected too. Talerco has a woman with him, redhead, midtwenties... Yeah, she's their target... Don't know how many, but I want to get answers first if we can... I know. Copy that, I won't." Luna hung up.

"You know and you won't what?"

Luna spared me a glance as he slowed down. "I know that gang members will shoot first, ask questions never." Luna turned down a dirt road I hadn't even seen, the entrance almost completely masked my overgrown trees. "And Marek said not to approach his place using the main road."

So it was Marek. The SUV dipped and bounced on the lane that was little more than washed-out tire indents with potholes.

"Talerco told Marek he was coming?"

Luna focused on the path ahead, the headlights the only source of light as we drove deeper into the woods. "Yeah, called him a few minutes ago." He dialed his phone using the car's speakers again.

Tyler answered. "What's up, boss?"

"Call everyone back," Luna ordered.

"You found them?" Tyler asked.

"I'm taking it from here. See you tomorrow."

"Boss." Tyler's tone said it all. "This doesn't sound good."

"Got it handled. Let the others know."

There was a shuffling sound, then the background noise lessened and Tyler spoke again. "You need me? Just me?"

"Negative, but appreciate the offer. Later." Luna hung up.

I read between the lines. "Marek doesn't want anyone else knowing where he lives."

"Nope," Luna confirmed.

"Then why'd Talerco go to him?"

Luna slowed to a crawl and turned the vehicle down an even smaller lane. Then he brought the SUV to a halt and leveled me with a look. "Because Marek has better security than all of us combined, the skills to make shit disappear permanently, and these pendejos won't be the only bodies buried out here if it comes to that."

Jesus Christ. "How good of a security system?" Because camera feeds meant evidence.

My door flew open.

"Good enough to know you're here," a deep voice clipped.

My instincts intact, I whipped my 9mm out and aimed dead center on the man's chest who was holding my door open.

Dane Marek, dressed in all black with a black ball cap pulled low over his face, stood in the open door with his piece already aimed at me.

If he'd been one of the gang members, I would've been dead.

"Christ." My heart fucking ricocheted around inside my chest. I hadn't been taken off guard like that since my first IED in Afghanistan. "How did you hear what I said?"

He touched his ear, then tipped his chin at the comm in

mine in response.

"I don't have my comm turned on." There was no way he heard me through the heavy, closed car door. Luna's SUV was armored.

"Doesn't have to be on. Not with the equipment I have."

"Which is gonna be useless as soon as Talerco shows up with the pendejos and their jammer in tow," Luna cut in as he took his tactical vest from the back seat. Stepping out of the SUV and strapping it on, he grabbed another handgun, then hefted his sniper rifle from the floor behind his seat before asking Marek about Ty. "You see my other man yet?"

"Negative." Marek stepped back enough to let me out. "No sign of him on any of my security feeds."

Luna swore in Spanish, then English. "Shit." Sparing me a glance, he nodded toward the cargo area of the Escalade where I'd stowed my guns. "Gear up. We're going in on foot from here."

CHAPTER TWENTY-FIVE

Genevieve

T ALON TURNED OFF THE COUNTY ROAD AND FLOORED IT DOWN A dirt lane in the middle of nowhere. Cutting the headlights, he glanced in the rearview mirror. "Okay, darlin', listen up. I'm gonna pull in front of the house and you're gonna jump out. Head straight down the hallway on the left, past the kitchen. The second bedroom on the right, go to the closet and open it. On the back wall, about chest high, is a handle—"

"Wait." I glanced behind us in a panic. The van was barely fifty yards back. "You're not coming with me?"

"Darlin'," he stated with total authority, "we're out of time. Ten seconds I'm gonna be on the house, and you're gonna be jumpin' out. I'm gonna have a mess of pissed-off, armed gang-bangers on me, and you're gonna be in the panic room while I do my thing. You get me?"

Oh God, oh God, oh God. "Talon…." I couldn't do this.

"Back bedroom, closet, chest-high handle. Pull it open, get the fuck inside and lock the door after you. You don't open that door for *anyone* 'cept me or Playboy, you hear me?" He slowed the Challenger.

I started to hyperventilate.

His hand gripped my chin, and he barked words at me. "You hear me?"

"Ba-back bedroom," I stuttered.

Floodlights outside a ranch home a few dozen yards ahead of us cast his face in shadows as he clipped out a nod. "Closet, handle, panic room, lock the door. You got it?" Holding the steering wheel in one hand, he dropped my chin and reached behind our seats. Hefting a giant automatic-looking rifle, he flipped it one-handed and laid it across his lap, his hand already on the trigger.

My eyes bugging out, my heart faltering, I nodded.

"Tell me," he demanded, yanking the steering wheel and sliding the car into a half spin.

I grabbed for the oh Jesus handle as my ass slid across the seat. "Back bedroom, closet, handle, lock myself in," I rattled off as the Challenger jerked to a stop inches from the front steps to the house.

Talon reached across me and threw my door open. "Go, go, go!"

I jumped out.

But my foot caught.

I lurched forward, my hands hit the steps, and one foot twisted under me as the other caught on the low doorframe of the Challenger.

A half cry, half grunt squeaked out as pain shot up my wrists. Panicked, I glanced over my shoulder.

Talon was already out of the car, aiming his rifle as the van pulled up. "*Run*," he yelled at me.

I jerked my leg out of the Challenger as the first shots rang out in the cicada-laced night air. Splitting the evening's silence, an explosion of gunfire rained out of Talon's rifle, plucking in to the van.

A split second later, bullets were whipping past me, plinking off the house's siding.

On all fours, I scrambled up the steps and shoved the front door open with all my strength.

My heart in my throat, my stomach outside on the ground, I fell into the house.

It was dark.

Pitch dark.

"Oh God, oh God, oh God," I cried, fumbling to slam the door shut behind me. But as I shoved it, three bullets hit the solid wood and I jerked back, leaving it partially open.

Hallway.

Hallway, hallway, hallway.

Oh my God, *where was the hallway?*

The house darker than hell, I glanced around in a complete panic-fueled terror as gunshots rained down outside like the second coming.

A clock on the oven glowed and my brain scrambled.

Past the kitchen?

Around the kitchen?

Opposite the kitchen?

Oh my fucking God, which way was I supposed to go?

The front door was kicked open.

I ran.

Blind, I ran like I've never run before…

For five whole erratic heartbeats and not enough strides.

My shoulder was grabbed a split second before an arm flew around my neck.

"Got you, bitch," a deep voice growled.

My feet left the ground.

I screamed.

And screamed and screamed and screamed.

But nothing came out past the arm crushing my windpipe.

CHAPTER TWENTY-SIX

Sawyer

MAREK LED, I FOLLOWED, AND LUNA TRAILED MY SIX.

Dark as shit, mosquitoes swarming, their buzzing rivaling the high pitch of the cicadas as they dive-bombed us, I couldn't see ten feet in front of me.

Only a yard ahead, I could barely make out Marek past the heavy overgrowth of palmettos, scrub pines, vining shit, and about a hundred other plants and trees I couldn't name. "How much further?" Talerco had to be at the house by now. I'd heard tires in the distance five minutes ago.

Marek stopped walking, and if it weren't for the screen of his cell lighting up as he glanced at it, I would've run into him. "Security feeds just went down."

Fuck. "Did Talerco tell you his plan for when he got here?"

"His call cut out before we could discuss anything." Marek shoved his cell back in his pocket.

"Then why are we approaching on foot?" Why the fuck weren't we at the house waiting for him. "He needs backup now." Not when we get there after trekking through fucking swampy forest.

Marek cut left like he knew where he was going. "He knows what to do."

What the fuck was that supposed to mean? "Meaning?" I demanded.

Throwing me a look over his shoulder that was meant to intimidate, he didn't respond.

Goddamn it. "He has a civilian with him."

"I know who he has."

I turned and looked at Luna for help. "Do you know what Talerco's planning?"

Luna used his rifle to shove a hanging palm frond out of his face as he stepped over a fallen branch. "Talon doesn't need a plan. All he needs to do is get her into Marek's house. They won't penetrate Marek's security if he gets her inside."

That didn't make me feel any better. "*If* being the operative word."

Marek threw up his arm, elbow bent, fist clenched. Both Luna and I halted.

A second later, gunfire erupted.

I shoved past Marek, and I was running.

Dodging between the trees, jumping over branches, palms lashed at my face and arms, but I kept running until I hit a clearing.

Talerco was behind the open door of his Challenger unloading his AR15 at the gray van as Genevieve scrambled up the front steps of the house on all fours. She hit the top step, shoved the front door open and fell inside.

But she didn't close the door behind her.

Goddamn it, she didn't close the door.

My rifle trained, I stepped out of the tree line and moved toward the front of the van.

The driver was dead, a masked man was returning fire from the opposite side of the van and another took off toward the house, skirting behind Talerco.

I raised my gun at the man running for the house.

Marek came out of nowhere, his hand slamming down on my piece. "Take care of the remaining shooter." He strode toward the house.

Enraged, I cursed and redirected my aim.

"Leave him alive so we can question him," Luna clipped, moving to my right, his gun trained on the closed back doors of the van.

Fuck. I fired off a single shot.

The asshole dropped, grabbing his thigh.

I didn't spare him a second glance. I sprinted toward the house just as Talerco saw Marek.

Talerco stood up from behind his car door and grinned. "Damn, Ink, 'bout time you showed up."

I ran past the van toward the front steps of the house and the still-open door. "One made it inside!"

"*Motherfucker*," Talerco swore as Ty came around the last bend in the driveway, gunning the Escalade.

I hit the porch steps and flew into the house as the rear doors of the van burst open and gangbangers spilled out.

Gunfire sprayed across the front of the house.

"Ambush!" Luna yelled.

CHAPTER TWENTY-SEVEN

Genevieve

THE STENCH OF ACRID, PANIC-LACED SWEAT FILLED MY NOSTRILS.

"Shut the fuck up, bitch." Choking me with his arm around my throat, he jammed his gun into my ribs. "Shut the fuck up right now, or I'll pump you full of holes and make you shut the fuck up."

"Try it and you're dead," Sawyer's lethally calm voice penetrated the darkened house.

A sob stuck in my throat.

My captor jerked us back a foot. "Who the fuck is that?"

A cacophony of gunfire erupted from out front, splitting the artificial silence of fear a split second before someone outside yelled, *"Ambush!"*

Fight-or-flight instinct kicked in, and I tried to drop to the ground.

The captor's arm around my neck tightened to suffocating strength as my knees hit the ground.

"What the fuck, bitch?" He yanked me back up.

"Marek," Sawyer snapped. "In position?"

"Copy," a deep voice sounded from behind us.

The captor jerked us away from the last voice as the front door was kicked shut and the room exploded with light.

Blinking away the brightness and tears, my eyes focused, and when they did, my heart jammed itself into my throat.

Sawyer.

Oh my God, Sawyer.

His rifle aimed, his feet apart, his eyes were glued just over my shoulder on the man holding me in a headlock.

He tipped his chin at me but spoke to my captor. "Let her go or you die."

"You shoot me, *either* of you shoot me, she dies," my captor spit, grinding his gun into my ribs.

I started to shake.

Gunshots rained down outside, plinking against the house.

Every second of the last time I had a gun pulled on me came back, and I couldn't breathe.

"All of you are dead," my captor spewed. "You hear me? *Dead.*"

Sawyer didn't respond. His aim moved from my captor's shoulder to his head.

I couldn't breathe.

"Not in the house," the deep voice behind me warned Sawyer. "Outside."

My knees started to shake.

"Yeah," my captor taunted. "Let's take this outside. See how you pendejos like that."

Shouting in Spanish erupted from outside.

Ears ringing. Arms heavy.

My captor forced a laugh. "See? Told you. Muerte, pendejo. *Muerte.*"

No air, heart pounding, shaking—everything shaking.

Don't fall.

Don't fall.

My head swam, and my knees buckled.

"*Fucking bitch!*" He yanked me upright.

The pressure on my neck increased, and my vision tunneled.

"Let go of her neck," Sawyer growled.

Don't stumble.

"Outside," the deep voice snapped.

Staples, staples, staples. Do not stumble. Do not stumble.

"You choke her out, *you're dead*," Sawyer roared.

Do not stumble.

The pressure on my neck eased a fraction.

"Three o'clock, two paces," the voice behind me clipped.

Burning, wheezing, one breath, not enough.

Sawyer reached out, slow motion, and opened the front door. He stepped to his right.

Need more air.

"That's it," my captor sneered. "Move the fuck outta my way if you want her to live."

Need more air.

Sawyer took another step to his right. A step away from the front door.

Oh God.

My captor moved.

Dragging me, pressing the gun into my side, he covered half the living room.

Fire, burning, breaths in short spurts. Oh God.

Tears welled.

Oh God.

"Genevieve," Sawyer snapped from somewhere far away. "Eyes on me!"

I couldn't hear.

I couldn't breathe.

Gunfire played in my head and outside.

Gunfire everywhere.

Shots, so many shots, the sound of death.

Oh.

My.

God.

We were moving right for the door.

I was dead.

I didn't have a chance outside.

No chance.

Too many bullets.

No chance.

Muffled, distant terror-driven screaming filled my ears.

Thoughts spun.

Head spun.

Staples don't matter if you're dead.

Filthy dirt-sweat taste on my tongue.

Bullets were going to rip through my flesh.

Sawyer was going to die.

Talon was going to die.

The man behind me was going to die.

I was going to die.

"Stop fucking screaming, bitch!" Cold metal pressed into my temple.

Sawyer roared.

"Get him outside," the other man ordered.

"I'm fucking going and taking her with me!"

I was yanked over the threshold, and my world spun to a stop.

Bodies.

Red, blood, flesh, face-up, facedown, eyes open, eyes closed, dead.

Dead, dead, dead.

One, two… five.

Bodies lying everywhere.

Except for three men standing.

Talon.

André.

Ty.

All pointing guns at us.

The world went dead quiet.

Except for one last word.

"Motherfucker," my captor whispered.

Wind rushed past my face a split second before his head exploded and a blood bath washed over me like hell on earth.

His body dropped, thumping halfway down the steps.

I fell to my knees as a keening filled the night's silence.

CHAPTER TWENTY-EIGHT

Sawyer

MAREK PULLED THE TRIGGER.

The asshole's head exploded, covering Genevieve in his blood before his body thudded down the steps face-first.

"He could have shot her," I snarled, pissed beyond words.

A sound, part scream, part cry, and all terror crawled up her throat and let loose.

"Wouldn't have happened," Marek stated, like he knew exactly how it was going to go down before he'd pulled the trigger. "Clean her up." He pushed past me. "Shower out back."

Using the strap on my rifle, I swung it to my back and reached for her.

"Hot damn." Talerco shook his head. "Nice shot, Ink."

"*Dios Mio*," Luna muttered.

Ty kicked one of the gangbangers lying near the van. "Got one still alive."

I lifted Genevieve to her feet, only to have her knees buckle.

Marek grabbed the dead carjacker by the back of his shirt and single-handedly dragged him toward the van. There was a brace on his wrist and the side of his head that wasn't blown away sported a bruise where I'd kicked him—it was the same guy Genevieve had pulled the mask off.

Pushing my hands away, Genevieve cried harder.

Talerco glanced at the mess on the steps. "Ink, where ya keep the bleach?"

Ignoring her attempts to block me, I scooped her up.

"Garage," Marek clipped, tossing the body into the van.

Covered in blood splatter himself, Luna came up the steps. "I'll find you some clothes. Shower's by the south end of the pool." He nodded toward the side of the house, then walked inside.

I carried a keening, shaking woman in shock down the steps and around the side of the bullet-ridden house.

I hated myself.

I hated every one of her tears. And I hated the goddamn blood staining her innocence. I didn't have words of comfort. I was angrier than the day my mother shed tears for her cheating husband. Except that wasn't my fault. This was. Everything that'd happened to Genevieve since she'd walked in that diner was my fault.

I carried her past the pool and to an enclosed outdoor shower. Turning the water on to full heat, I set her on her feet, only to have her slip toward the ground. Already covered in the same blood that was all over her, I wrapped an arm around her and held her to my chest. Sliding my rifle off my shoulder, I leaned it against the fencing enclosing the shower and unholstered my other guns, tossing them on an adjacent bench.

Her voice hoarse, her cries growing quieter, she leaned into me like she had nothing left.

"Come on," I muttered, stepping her toward the spray. "Let's get you cleaned up."

No reply, no response, as if she didn't hear me, she continued to shake and mew like a wounded animal.

I stepped us under the spray.

Water cascaded over her face, and she sputtered out a cough.

I swept my hand over her face, pushing her hair back. "Come on, baby. Let's wash this off." I adjusted the water temperature.

She sucked in a breath and looked at me for the first time since I'd walked into Marek's living room. "It-it's not *this*."

"I know." I ran my hand over her bloody hair for the second time since I'd known her. "You're okay, though."

"No." She shook her head as a fresh wave of tears welled in her eyes. "No no no no—"

I grasped her face. "You're safe now. You hear me? Safe," I enunciated.

A new sob broke free.

I pulled her into my arms.

"Yo, Playboy," Talerco called from outside the enclosure. "I got clothes for her from her suitcase, a shirt for you, and some towels and soap from Luna."

"Set them on the bench." I wasn't letting go of her right now.

"Y'all decent?" he asked.

"Yeah." I held her to me, wishing like hell she hadn't seen what she saw. In the same breath, I wasn't sorry a single one of those fucks were dead.

Talerco stepped in and set the shit on the bench behind us. Wearing a clean shirt, he eyed Genevieve. "How's she doin'?"

I pulled her away from my chest just enough to tip her chin. I was an asshole for not checking to make sure she wasn't physically injured beyond being choked. "Did he hurt you?"

Her gaze distant, she didn't say anything.

"Hey, darlin', how ya doin'?" Talerco asked. "We just

wanna make sure you're not injured."

Leaning against me, her arms still at her sides, she blinked, then inhaled. Pulling her chin out of my grasp, her gaze cut to Talerco. "I'm fine," she rasped.

Talon smiled as he winked at her. "You're tough as nails, darlin', you know that?" His expression sobered. "But if anythin' changes, you tell me or Playboy, okay?"

She nodded, then dropped her gaze, settling her head against my chest.

Talerco glanced at me. "Garbage bag's there for your clothes."

"Copy." I ran my hand over her hair again.

He looked back at Genevieve. "Darlin', let me know when you're ready to get those staples out."

I answered for her. "After I get her cleaned up."

Talerco nodded. "Back door's open. I'll be inside." He retreated.

She looked at her shirt, then back up at me. Her voice came out small and rough. "My clothes are ruined."

"I know." But not for the reason she thought. The blood would wash off. Trace evidence wouldn't.

"Did…." She swallowed. "Did you shoot him?"

"No."

Her shoulders dropped as if she were relieved.

She had to know the truth of who I was. "I didn't shoot him only because someone else beat me to it." I grasped the hem of her pink shirt. "Arms up." She did as I said, and I pulled her shirt over her head.

In an olive-green bra that matched her eyes, her full breasts and hardened nipples stretching the lace material, she looked so damn vulnerable as her arms fell to her sides. "Then who killed him?"

Covered in blood and shed tears, she was still stunning. "I'm not going to tell you that." Every curve of her body played on my conscience.

"Why?"

"It's over now. You can get on with your life." I slid my hands over her hips as my fingers sank into the waistband of her pants.

"But the police—"

"The police will never know about this." Dropping to one knee, I dragged her leggings down her thighs. Fuck my life, she wasn't wearing any underwear. "Hands on my shoulders," I ordered, my voice hoarser than it should've been.

Still trembling, but not outright shaking, she did exactly as I told her.

My honor gone to shit, my cock grew hard as fuck. I pushed her pants to her ankles, shamelessly taking in the sight of her. "Lift." Ivory smooth legs, full hips, a small patch of lighter red curls between her legs, I wanted to sink inside her and make her forget, if even for a moment.

She lifted one foot.

I slid one of her flats off, then the other before pulling her pants all the way off. Blood-soaked water cascaded down her legs and washed over her bright yellow toenail polish. Guilt hit me all over again as I stood.

Stripping out of my shirt, I grabbed the bottle of shower gel and squirted some into my hand as she stared down at her chest.

"There's blood on my bra," she whispered.

Jesus. I couldn't take her bra off. If I fucking did, I'd touch her. "I know, baby." I lathered the soap into her hair.

She looked up at me, and her voice dropped to a hushed whisper. "You called me baby twice."

"I did." I had a hundred names I wanted to call her, but none of them made her mine. I rinsed her hair.

"Please," she barely breathed, leaning into me harder. "Take it off."

Fuck. "Turn around," I ordered.

Without hesitation, she turned.

I undid her bra and pushed it off her shoulders. "Rinse," I clipped.

The bra fell to the ground, and she stepped under the spray completely naked.

My eyes on her, I grabbed the soap and washed my arms and chest. Dragging my gaze over her perfect ass and the soft swell of her hips, I stepped behind her and angled the shower-head to rinse myself off.

Standing in the protection of my body, her head down, her back to me, she reached back and her hands landed on the outsides of my thighs.

Then she pressed her ass into me.

I'd seen death. I'd felt what she was feeling right now. I knew what she wanted.

I wanted it more.

So goddamn much more.

But she didn't know what she was asking.

Rinsing my face, then angling the spray to our right, I reached to turn off the water.

Her hand covered mine. *"Wait."*

CHAPTER TWENTY-NINE

Genevieve

IS IMPOSSIBLY HARD, WARM BODY COCOONING ME, I SUCKED IN A breath full of anxiety, fear, and unspeakably disgraceful relief. But I needed more. I need more of what I felt pressing into my lower back.

My hand landed on his, and I pleaded. *"Wait."*

Every muscle in his body stiffened. "You don't know what you're asking."

I knew exactly what I was asking.

I wanted to feel the very breath going in and out of my lungs. I wanted my soul not to weep. I wanted my eyes not to see. I wanted my body to feel the very essence of what life should be about. I wanted to feel warmth, deep in my veins, and I wanted to feel him.

I wanted to feel him inside me.

Warm water running down my naked body, his breath on my shoulder, my hands trembling, I turned.

But I didn't look at him.

Not at his eyes.

I couldn't.

I ran my hands over the muscles he worked on every day. My fingers tracing the ridges and valleys of every defined inch of his abs, I touched him.

I touched him how I wanted him to touch me.

And for two whole heartbeats, he let me before he grasped my wrist in a punishing grip and yanked my hand off his body. *"Genevieve."*

Expecting his stark blue gaze, I looked up.

Except there was nothing stark about the fierceness in his eyes.

My lips parted on a half gasp, half moan as awareness shot up my arm from his grip and traveled over every needy inch of my heated flesh.

My wet hair soaking my back, water running down my chest and over my achingly hard nipples, my feet standing in a puddle of another man's death, my mouth suddenly went dry.

I licked my lips.

His nostrils flared. "Ask."

"Please," I begged.

Grabbing my other hand, shoving me against the fenced wall of the shower enclosure, he threw my arms above my head and took both wrists in one hand. "Say it," he growled, low and demanding, as he cupped me between my legs.

My entire body shuddered, and he dragged his fingers through my heat.

My head fell back, my eyes closed and I groaned.

As abruptly and as dominantly as he'd cupped me, his hand left my core and he grasped my jaw. "Eyes on me," he barked, tilting my head back up.

Oh God, I wanted him. Spreading my legs, I gripped the top of the fence. "More."

"Say it."

"Take me." I thrust my hips toward him. "Fuck me, own me, make me feel good." *Please, please, please.*

His chest heaving, his glare ruthless, he let go of my face

and unbuckled his pants. "Birth control?" he ground out, freeing himself.

Oh God, *no, no, no*. I wasn't on anything, but I needed him. I needed him right now more than I needed to breathe. "It doesn't matter," I stupidly, foolishly blurted.

Grasping the back of my thigh, his jaw ticked as he lifted my leg around his waist. "It matters," he bit out, fisting himself.

My heart pounded, my core pulsed, and my nails dug into the fence as I lifted my other leg around his waist. "Sawyer," I begged.

He dragged his hard length through my desperate need and pressed against my clit.

"Oh God."

"*It fucking matters*." He thrust into me.

My mouth opened with a silent cry of shock at the sheer size of him as pain ripped through my core.

A guttural growl, low and dominant, tore from his chest as he pulled out and slammed back into me.

"Is that what you wanted?" he bit out.

Tears welled. I nodded.

"Say it," he demanded, bringing his lips within a breath of mine. "*Say it*."

"Fuck me," I whispered as the last of my dignity slid down my face.

Roaring, he pulled out, then shoved into me harder. My back slammed against the fence, and his thumb went to my clit, mercilessly grinding in a circle.

Desire exploded and my tight, unused muscles released, opening my body for him.

Grunting, he ground one more tight circle. Then he started to fuck me in earnest.

Pounding into me fast and slow, thrusting as deep as he could go, grinding his hips—I'd never been fucked like this. Pain morphed into pleasure and stole not only my breath but every thought except of him and his next thrust.

"More," I cried, words bleeding out of my mouth. "More, oh God, *more.*"

Holding my arms above my head, circling my clit, staring me down, he gave me more.

He fucked me, and he gave me more.

"Oh, God." My body started to shake for an entirely different reason. "I'm going to come."

His eyes locked on mine, his chest heaving, his jaw locked, he increased his speed.

Then he did the last thing I was expecting.

He pinched my clit.

Hard.

My release burst from every nerve ending in my entire body, mocking every single sexual experience, every expectation, and every orgasm I'd ever had in my entire life. My eyes closed, my head fell back, and my arms burned as his huge, giant cock slammed into me and ground the same circle as his merciless torment of my clit.

My core pulsing so forcefully it was painful, my muscles squeezed around his hard length, a length that already barely fit inside me. The sensation of his body being too big and mine being too small only made my orgasm that much more intense.

As the last wave of intensity trailed away, he pulled out halfway and shifted his hips, tilting up.

A new sensation, not entirely pleasurable, made my womb contract, and my eyes flew open in alarm as something deep inside me woke up.

Fierce blue eyes, darkened with intent, met my alarmed confusion.

"What are you doing?" I panted.

With his voice sex-rough and demanding, he issued an order. "Arms around my neck."

I didn't question him. I didn't even hesitate. Releasing my cramped hands, I wrapped my arms around his neck.

He grasped the backs of my thighs, pulled out halfway, then slammed home.

The spot deep inside me that he'd merely brushed past before, he drove against hard. Then, angling my thighs wide, watching me intently, he slowly pulled back only to drive into me again.

His cock slammed into me at an angle I'd never felt before, and he stole my breath. A cry of fear crawled up my throat, but before it escaped my lips, he drove into me again and the cry turned into a groan.

Watching me, he did it again.

And again.

I never saw the second orgasm coming.

Stars exploded across the night sky as I fell apart into a million pieces of submission.

Moaning, crying, begging for mercy, I came.

And I fell.

I fell so hard, I didn't notice his lips never touched mine.

His forehead hit the fence next to me, his hard length left my body, and he let go of one of my legs to grip himself. Pulse after hot pulse of his orgasm spread over the curls between my legs as he held his cock against me and released.

CHAPTER THIRTY

Sawyer

FUCK.

FUCK.

I was my goddamn father.

But Jesus fucking Christ.

Hot and tight and... *fuck.* My fist against the fence, my cock against her heat, my come all over her—Jesus Christ.

Pull it together, Savatier, fucking pull it together.

Dropping her other leg, setting her on her feet, I couldn't fucking look at her. If I did, my mouth would be on hers and I'd never let her go.

"Sawyer," she breathed, saying my name with reverence.

Goddamn it.

I turned her toward the still running water, now only luke-warm, and barked out a command like I was her CO. "Rinse."

I stepped away from her.

My pants soaked, my dick still hard, I reached for one of the towels, then turned back toward her.

Standing under the spray, her hair wet, her body made for mine, she looked up at me with her hazel eyes, and she stole my fucking breath.

She crossed her arms over her breasts. "Do you, um, need the water on?"

"No," I clipped, reaching around her to turn it off, then

handing her the towel.

Taking it, she wrapped it around her body.

I picked up our clothes and her shoes and tossed them in the garbage bag, then I grabbed the second towel and dried off before tossing it in as well.

She watched me take the shirt from the bench and pull it on. "My shoes too?"

"Yes, they have blood on them." I handed her the clothes Talerco had left for her.

She reached out from under her towel to take them, but she made no move to get dressed.

"Put the towel in the bag after you're done with it." I turned to give her some privacy.

"That's it?" she asked.

I turned back around, but I didn't say anything. I fucking couldn't.

Hurt clouded her features. "That's all you're going to say?"

"What would you like me to say?" That I'd never failed someone more? That she felt better than any woman I'd ever been inside? That I broke my only rule for her?

Her eyes went wide, like she couldn't believe what I'd said. "Why are you acting this way?"

"What way?" I knew exactly what I was doing.

"Distant."

"We were never close." I hated myself. I'd thought the past five days of keeping my hands off her had been hell, but it was nothing compared to this.

A temper I'd only seen her unleash a couple times came out. "That…" She waved behind her at the shower. "*That* wasn't close? Because it felt pretty damn close to me. Two people can't get any closer." Color flooded her cheeks, and as quickly as her temper had flared, it died. "And just so you know, I've only ever done that with one other person." Her voice small, her eyes welled with tears. "So maybe that means nothing to you, but to me?" Her closed fist holding her towel thumped against her chest. "To me, *that felt close.*"

My head a mess, my chest feeling like it was in a vise grip, I wanted to walk away as much as I wanted to lift her up and sink inside her tight heat again and again. But she deserved more, and despite her words before I'd let shit go too far, she'd walked out of my place.

Taking the fucking high road, I nodded toward the clothes in her hand. "Get dressed and we'll have Talerco remove your staples. Then we can talk back at my place."

"Talk," she stated, like it was a four-letter word.

I tipped my chin, telling myself that her pissed off at me was better than her shaking with shock and fear.

"Sure, okay." All of the emotion from earlier left her voice. "*Talk.* Dead bodies, a bunch of men with guns, and"—she held up her clothes as sarcasm crept into her tone—"a new outfit because the one I was wearing moments ago is now covered in someone else's blood and brain matter, which also got in my hair, and which I had to wash off in a stranger's shower. But you want to talk. Sounds great."

"It's Marek's shower." I gave her some information.

"Marek," she stated.

"The one who was inside with me. Dane Marek. This is his house."

"Seems like a perfectly reasonable explanation." She turned and dropped the towel. "If I knew why the hell I was here in the first place." Careful of her staples, she pulled a green shirt over her head.

I tried not to stare at her curves and failed. "You were being followed. This is a remote location where Talon knew the terrain."

"Terrain. Right." She pulled on a pair of green, pink, and gray leggings, then used the towel to swipe at her hair one more time before reaching for the garbage bag.

I grabbed the bag and took the towel from her, shoving it inside and tying it closed.

"Playboy!" Talon yelled from the back porch. "Time's a wastin'. Get in here."

Stepping toward Genevieve, I reached for her.

She jerked away from me. "What are you doing?"

"You don't have shoes. Carrying you inside."

"It's not the first time I've gone without shoes, and I'm sure it won't be the last," she clipped, walking around me.

Jesus. I stood there a beat, feeling even guiltier before grabbing my rifle, handguns, and the garbage bag, and following her to the house.

Talerco stood on the back porch, holding the door open. "Hey, darlin'. Ready to get those staples out?"

"Yes." She walked up the steps.

A guttural howl of pain sounded from the front yard.

Genevieve froze in her tracks.

"Damn." Talerco shook his head. "Trigger is crazy as fuck."

I was almost afraid to ask. "Trigger?"

"Yeah." Talerco smirked. "The latecomer to the party. What's his name? Ty, or some shit like that? You ask me, his momma missed the mark on that one. She shoulda named him Trigger. Fittin' all the way 'round far as I can tell. Trigger happy, trigger temper." He shrugged and glanced at Genevieve. "Come on, darlin'."

Whoever Ty was working over yelled out again in pain.

Her back stiff, Genevieve glanced toward the front yard.

Talerco let go of the door and stepped beside her, putting his arm around her. "Ignore it. It's all good." He led her inside.

I followed.

Sitting at the kitchen table, his laptop in front of him, Luna looked up. "Hey, chica, come have a seat."

Genevieve looked to Talerco.

Talerco smiled, pulling the chair next to Luna out for her. "Nothin' doin', darlin', nothin' doin'. Just a little chat."

These pricks planned this? "Hey," I warned Luna. "She's been through enough tonight."

Luna leveled me with a look I knew well, one that made him the boss, before he turned to Genevieve as she sat. "All right, chica, here's the hard truth. I want to walk away from tonight and take my men with me." He paused for effect. "I'm in a position to do that." He waited, giving her a chance to respond.

She said nothing.

"So here's the deal," Luna continued. "I've cleaned this up. There're no loose ends on my part. A rival gang is taking credit for the kills, and none of my men will talk." He studied her a beat. "That leaves one wild card. You."

Genevieve shifted in her seat. "I'm not a wild card."

"You are if you go to the police," Luna said bluntly.

I opened my mouth to tell him to back the fuck off, but Luna held a hand up to me.

"Which is your right," Luna continued. "We broke no laws. They were trespassing on private property with deadly intent. We defended ourselves, and we—"

A bloodcurdling scream sounded from the front of the house.

Luna cleared his throat. "We defended ourselves, and we got the information we needed."

The front door burst open, and Ty strode in covered in sweat and out of breath. He beelined for the kitchen, grabbed a knife out of a butcher's block, and rushed back out, slamming the door behind him.

"*Jesus Christ*," Talerco muttered, crossing his arms as he leaned on the kitchen island. "I'm not triaging whatever the hell mess he leaves behind."

Ignoring Talerco, Luna spoke to Genevieve. "If you decide you want the cops involved, tell me now. I'll make a phone call, and we'll do it by the book. My way is more expedient, but either way, the end result is the same. You no longer have to worry about looking over your shoulder."

"How do you know that?" Genevieve's voice had a slight tremor. "There could be a hundred gang members still looking for me."

"To what end?" Luna asked. "The man you could identify is dead."

Genevieve sucked in a sharp breath.

"Trust me, I would not lie about your safety," Luna promised. "My word is my reputation. But you need to make a decision one way or another and stick to it, understand? Because if we bury this, we don't speak about it again." He gave her a hard, warning stare. "Ever."

Genevieve nodded.

Luna pushed. "So what's your decision?"

The woman I'd come to know over the past five days pushed back. "Why is this my decision? I'm not the only one involved. I'm not going to decide everyone's fate."

"First, no one's fate is at stake. Second, we're all in

agreement the best way to handle this is to let a rival gang step in and take credit, which they are more than willing to do."

"Which sounds fine in theory, until one of those gang members leaks the truth or my name." Her voice was stronger, but Genevieve's hands twisted in her lap. "They took my purse. They have my wallet, my license. They know where I live."

Luna nodded. "I know. And we're finding out right now who else knows your personal information. Then, I am making you a promise that I will personally deal with it."

"If you could personally deal with it, then why after five days have you still not found your stolen SUV?" Genevieve blatantly asked.

The front door opened again and Ty walked in carrying the knife. Putting it back in the butcher block, he glanced at Luna. "It's contained. You're all set."

"He still breathin'?" Talerco asked Ty.

Ty rolled his shoulders and stretched his neck. "Is that a rhetorical question?"

Jesus Christ. "Luna," I snapped. "Outside, now." I threw Ty a warning look. "You too." I pointed at Talerco. "Stay here with her." I walked out the front door to the overwhelming smell of bleach.

Luna followed, and I spun on him as soon as Ty closed the door behind them. "What the hell were you thinking?" I jerked my chin toward Ty. "Hiring him wasn't a fucking mistake, it was outright ignorant, not to mention you've given her enough rope to hang every one of us."

"Watch your fucking mouth, Savatier," Ty bit out, pulling a pack of cigarettes from his pocket. "We're all here because of your rich, stupid ass." He put one in his mouth and pulled out a lighter.

Luna held a hand up to Ty. "You light that shit up in front of me, I'm gonna break your fucking arm off. And you know damn well we're all here because some Tres Angulos assholes decided to take my property. The fact that it was Sawyer's vehicle was bad luck, and his lady getting a visual on one of them was pure accident. You want to blame someone, then blame me and my company vehicle."

My back teeth ground, but I didn't say shit.

Ty tucked his smoke behind his ear and pocketed his lighter, but he didn't say shit either.

Luna glanced at me then back at Ty. "How contained is this?"

Ty glared at me, then answered Luna. "We're good. He said no one but the six assholes in the van knew about the chick. The one still alive didn't even know her name, only her hair color. They'd been taking shifts sitting on Savatier's place since we left the hospital with her, waiting for an opening."

"You were outside the hospital that night. How the hell did you miss them?" I accused.

"Same way you did, prick," Ty snapped back. "They've been using three vehicles, rotating out, and they were parked behind the privacy fence at the construction site across the street. I don't have X-ray vision."

Luna shook his head. "They should've been spotted, by both of you."

Goddamn it. "I wasn't the one on duty."

Ty glared at me. "That's because—"

"Enough," Luna cut in. "What's done is done." He looked at Ty. "What else did you get?"

"Nothing important," he ground out. "They were doing two-man shifts, but today one of them spotted Talerco's ride pull in, and on a hunch, called the mask-losing prick. He then called the rest of his gang buddies, grabbed his signal jammer, and they were all waiting when Talerco came out. They saw the redhead in the front seat. You know the rest."

"Why'd they target the company vehicle in the first place?" Luna asked.

"They didn't target it. It was dumb fucking luck. They'd stolen the jammer that night, were going to the diner to eat, and saw the vehicle in the lot. One of them knew it was an L&A ride, and they decided to boost it and test the jammer. They knew you tracked your fleet."

Luna swore. "How'd they know that?"

"Hell if I know. I didn't fucking ask that."

Luna's voice dropped to a lethal calm. "And did you ask where my Escalade was?"

Ty stared at him a moment, like he was trying to gage Luna's sudden shift in tone. "Northwest Miami, somewhere in their territory is all I know. They used the jammer until they found your tracking device and disabled it."

Shaking his head, Luna looked pissed.

Marek came up the front steps holding a black box with antennas coming out of it. "I'm keeping the jammer. Van's loaded with the bodies." He glanced over his shoulder and went still for a moment, like he was listening to something. "Company's coming. Two, three minutes." He glanced at Luna. "Need backup?"

"No, gracias," Luna answered.

Marek eyed Luna. "If they remember this address or ever show up here again, they're dead."

"Understood," Luna acknowledged. "I'll relay the message."

Marek walked into his house without so much as a nod.

Luna glanced at me, then Ty. "Both of you get out of here. I'll handle this."

"I'll wait in the SUV until they're gone. Give me the signal if you need any more of these fucks taken out." Carrying his rifle, Ty walked toward his Escalade.

I watched him skirt the van that was riddled with bullet holes and get in his SUV. "You gave her a choice," I reminded Luna.

"That choice had a time limit." He tipped his chin toward the van. "Now I've got a van full of dead Tres Angulos and two rival gang members pulling up that are willing to take credit and haul them away. I'm making a command decision. Go inside if you don't want them to put a face to this mess."

Tires sounded on the dirt lane as I leveled Luna with a look. "You sure about this?"

Looking tired as fuck, Luna exhaled. "Are we ever sure about anything?"

CHAPTER THIRTY-ONE

Genevieve

"Last one," Talon murmured as he used the plier things and took the final staple out. "All done, darlin'." He set the tool down and turned my chair back to face his. His green eyes roamed over my face. "I can definitely see it."

I blushed under his scrutiny. Blond hair, muscles, and the way he smelled like the beach and coconuts, he was gorgeous. But he wasn't Sawyer. "See what?"

"Why Playboy's got it so bad." He winked at me without smiling. "But I'm missing somethin'."

I dropped my gaze. "He doesn't have it bad." I did, or I had, until I'd stupidly, *stupidly* begged him for sex in the shower.

"Now you're blushin' even harder." Talon chuckled, tossing stuff back in his first aid kit. Then he tipped my chin. "For real, you good?"

"Yes." No.

Lacing his hands and resting his arms on his legs, he leaned toward me and dropped his voice. "Know what I figured out a little too late in life?"

"What?"

"Talkin' helps."

Touching the back of my neck, I avoided his gaze and lied again, "Besides thank you, I have nothing to say."

Slow, not taking his gaze off me, he nodded. "Okay, well,

not judgin', but a woman who asks me to get her away from her man only to play hide the sausage with him six dead bodies later probably has at least one somethin' to say."

I was both all at once mortified and angry, and my anxiety bled out all over Sawyer's friend. "He's not my man, and he doesn't want me. He made that perfectly clear." I made to stand. "So you can tell him to go… go jump off a cliff."

Talon took my wrist, the same wrist Sawyer had held, and pulled me back down. "Sit," he commanded, being just as bossy as his jerk of a friend.

"I don't have to do what you say," I snapped, fighting tears and a coming tide of emotions I had desperately packed away, not to mention the emotions that had made me run from Sawyer's penthouse in the first place.

"No, you don't have to do what I say," he conceded. "And I'm not gonna tell you one way or another how to manage your love life, darlin', but I am gonna tell you you're dead wrong." He let go of my wrist, only to take my hand. "A man doesn't get spittin' mad when a woman he cares nothin' for walks out. You hear me?" He squeezed my hand. "Savatier cares, darlin'. A whole lot."

Tears welled, threatening to let loose. "You're wrong." Sawyer didn't forgive me for lying to him about being married. I got that. He probably had all sorts of women lie to him to get his attention. And I'd been no better, but in my mind, I wasn't seeing anyone. My marriage was over, and I knew that, I just hadn't had the strength to move on yet.

"I'm so right, there ain't no room for wrong." Talon's thumb stroked over my hand. "So do with that information what you will. I'm not here to play matchmaker. But I do have another concern, one that's got even me worried."

"What?" I asked, barely holding it together.

He stared at me for a moment. Then his Southern accent disappeared. "You saw a lot of violence tonight, more than most people see in a lifetime. That's going to play on your conscience."

"They shot first," I blurted, telling him the thought I'd been chanting over and over as I desperately tried to stuff every single second of the past hour down deep where I didn't have to think about it. "They were going to kill me."

He didn't hesitate. "Yes, they were."

The shoddy wall holding all my emotions in started to crack. "I'm alive." My voice shook.

"Yes, you are."

My voice dropped to a whisper. "It was justified."

"Yes, it was."

A tear escaped and spilled over. "I didn't pull the trigger."

"No, you didn't. I did, and I'd do it again in a heartbeat."

Tears started flowing freely, but he wasn't finished.

"So would Savatier, so would all of us here today." He took my hand in both of his. "We were all trained to protect, and that's what we did. You have nothing to feel guilty about."

I couldn't swallow past the lump in my throat. "It was *all* my fault," I sobbed. "I pulled his mask off!"

A man who smelled like the ocean pulled me into his arms. "No, none of it was your fault."

I cried harder. I didn't even hear the front door open.

"What the hell did you do to her?" Sawyer barked.

Talon eased back, but he held my arm and ignored Sawyer as his Southern accent came rushing back. "You remember what I said, darlin'." He stood and tipped his chin at Sawyer. "No time like the present to man up, Playboy." Grabbing his medical kit, Talon walked toward the front door.

Eyebrows drawn together, jaw set, Sawyer glared after Talon. "I need her stuff."

"Already in Patrol's ride," Talon threw over his shoulder before opening the door and walking out.

Sawyer watched Talon leave before looking back at me. "Why were you in his arms?" he accused.

It was as if a switch had been flipped.

The foster girl who married Brian was gone, and the girl in the diner who owned her own business and told Sawyer Savatier's supermodel ex-girlfriend off came out. "For real? You're going to stand there and ask me that? After what happened outside? After *everything*?" I stood. "You know what, forget it. Forget *you*." I pushed my way around him. "Talon!"

"You're still married," he ground out.

The weight of humiliation slammed into my chest and I spun. "I'm separated, big difference. Get over yourself!"

"There is no—"

"No." I held my hand up. "Don't you dare. You were there in that shower as much as I was, and I'm not going to let you turn me into some villain or into some... some... *bad person* like those... those..." I hit a wall. The breadth of my emotional tolerance stretched to the very last shred of dignity I had left, and a sob, half mortification, half nervous breakdown, and all frustration broke free. "Carjackers," I managed.

"This isn't about a carjacking!" he roared.

I lost it. "How easy for you to say," I yelled back. "You didn't get staples, you didn't get shot at, you didn't get locked up for five days while crazy-scary gang members hunted you down. You have no idea what it's like!" As soon as the words left my mouth, I realized what a complete jerk I was. Of course he knew. He knew what every one of those things was like.

But I wasn't taking it back.

Not one word.

I yanked open the front door of the house I almost died in just as Talon was getting in his Challenger. "Talon!"

CHAPTER THIRTY-TWO

Sawyer

PARALYZED WITH DISBELIEF FOR A SECOND, I DIDN'T MOVE.

Then I made for the front door.

Dane Marek came out of nowhere. "Let her go."

"Fuck you." I reached for the door. "The last time she got in a car with him, she almost died."

He stepped in front of me. "But she didn't."

"Move," I warned.

He studied me. "What does it matter if she's married?"

My nostrils flared. "None of your goddamn business." I was not my father.

"Try again."

I didn't give a shit about the rumors about him. Mercenary or not, I stepped up to him, toe to toe, eye to eye. "Last time I'll say it. *Move.*"

"She is not your past."

She wasn't my future either. And now I was everything I swore I would never be. "Get out of my way, Marek."

"Give me a reason to."

Goddamn it. "I am not my fucking father!"

"Did you tell her?"

"Tell her what?" That I fucked up? That I was enraged she was in Talerco's arms? That I wanted back inside her so goddamn bad, I couldn't see a single thing except anger?

"That you want her."

"It isn't that simple," I ground out.

"It's exactly that simple."

"Get out *of my way.*"

Stepping aside, Marek glanced out the window by the door. "We get what we deserve. Remember that." He walked the fuck off.

I yanked the door open and flew down the front steps. I was across the drive and grabbing her as she was getting in Talerco's car before I had a plan.

I didn't think.

I didn't calculate.

I didn't measure every angle and scenario and compensate for variables.

I was turning her, taking her face in my hands, and I was crushing my mouth over hers.

I kissed her like I'd wanted to in the shower, and her shocked gasp gave me the in I needed. I devoured her mouth like I'd devoured her body, and goddamn it, I kissed her.

I fucking kissed her.

For two strokes through the maddening, infuriating, diabolical temptation that was all her, she let me.

But then she pushed me away, and the back of her hand wiped across her lips. "Too little, too late." She got one leg in the car.

Reactively, I grabbed her arm. *"Genevieve."*

All of a sudden, Luna, Talerco and Ty were on me. Luna to my right, Ty to my left, it was Talerco who spoke.

Standing on the opposite side of his Challenger, he leveled me with a look. "Don't make me come over there, Playboy," he warned. "Let her go."

Adrenaline fueling irrational thoughts, I glared back at Talerco. "Stand down."

"You stand the fuck down," Talerco countered.

"Enough," Luna barked in Spanish.

I spun on Luna. "It'll be *enough* when all of you mind your own fucking business."

"That's it!" Genevieve yelled, yanking out of my grasp. "Talon, take me home, *now*." She got in the car and slammed the door.

Talerco eyed me before getting behind the wheel, cranking the engine and flooring it.

Luna's hand landed on my shoulder. "Give her some breathing room."

Jerking away from his touch, I glared at him. "This is none of your business. I stay out of everyone's goddamn shit. I expect the same fucking courtesy."

Expression neutral, Luna's hands went to his hips. "You done?"

No, I wasn't fucking done. I'd fucked her and she'd left, and my head was goddamn spinning, and I'd turned into every piece of shit thing I hated about my father. I wasn't *done*. I was irate.

"Good," Luna said, without waiting for an answer. "I got a lead on your SUV. Some Tres Angulos prick has it." He rattled off an address. "Go with Ty and get my vehicle back." Luna eyed Ty. "Don't fucking kill anyone."

"Too late for today," Ty clipped. "Maybe you'll get lucky tomorrow." He glanced at the bloodstains still on the dirt driveway near where the gray van had been. "Might want to make sure Marek does something about that."

Luna cussed in Spanish, but I was already walking to Ty's SUV and yanking the passenger door open.

A few seconds later, Ty got behind the wheel and punched in the address Luna had given us. "So what's the real plan?" he asked as he pulled down Marek's driveway. "You really want to leave any potential witnesses and just retrieve the vehicle?"

My nostrils still flaring with every inhale, I didn't comment.

Ty smirked. "Read you loud and clear." He pulled onto the main road. "Wouldn't be my first choice either."

Fucking prick. "Don't mistake my silence for consent to anything you say."

"Whatever, asshole."

His phone rang, and instead of answering on the car's speaker system, he looked at the display. "Shit." He yanked the wheel and pulled off the road. Slamming on the brakes, he threw the SUV into park, then swept across his screen.

A small boy appeared on the screen, his hands gesticulating.

"Hold on," Ty said to the kid before balancing his phone on the steering wheel.

The kid gesticulated again.

"I said hold on. I'm in the car." As Ty spoke, he also signed out his words in ASL.

The kid signed back.

"Why the hell are you up so late?"

The kid said something to him.

Ty started signing and speaking again. "I can't pick you up. I'm at work, and hell is not a swear word. It's a place."

The kid said something back.

"Motherfucker," Ty muttered under his breath. "Okay, fine, a dollar for the swear jar. Now, why are you up?"

Ty frowned as the kid signed back.

"Your mom always works nights. This is nothing new, little man."

The kid rolled his eyes, then signed again.

"What?" Ty sat up straighter. "Where the hell is the babysitter?"

The kid signed again.

"She said that?" Ty swore under his breath, then started signing again. "You let her know next time I see her, I'm gonna kick her ass. And yes, ass is a swear word. Don't use it with your mother."

The kid let out a silent laugh.

Ty grinned, then got serious again. "Crawl back into bed, take your phone and play a game until you fall asleep. I'll text your mother and let her know what happened with the babysitter, and in the meantime, I'll get there as soon as I can. Is the front door locked? Did you use the chain?"

The kid nodded.

"Good." Ty signed the word out as he spoke it. "I'll come in the back door. Call me back if you get scared."

The boy flexed his little arm, then signed.

Ty smiled. "I know, rug rat, you're strong as hell and brave. Get some sleep."

The boy signed the only thing I knew in ASL. *I love you.*

"Love you too." Ty hung up and fired off a text before pocketing his phone and pulling back on the road.

My impression of him had done almost a one-eighty. "Your son?"

"None of your goddamn business."

"He's smart." He signed twice as fast as Ty.

Ty eased off the gas and leveled me with a look. "My personal life's personal, got it?"

More than he'd ever know. "Copy."

We drove the rest of the way in silence, except for the GPS

spewing directions. When we got close, Ty pulled down an alley behind a strip mall where half the storefronts were boarded up.

Glancing at the GPS one last time, he cut the engine and reached behind his seat. "A block over and half a block east. Looks like it'll be residential." He pulled two 9mms from the back seat. "My vote is a surprise approach on foot." He rummaged around in a duffle behind my seat before coming away with two silencers.

"Fine." I checked the magazine on my gun out of habit.

"Put your shit away." Ty handed me one of his 9mms and one of the silencers. "Fully loaded." He eyed me as he screwed the other silencer on his gun. "And untraceable." He raised an eyebrow. "We cleaning house?"

My jaw ticked, and I holstered my own gun. Screwing the silencer on the gun he gave me, I glanced around the alley and the street beyond. Gang territory at night, there were no people out. "How untraceable?"

Dead serious, Ty looked at me. "'Leave-it-at-the-scene untraceable.'"

I didn't trust him as far as I could throw him, but if anyone was going to have an untraceable piece, it'd be him. Without a word, I got out of the SUV.

Ty followed suit and locked the doors, then everything the Marines trained us to be kicked in.

Weapons drawn, sticking to the shadows, I led and Ty took my six. We covered the first block in under three minutes, and a minute later I had a visual on my Escalade in the driveway of a rundown, south Florida bungalow. A ratty screen door in place, the front door wide open, a TV was blaring from the house.

I stepped behind the vehicle and looked for the small

indents on the passenger side where I'd fired rounds at the SUV five days ago. Even though the Escalade now had tricked-out rims, the circular dents were right where I'd shot at the vehicle. I looked through the windows on the off chance her purse would still be there, but I couldn't see shit past the limo tint. As much as I hated to agree with anything Ty said, he'd been right earlier about not leaving any potential witnesses. That shit would follow Genevieve for life, and I wasn't going to let that happen.

I nodded at Ty.

Shaking his head, he kicked the rims. "Fucking gangbangers," he whispered. "They got no class."

"Recon the west side of the house, I'll take the east. Let's find out what we're dealing with."

"Copy." Ty took off toward the west side of the house.

Hunched over, I skirted the east side and checked all three of the windows. First room had four men drinking and staring at a TV. Middle window was dark, but I could see enough to tell it was an empty bathroom, and the last window was a kitchen with another guy at the stove.

I made my way back to the SUV.

Ty was already there. "Two bedrooms, one empty, two people fucking in the other."

Damn it, a female. "Four men in front room. Three are on the couch, one's on a chair, all facing west. Guns on the coffee table. A fifth man in the kitchen at the stove."

Ty nodded. "We'll breach the front door, and you take the first two on the couch. I'll get the third and the guy on the chair. You cover the kitchen, and I'll take the bedroom."

"No." He'd kill the female. "I'll cover the bedroom, you take the kitchen."

Ty smirked. "Just have to see them fucking, huh?"

"Screw you. You'll kill the female."

He looked at me like I was an idiot. "Cleaning house means cleaning house, not leaving a witness."

"I'm not shooting the female."

"You think women aren't gangbangers? You're gonna risk leaving someone alive who saw your woman's shit? Memorized her address from her ID they stole?" He shook his head. "Fuck, dude. Get real."

"We don't know if they know anything, or if her ID is even in there."

Ty snorted. "First, they're all gang brothers, they talk. Second, there were two purses in the bedroom and this house doesn't look a damn thing like a woman lives here. There's a fucking dude at the stove, bro."

I didn't have time to argue.

Shouting erupted from the living room, and we were out of time.

Ty sprinted toward the house, and I followed. He paused for one second outside the front door to glance at me and mouth, *three, two, one.*

We moved.

Ty breached first, and I was in immediately after.

Except nothing was how it was a few minutes ago. All four men were on their feet grabbing for their guns, and the fifth guy was standing at the door from the kitchen into the living room, with a cell phone to his ear, yelling at the other men.

None of them had a chance.

Two double taps and a single shot later, all five men were dead on the floor.

The sixth man, pulling on shorts, ran from the bedroom,

and Ty pulled the trigger.

A woman behind him started screaming.

Ty took aim.

"No!" I warned.

Ty pulled the trigger anyway.

A single shot to her forehead, and just like the others, she hit the floor.

"Goddamn it, Ty!"

He shrugged. "If I'm wrong about that purse, I'll pay when I meet my maker." He kicked the front door shut behind him then stepped over the dead couple. "I'm already going to hell."

Jesus fuck.

"What color's her purse?" Ty asked over his shoulder as he walked toward the bedroom.

I looked around at the bodies. "Yellow." *God-fucking-damn it.*

Ty came back into the living room wearing a smug smile and holding up Genevieve's purse. "Bingo. What'd I say?" He tossed it at me.

I grabbed it. "That you're going to hell." I did a cursory check of her purse. Wallet, ID, girl shit, it seemed to be all there, but no Escalade keys.

"In due time." Ty scanned the living room.

"No Escalade keys. Was there anything else in the bedroom?"

"Besides a crack pipe and forty-o on the nightstand, not that I saw, but you can check." He pulled one of the dead guys in the living room closer to the front door. "Give me your gun."

What the fuck? "Why?"

He stepped over the guy and moved another one opposite of where he'd laid the first one. "C-Y-A." Wiping his gun down with his shirt, he then put it in the hand of the first guy he'd moved and used the dead guy's finger to pull the trigger twice before removing the silencer and leaving the gun in his hand.

"*Jesus Christ*, Ty." I stared at the two new bullet holes in the second guy's chest.

"What?" He stepped around me. "Like you've never had to cover your tracks before."

I hadn't.

He took my gun and wiped it down and repeated the same process but with the second guy he'd moved, having him shoot the first guy.

When he was done, Ty shoved the silencers in his cargo pocket and surveyed his handiwork. "That'll do. Now the kitchen." Stepping over the guy I'd seen at the stove, Ty headed down the hallway.

I did a sweep through both bedrooms then made my way to the kitchen. "No keys."

Ty absently looked around the kitchen. "They're here somewhere."

Shit. "Probably in a pocket of one of the dead assholes."

"Check the guy who was in the kitchen first. He's the oldest, my vote's on him." Ty pulled a dishtowel off the oven door and used it to turn the burner back on under a pan of food on the stove.

"What are you doing?"

"Insurance," he muttered, looking through the cupboards. "Go find the keys."

I went back to the guy from the kitchen, and in the second pocket I checked, I found the Escalade's key fob. "Got it," I called as I walked back to Ty.

"Great." Pulling a fifth of tequila out of the cupboard, he

unscrewed the top and started pouring it all over the counter and floor.

I jumped back to avoid getting that shit on my boots. "What the fuck?"

"Like I said, insurance." Ty settled the empty bottle on its side on the counter and pulled the dishrag off his shoulder. Placing one end of the towel near the bottle and spilled liquor, he put the other near the open flame of the stove, then he glanced up at me. "Okay, ready?"

"That's your insurance? Burning the place down?"

"You got a better idea?"

Fuck. "No."

He smirked. "Hang out with me more and you might learn a few things, pretty boy."

Asshole. "Just do it. We need to get out of here." We'd already been here too long. Someone had probably seen us and tipped off the guy in the kitchen, or one of them had spotted us when we'd reconned. Either way, I wasn't sticking around to find out.

Ty shoved the edge of the cloth just close enough to the flame, and the rag caught fire. "Aaand my work here is done." He stepped back from the stove and turned toward the back door. Using his shirt like a glove, he opened it. "I love a clean break."

"Until someone reports us to the police."

Ty smirked. "In gang central? They hate the pigs more than they hate rival gangs. Trust me, if anyone did see us, no one's gonna say shit."

"There could still be trace evidence the cops find that links back to us," I argued.

Ty stepped outside, holding the door for me to follow, then

he closed it using his shirt so his prints weren't on anything. "If that happens, Luna will cover it up."

"He doesn't interfere with police investigations."

Ty laughed. Quietly, but he still laughed. "First, there won't be an investigation. Dead gangbangers killing each other, same narrative, different day, end of story. Second, why the fuck do you think Luna keeps half of Miami PD on his Christmas list? Let me clue you in, pretty boy, it ain't because they're all bros." He shook his head. "Shit, man." He scanned the backyard, same as me. "I'll wipe the front door down, you get the Escalade back to base. Stay pretty." He tipped his chin and disappeared around the west side of the house.

I took the east, glancing in the kitchen window.

The fire was already across the entire floor and had ignited the carpet in the hall.

Keeping to the shadows, I made my way to the SUV and got behind the wheel. The interior smelled like cheap cologne and desperation. Cursing, I put the seat all the way back and glanced around for Ty.

No sign of him, I drove to Luna and Associates.

CHAPTER THIRTY-THREE

Genevieve

Talon pulled up in front of my apartment complex. Scanning the parking lot, he threw the Challenger in park. "Need me to come up and get you settled, darlin'?"

"No, thank you." I spotted my Jeep a few parking spaces over.

"You got keys?"

I shook my head. "Don't need them." I'd dropped or lost mine enough times to have a spare hidden. Suddenly more tired than I'd ever been, I pushed the car door open.

"Hey." Talon stopped me.

I glanced back at him. The streetlights shone on his face, highlighting his angular jaw, and for the first time since I'd met him, he didn't look like an easygoing surfer. He looked like a hardened Marine. "What?"

"Playboy ain't a bad man. You could do way worse, just sayin'."

"Whether he's a good man or not is irrelevant." I was done with men who didn't want me, or were only with me out of obligation or worse, pity. I was better than that.

"Fair enough. Take care, darlin'."

Since it was probably the last time I'd see him, I reached over and gave him a quick hug. "Thank you for saving my life."

Returning the hug, he chuckled. "Nothin' doin', darlin',

nothin' doin'. All in a day's work."

"This is your job?" Making house calls and saving women from peril?

He laughed. The sound, rich and honest, filled the interior of his car, then spilled out into the night as if it couldn't be contained.

"No, darlin', I'm retired." He winked, like it was an inside joke. "But seems as if the man upstairs wants more outta me than just catchin' waves and livin' the good life. I get called into action every time one of Patrol's men, or women, needs medical attention."

"Patrol?"

"Luna."

"Why do you call him Patrol?"

Talon's expression sobered. "Best Marine sniper I ever met. No one died when he was on patrol, me included."

Wow. Nothing like the reality of war to make your own problems feel insignificant. "Thank you for your service."

This time his smile was reserved. "You are entirely welcome."

"So you really are a doctor?"

"Nah, I just play one on TV." He winked again. "Now get, I gotta get home to my women."

"Women?" As in plural? *Wow.* I felt thoroughly out of my element.

Talon chuckled, but his hand went to his heart, and happiness spread across his face. "Yeah, two to call my own."

Intimidated, my cheeks heated. "Take care, Talon." I got out of his car.

"You too, darlin'."

I closed the door, and it wasn't until I walked in to the foyer that I heard his Challenger pull away.

Exhaling, trying to calm my nerves, I looked over my shoulder and fidgeted as I waited for the elevator. Too soon I was on my floor and retrieving my hide-a-key from a neighbor's potted plant outside their front door.

I wanted to be home. I wanted it more than anything right now, but I knew before I even inserted the key that it wouldn't feel like home ever again.

I was a different person the last time I was here. My whole world was different now. I had deaths on my conscience. My soul had taken a beating. My pride was damaged, and my heart was more wounded than when I thought of a mother who'd given up on me.

Everything was different.

But when I pushed my front door open, the smell of home hit me. Incense, the soap on the kitchen sink, the perfume I wore for client meetings, coffee—it all greeted me, and for a single moment, I breathed it in.

Then I stepped inside, shut the door and turned on the lights.

I was right.

Nothing was the same.

For the first time, I was looking at my apartment the way Brian had seen it. It wasn't my beloved safe space full of nonexistent memories and homey comfort. Dishes in the sink, ratty fabric hanging on the walls, too many scarves thrown all over the lamps, shit all over the bookshelves that wasn't books—it was a mess.

Everything was a mess.

Me, my apartment, my life, my heart, my mind.

I snapped.

Energy I didn't know I had surged, and I was rushing into the kitchen to grab trash bags. Amped on frantic adrenaline, anger and guilt, I stormed to my bedroom and began ripping every colorful, ridiculous piece of clothing off hangers and stuffing them in trash bags. Three bags later, I was on to my drawers, pulling out all my stupid flowered, printed, colorful underwear and bright tank tops and T-shirts and shoving them in trash bags.

Dragging the bags to the front door, I didn't stop there.

I took them all to the elevator, then carried them to the apartment complex dumpster. The bin already full like it usually was, I dumped the bags next to the dumpster and made my way back upstairs.

Two feet inside my place and my gaze landed on the pile of clothes I had on a side chair near the TV that I never sat in. A dumping ground for discarded clothes and laundry I hadn't yet folded, it gave me the same itch.

Grabbing a fresh bag, I was walking toward the chair when a knock sounded at the front door.

Startled, my entire body froze.

Acute fear crawled up my back and spread like ice in my veins. There are no gangbangers left, I told myself. No one is after me. *I am safe, I am fine,* I silently chanted the affirmations as the knock sounded again, crippling me with panic.

Oh God. *Oh God, oh God, oh God.*

"Genevieve," Sawyer called through the door. "It's me. I have your things."

I sank to the floor in the middle of the living room.

No. No, no, no, I couldn't see him.

Panicked, not thinking straight, I didn't tell him to take a hike, and I didn't tell him to go pick on some other woman he wanted to screw, then treat like shit. I didn't even reply. I was too busy struggling to pull enough air into my lungs as my heart crushed in on itself.

"Genevieve." He knocked again. "I see the light. I know you're in there."

Oh dear God, please go away.

When I continued my panicked silence, he upped the ante.

"Open the door, Genevieve. *Now*," he ordered, putting all the dominance in his voice I knew he was capable of.

Open the door, I told myself. Get your suitcase, then close the door. You don't have to talk to him. Clean break. Get your shit and move on.

I stood and the plastic trash bag in my hand crinkled, and it hit me.

I didn't want my stuff.

All that suitcase had was colorful bras and silly little girl T-shirts and ridiculously printed leggings. Happy clothes. For a girl who had been trying to *fake it 'til she made it*. But I wasn't her anymore.

So I sucked in a breath.

Then another.

I didn't have to answer that door.

Not to him. Not ever.

Being as quiet as possible, I opened the trash bag and moved toward the chair.

"All right, fine," he said through the door. "If you're not going to open the door, I'm coming in."

I froze.

A key sounded in the lock.

I unfroze.

At warp speed, I tiptoe-ran all the way down the hall,

making it into my bedroom before I heard the front door open, then close.

"Genevieve?"

I spun in panic.

Heavy footsteps sounded across the entry hall, then I heard my keys being dropped on the kitchen counter. "I have your suitcase." A small thud sounded on the tiled floor.

As silently as possible, I flew into my walk-in, pulled the door halfway shut, and crouched down low in the back behind hanging dresses I'd thankfully left alone. Then I did what every self-respecting coward does. I hid.

My heart beat so loudly in my ears, I could barely hear his footsteps as he came down the hall.

The distinctive sound of my bedroom door being pushed open across the carpeting ricocheted around in my head, fighting with the sound of my own quickened breath.

A second later the closet door made its tiny squeak of protest as it was pushed open.

Squeezing my eyes shut, I held my breath.

One heartbeat.

Two…

Three…

Oh God.

Four…

The floor squeaked as his footsteps retreated.

His boots hit the tiled hallway, and I bit my cheek as tears welled.

The front door opened, and everything went still. Then three long seconds later, my front door shut.

Suspended in anxiety, I waited.

One minute.

Two.

Five.

I pushed the dresses aside and got up.

The second I stepped into my bedroom, I smelled him.

Sandalwood. Soap. Musk. *So much musk.*

My feet moved me toward the entryway.

There sat my flowered suitcase.

But it wasn't alone.

On top of the printed suitcase I used to think was cheerful and fun, but now only looked pathetic with its broken wheel, sat my bright yellow purse, the one I'd had stolen when the Escalade was carjacked. The night my life changed forever. The night a man told me to have dinner with him at three o'clock in the morning.

I broke down in tears.

Big, ugly, soul-aching tears.

A minute, an hour, a lifetime later, they stopped to make room for a crushing headache.

I took my garbage bags and went after the chair, but I didn't stop there. The wall hangings, the scarves, the knickknacks on the shelves, the dishes in the sink, all of it went into garbage bags, and when I ran out of bags, I used boxes.

Like a crazy person, I dragged it all to the dumpster in the middle of the night.

Then I fished a tablet I hadn't bought out of the offensively cheerful flower-patterned suitcase, and I emailed every single current and pending client, giving them a competitor's contact information.

Then I did the only thing left there was to do.

I pulled out the divorce papers, signed them, and walked them down to the mail drop in the lobby.

Nothing of my old life left, I crawled into bed.

My body spent, my mind shot, I prayed for sleep.

It didn't come.

Making my way to the couch with my comforter in tow, I turned on the TV and mindlessly stared at it until the sun came up on my new life.

CHAPTER THIRTY-FOUR

Sawyer

I COULDN'T SLEEP.

It was a dick move going into her apartment, but Preston had been right, the place was a disaster. More, I could smell her. Her shampoo, the faint smell of perfume, and just... her. Her skin, the scent of her neck, the smell of her body—I could've sworn she was there, hiding in her closet behind the hanging clothes, but I couldn't bring myself to look.

Instead, like a pathetic asshole, I'd sat in her parking lot for an hour. Her Jeep didn't move, and she never showed up on foot. I'd finally had to call it. But now a few hours later, the sun was rising, and I couldn't lie in bed another minute.

Forgoing the gym, I showered and dressed for work, but then I went to a coffee shop chain where I knew I could get a damn lemonade.

Bearing sustenance in the form of a bribe, I drove to her place. Thirty-one years old, and I'd never chased a woman. I'd never had to. My last name and genetics were all I usually needed.

But here I was at seven a.m. because a five-foot-nothing redhead who drove me absolutely insane had sucker punched me with her own brand of innocence and strength, and I didn't know who the fuck I was anymore.

Bypassing the elevator, I took the stairs and strode to her

door. Hearing a TV on inside, I exhaled and knocked.

Nothing.

Impatient, I knocked again.

Still nothing. No shuffling sounds, no shadow passing across the peephole, no turning down of the TV.

Fuck.

"Genevieve." I knocked again. "Open up."

Ten seconds… twenty.

Goddamn it. "I brought you breakfast." I knocked again, then I did something I'd never fucking done in my whole damn life. I begged. *"Please.* Open the door."

Forty-five seconds, no response.

I counted down another fifteen seconds, but she still didn't answer. I put the lemonade, hot tea and carrot muffin on the floor. "Fine. If you don't want to talk to me, at least eat the food I brought. It's outside the door." I waited a beat, then headed back to my car.

Once I was behind the wheel, I cranked the engine, but I didn't pull out. I glanced at the clock on the dashboard. I had fifty-two minutes before I was due at work. Not that any of us had set schedules, but I rolled in at the same time every day I wasn't out on assignment. You could take the Marine out of active duty, but you couldn't take the Marine out of the man. I liked routine. I craved it. Until I'd met Genevieve, routine had kept my head straight. But sitting my ass in my Range Rover parked outside a woman's house I'd been cock deep in was anything but routine.

I still fucking sat.

I sat for forty-five minutes, silently berating myself for every damn thing I'd done wrong with her. Not the least of which was blaming her for me having sex with her. I could've turned her down, kept my damn dick in my pants, but the simple truth was I didn't want to. I'd wanted to dominate her since the second I'd laid eyes on her.

It was no excuse for breaking the promise I made to myself all those years ago to never be a damn thing like my father, but maybe, just maybe Luna had been right. Maybe there were shades of married. I wasn't ignorant, I knew I had nothing to do with breaking her marriage apart, but I'd always thought if temptation did arise, I'd be a stronger man, an honorable man.

But there was no honor in stalking a woman who didn't want to speak to you.

CHAPTER THIRTY-FIVE

Genevieve

A KNOCK SOUNDED ON THE FRONT DOOR.

It wasn't the usual early morning knock that I'd been getting and ignoring every day for a week. That knock came complete with a one-sided conversation, breakfast food, lemonade and tea, and it was all neatly delivered on time and left outside my door. This knock, at night, wasn't that knock, but I ignored it just the same.

Another knock sounded.

I stared at the TV. A couple was house hunting. I pitied them.

A third and fourth knock sounded, then it turned into outright rude banging.

The couple chose the shittiest house possible.

The banging kept up.

Rousing myself, I got up and went to the door, but I didn't bother looking in the peephole. Safety didn't matter anymore. I now knew you could die anytime, all it took was someone with a gun.

My dirty hair falling in my face, I opened the door.

His scent hit me before my eyes adjusted to the bright light of the hallway. Wearing jeans, a fitted T-shirt, and a baseball cap pulled low over his face, Sawyer shoved his offending knock-slash-banging hands in his pockets.

"My father cheated on my mother," he admitted without preamble.

I hadn't slept in a week. I didn't give a shit what his father did.

"I swore to myself I would never be like him," he continued. "He's a fucking bastard all the way around."

A strange thing about not talking all the time? I realized other people were just as quick to fill that silence I used to so desperately avoid. I'd spent my entire childhood in silence. Even in a house full of foster kids where the foster parents were only in it for the state funds, my world was silent. I'd had no one to talk to. Not about me or my fears or my crippling anxiety. No one wanted to know how I was, what I was thinking, or what I was feeling.

I learned quick that true words meant nothing.

So I never said any.

I smiled and talked about nothing, and all that nothingness took so much energy that I didn't have to think about the hole in my chest that grew every day.

One that was still growing.

Stark blue eyes studied me, and for a second, I thought maybe, just maybe, for the first time someone was seeing that hole.

Then he spoke and crushed the hope.

"Did you hear me?"

He'd missed the boat. The tide had shifted. I no longer had the energy to speak about nothing and listen to nothing. And his words, they were nothing. I didn't want to hear them, and I didn't want to give any back. Those six dead men, gang members or not, they'd never speak again. Why did I get to? Because my desperate beginnings in life didn't culminate in joining a gang just so I could belong to something other than my thoughts?

No, I didn't want to speak.

Or listen.

I shut the door and turned to go back to my couch.

Unfortunately, I didn't check to make sure the door closed all the way. I didn't even bother to lock it. What was the point? If I'd learned nothing else, I'd learned that I had no control over when I died, and locks weren't going to change that.

So I hadn't checked.

But I probably should have, because every other time I'd closed a door on him, he'd done the opposite of what he was supposed to.

This time was no exception.

No boundaries, he followed me inside, but unlike me, he locked the door behind him. I probably should've clued him in that it was pointless, but he was one of the people in life who carried one of those guns that took away life, so… lucky him. He probably had an advantage in that regard.

I silently snorted to myself. *Advantage.* Right. He had all the advantages. Funny how it never made him smile.

Like now, no smile, he strode in and stopped short, looking around my teeny, tiny living room. "Where is everything?" he bit the question out, making it sound like a demand.

Too bad for him I was done taking orders from anyone, clients especially.

I sat on my couch that now only had two pillows, two matching pillows, and I stared at the TV. "I have everything I need." Until rent was due next month, then I might not. But my last client had offered me a job in her art gallery. Maybe I should call her.

His hands went to his hips and his voice came out accusing. "Where are the scarves, the wall hangings, the clothes on the chair?"

"Gone." All of it, even the dishes in the sink, and it was all his fault.

"Why?" he demanded.

Short and clipped, it was the same voice he'd used on me in the shower. *Say it,* he'd demanded that day, and the two words had replayed in my head on a daily cycle like a curse. *Say it, say it, say it.*

I picked up the remote and turned the volume on the TV louder, drowning out him and his memories.

"I'm talking to you," he barked.

I hit the volume another level higher.

I didn't want to talk.

I was done talking.

I was done listening too.

"*Genevieve,*" he snapped as the old lady who lived below me banged the handle of her broom on her ceiling.

Leaning over, I picked up the single bookend I still owned. Ceramic and heavy and shaped like an owl, it was a stupid bright glossy yellow. I slammed it on the wood floor four times. Then I sat back on the couch and leaned my head on the even stupider plain-colored throw pillow as I curled into a ball.

The old lady banged on the ceiling again. But this time, she didn't stop.

I turned my TV up to full volume, blasting the home renovation show.

For two whole ear-splitting heartbeats, he stood there.

Like a sentry, like a giant crusader of judgment, like a glowing neon sign of everything I never was and could never have, he stood there. Hands on his hips, baseball cap pulled low, an angry frown perfected by wealth and privilege and the Marines, he stupidly, crushingly, stood there and stared at me like I was the crazy one.

Then he moved.

One second he was a statue. The next he was scooping me up.

Except unlike the last time he'd picked me up, I didn't go willingly.

"No!" I kicked out, making a solid connection with his thigh.

He didn't even flinch. His maddeningly giant, muscular arms slid around me like vise grips and he lifted.

My body left my couch and, sanity be damned, I let loose. "NO!"

I screamed.

I kicked.

I hit.

I called him every swear word that my brain could feed my mouth. "Put me down, you asshole, motherfucker, jerkface, shithead!"

He didn't even flinch.

So I said the very last words I meant and the only ones I could say. "I hate you!" I hated him for everything he'd shown me. I hated him for giving me a whiskey. I hated him for taking me to that diner. I hated him for his perfectly perfect penthouse. I hated him for his stupidly ridiculous cooking skills, and I hated every kind thing he'd ever done for me. "I hate you, I hate you, *I hate you!*"

I loved him.

Giant sobs broke a week-long dam.

"I hate you," I choke-cried, hitting his chest.

His giant strides eating up my living room and hallway, he strode into my bathroom like he'd been there before. Setting me on my feet, but not letting go of me, he threw on the water.

His giant arm clamped around me, holding me to his chest, didn't give me much room. But one leg free and one arm loose, I gave it my all. I kicked and I hit him. "Let me go! I hate you!"

Holding me even tighter, he reached in his pocket and retrieved his keys, wallet and cell. He tossed them all in my bathroom sink, along with his baseball cap, while I continued to uselessly beat against his stupidly big muscles.

I didn't think about why we were in the bathroom.

I didn't think about anything except the unbearable last seven days.

I wanted out of my head, and I wanted out of his arms.

But nothing had felt this solid in a week. Nothing had felt this solid ever. His hard muscles, his rising and falling chest, his musk-laced sandalwood and soap scent, his unbreakable demeanor, he was solid. Too solid.

And I was nothing.

"Nothing, nothing, nothing," I chanted, pounding my fist against his chest.

My feet left the ground.

Cold water hit my face, my arms, my chest, and I screamed.

Huge hands, gripping me firmly, held me in place.

I kicked out and screamed louder as water sluiced down my shivering body, drenching my three-day-old outfit.

"That's it," his deep voice calmly encouraged. "Get it out."

I didn't want to get it out. I wanted to scream. I wanted to wail. I wanted to unsee dead bodies and unfeel his hands on me. I wanted my life back before I lived a week with no cluttered chaos and homemade dinners every night. I wanted to have never, *never* pulled off that man's face mask.

I killed him.

I killed a human being.

He was dead at my hands. They all were.

But they were going to kill me and not blink twice.

What was I supposed to do with that?

What was I supposed to do with the guilt eating at my stomach and the regret suffocating my heart?

I didn't know. So my soul screamed until my throat burned like fire, then I screamed some more.

I screamed until the bathroom door kicked open and a cop stood there, weapon drawn.

"Arms up!" he shouted. "*Arms up!*"

My screaming stopped, but I started to violently shake.

His eyes on me, Sawyer raised his arms. "My wallet is in the sink, officer. Look at my ID, and please lower your weapon. She has PTSD from an armed robbery."

The cop ignored him. "We got a call for a noise complaint. Why is she screaming?"

"She's upset," Sawyer calmly answered. "Wallet, my ID," he commanded. "Check it."

"Keep your hands where I can see them." The cop slowly lowered his weapon and holstered it to pick up Sawyer's wallet.

Sawyer turned the water to hot, then wrapped his arms around me.

The noise of the TV blaring from the living room stopped, and another cop appeared behind the first one. "Everything okay?"

No one answered.

The first cop opened Sawyer's wallet and looked at his

license, his shoulders visibly stiffening. "My apologies, Mr. Savatier. I didn't realize who you were."

"No apology necessary," Sawyer answered civilly.

Putting Sawyer's wallet down, the cop nodded at me. "Does she need medical attention?"

"No. I've got it handled."

"Understood." The first cop glanced at the cop behind him, and they started to leave.

"The front door?" Sawyer asked.

The first cop glanced back at him. "You can submit a claim to the department for any repair costs."

"That won't be necessary. Thank you for checking on us."

The first cop tipped his chin. "Thank you for your service. The downstairs neighbor requests that you please keep the noise to a minimum."

"Ten-four," Sawyer answered.

The cops left.

Sawyer's arms tightened around me. "They're gone."

Despite the warm water, my teeth chattered. "M-my fr-front door's br-broken?"

"I'll fix it."

"Wh-why are y-y-you here?"

"Let's get you dried off." He shut the water off and stepped out of the shower.

I stared at his soaked clothes as he grabbed a towel from the hook behind the door. "Y-you're soaked."

He wrapped the towel around me. "You have a dryer."

"Your sh-shoes."

"Waterproof boots. They're fine." He lifted me out of the shower like I was a child. Stepping out of his boots in my small bathroom, he undid his belt and pulled it free. Tossing it with his stuff already in the sink, he pulled off his T-shirt and undid his jeans.

Holding the towel around my shoulders, I watched his striptease.

No shyness, he took off his pants and fitted boxers. "Get your wet clothes off, and I'll grab you dry ones." He dried his shoulders, then wrapped the towel around his waist, but it did nothing to conceal the hard, full length of him.

All I could think was, how did that fit inside me?

"Genevieve?"

I wanted to hate the way he said my name, but I didn't. Every time I heard it, it was like I was hearing someone else's name. No one said my name like he did. Hearing it made me look up at his too handsome features and clear blue eyes. I'd stopped shivering, but my heart was hammering irregularly, and more than anything, I just wanted to fall asleep in his arms. I wasn't even mad at him for throwing me in the shower.

As if he could read my thoughts, he cupped my cheek and his thumb gently brushed under my eye. "When was the last time you slept?"

Did it matter? I shrugged.

"Okay." Inhaling, he pried the towel from my grasping hands. "Let's get these wet clothes off you." He tossed the towel over his shoulder and lifted the hem of my baby doll pajama tank. "Arms up."

The memory sandblasted me. "That's the second time you've said that to me."

The muscles in his jaw moved, but he didn't say anything. He lifted my shirt over my head, and I was suddenly acutely aware of my hardened nipples and no bra.

I reached for the towel over his shoulder.

Taking over, he whipped it off and wrapped it around my shoulders, but unlike me when he was undressing, he avoiding staring at my half-naked body.

I held the towel tight against my chest as he gripped the waistband of my black pajama shorts and slid them down my legs.

Gathering up all of our wet clothes, he stood and turned toward the door. "Wait here," he commanded before walking out.

I did what he said, but I made one mistake. I looked at myself in the mirror.

CHAPTER THIRTY-SIX

Sawyer

THE LOST LOOK ON HER FACE WASN'T ANYTHING I HADN'T SEEN A hundred times over in the Marines, but on her?

I shook my head and threw our clothes in her dryer.

I was an idiot for not immediately noticing all the shit missing from her place. I'd been so damn worried that she wasn't answering the door, that when she finally did, all I had was anger. Misplaced anger.

I walked into her bedroom and went for the closet. It was half empty like last time I'd seen it, but today I noticed it was all monochromatic. Blacks, whites, grays—all the pinks, yellows and greens she'd worn when she'd stayed with me were gone. I got angrier with myself. Yanking a gray shirt off a hanger, I found a pair of black leggings in a drawer and strode back to the bathroom.

She was exactly where I'd left her, except she was staring at herself in the mirror.

"I'm tired," she whispered.

Her voice, the look on her face—she crushed me. "I know." I took the towel from her again and dried her hair as best I could before slipping the shirt over her head. "We'll make a quick run to grab supplies to fix your door and some food, then you can sleep." I dropped to a squat and held her pants for her to step into.

"I can't go into a store." She stepped into one leg.

"Why not?"

She stepped into the other. "No bra."

Shit. "You can wait in the car if you want." I pulled her pants up for her.

Her gaze fixed on the mirror, she didn't comment about the car. "My hair's a mess."

I picked up her brush. Grasping her long locks in one land, I started at the bottom and worked my way up, brushing out the tangles.

"You've done this before."

"For my sister, when we were kids." Holding the top of her head, I worked through the section I'd had in my hand.

"She's lucky to have you."

"She wouldn't agree."

"Why?"

Thankful to have her talking, I answered even though discussing my family was my least favorite subject. "I left her with the burden of taking over my father's business when I enlisted."

"Having money is a burden?"

She had no idea. "It's not a simple life."

"Neither is going hungry."

Impotent anger at her past circumstances made my muscles stiffen, but I forced my voice to remain even. "Did you go hungry often?"

"Not once I was old enough to work."

I drew the brush through the entire length of her hair. "What was your first job?"

She exhaled as if releasing some tension. "Sweeping floors in a bakery. I was fourteen. At the end of the day, whatever didn't sell, I was supposed to bag and take to a nearby homeless shelter, but....” She trailed off.

“You kept it.”

“I did. Until I got fired.”

I did one more pass with the brush. “What happened?”

“I got sick, but I couldn’t call in because my foster parents wouldn’t let any of the kids use the house phone. So when I showed up the next day, barely well enough to stand up, let alone leave the house, they fired me for being a no-show.”

I put her brush down and looked at her in the mirror. “I’m sorry.”

Her gaze drifted. “One of the owners, Rusty, taught me how to decorate cakes. He never knew it, but I credit him for sparking my interest in parties.”

Nothing animated about her voice or story, she looked more sad than when I’d walked through the door. I wanted to pull her into my arms, but I didn’t. “I’m glad you had that experience then.” I took her hand. “Come on.”

She didn’t protest as I led her to her kitchen. She didn’t ask what I was doing when I sat her on a stool. She didn’t look at her front door, and she didn’t comment when I made her a cup of tea.

She watched my movements like she was both studying me and not seeing me as I set the mug in front of her. “Drink.”

Lifting her hands from her lap, she wrapped them around the mug, but she didn’t drink. She stared at the tea.

“I’ll check the dryer.” I made it two strides.

“You thought that made you like him? Like your father?”

I paused.

“Because of... what we did in the shower?”

I turned. “Yes.” I didn’t lie.

She picked the mug up. “I signed the papers.”

I stared at her profile.

She took a sip. "That night. I signed them."

I wanted to ask if it was because of me. It shouldn't have mattered, but it did. "I'm sorry your marriage dissolved."

Anger bled into her tone. "Stop apologizing to me."

"Stop blaming yourself for those gang members' deaths."

Her hands tightened on the mug. "We're not supposed to talk about that. *Ever*," she bit out.

"You can always talk to me. Anytime."

"I don't want to talk."

That's what worried me. "None of us had any reservations about pulling the trigger."

"I'm not you or one of your friends."

No, she wasn't. "That's what I like about you."

"You don't like me," she argued, holding the mug in front of her like a shield as she stared straight ahead. "I'm not stupid. You're angry around me."

"I'm angry with myself."

The mug paused halfway to her mouth then she put it back down, but she didn't say anything.

"Every step with you, I mishandled," I admitted.

She looked up at me, and her amber-green doe eyes took me in like the hero I wasn't. "I'm alive because of you."

"You were in danger because of me," I corrected.

Her full lips parted as if she were going to say something.

Like a fool, I waited, hoping for her forgiveness.

But she closed her mouth and dropped her gaze.

I went to get my clothes.

CHAPTER THIRTY-SEVEN

Genevieve

I PUT ON A BRA AS HE CHANGED BACK INTO HIS CLOTHES IN THE bathroom. When he came out with his baseball cap pulled low and told me to grab my purse, I grabbed it. When he wordlessly put his hand on the small of my back and led me past my splintered front doorjamb, I allowed it.

When he took us to his Range Rover and held open the passenger door, I got in. When he got behind the wheel and told me to buckle my seat belt, I buckled it.

Everything he told me to do, I did.

But my head was spinning.

He blamed himself.

Just like I was blaming myself.

But I knew it wasn't his fault.

Just as I should've realized it wasn't mine.

Two lives intertwined by happenstance, blaming themselves for a third person's horrible choices. When in truth, Sawyer was no more responsible for those six deaths than I was. Everything we did was in defense against their actions. None of us would have been in those situations if it weren't for that carjacker.

It was his fault.

Not mine.

Not Sawyer's.

The weight I'd been carrying lifted somewhat as he pulled into the parking lot of a home improvement store.

Putting his SUV in park, he left the engine and AC running. "Lock the doors after I get out."

"I'll come with you." I reached for my door handle but not before I saw a look flash across his face I couldn't decipher.

"Wait." He cut the engine and got out, rounding the front of the vehicle.

I watched him scan the parking lot, taking in every inch of our surroundings like he was cataloging everyone and everything.

It made me feel safe, safer than I'd felt in seven days.

Opening my door, his manners didn't waver. He held his hand out to me.

I took it.

He helped me out of the vehicle, and for the first time in days, I tasted, smelled and felt something other than guilt.

I felt his strong hand around mine. I smelled his clean scent. I tasted the mint tea he had made me, and sun warmed my face.

I felt safe.

"Thank you," I whispered, not trusting my voice.

His stark blue eyes cut from the surrounding parking lot to me. "For what?"

"Taking care of me." It made me feel so vulnerable to say the words, but I said them and more. "Feeding me all week." Every day I'd waited until he'd left, then I'd gotten up and retrieved his daily breakfast and eaten it. It was the only food I'd eaten all week.

For three whole heartbeats, he said nothing.

Then Sawyer Savatier leaned down, and his lips touched my forehead. "You're welcome."

I exhaled, releasing a breath I'd been holding since my first memory of foster care. I didn't think I'd ever felt less burdened, until I inhaled and the air wasn't weighted with every breath of my past.

Across the parking lot, through the entrance and until he pulled a cart out, Sawyer held my hand. Then he put me in front of him, grasped the cart and enclosed me in the circle of his protection.

My steps no longer heavy, I let him lead us through the store, quietly watching as he put stuff in the cart and answering his few brief questions about any tools I might have at home. It wasn't until we were in the checkout line that I realized I'd never done this with Brian. I'd never done it with anyone.

I was a home-improvement-store-as-a-couple virgin.

The thought almost made me smile, until I realized we weren't a couple.

My fragile mood plummeted as the young female cashier smiled wide at Sawyer despite him standing at my back with one hand on my hip as he unloaded stuff onto the counter to be rung up.

I reached for my purse to get my wallet, but his hand covered mine, stopping me.

His lips brushed my ear as his voice dropped. "I got it." He kissed my temple.

Three simple words, one single gesture, but I felt them race up my back and sink low in my belly, sending a shiver of awareness across my whole body.

I didn't argue with him about paying. Instead, I watched the muscles and veins in his forearms flex as he pulled his own wallet out and paid with a credit card.

Politely thanking the cashier, but not making eye contact,

he took the receipt, then his lips brushed past my ear again and he tapped my leg. "Step up. On the cart."

I didn't hesitate. I put both feet on the bottom rack of the cart.

His chest closed in on my back, his arms locked around my sides, and he sped up his stride.

He took me on a ride.

Fresh air and wind hit my face and something extraordinary happened. Something I didn't think I would be capable of again.

I smiled.

I smiled freely all the way to his SUV.

I smiled contentedly as he opened the back.

I smiled like a schoolgirl as he caught my gaze and winked.

And I smiled blissfully as he took me in his arms.

Pulling me in close, pressing me against his hard body, he hugged me.

He hugged me, and he made me feel.

"That smile." He kissed my hair. "That's what I was looking for."

CHAPTER THIRTY-EIGHT

Sawyer

HER SMILE, UNGUARDED AND BEAUTIFUL, SPREAD ACROSS HER FACE.
For the first time since she'd walked out of my place, I could breathe.

"That smile." Holding her in my arms, I kissed the top of her head. "That's what I was looking for."

Her arms wrapped around my waist. "Thank you," she breathed.

"You can thank me after I fix your front door." Regretfully, I let her go and held the passenger door of the Range Rover open for her.

"Maybe I will," she quipped, some of her spark coming back.

Closing her door, the corner of my mouth tipped up as I got behind the wheel. An easy silence fell between us on the way back to her place, and I couldn't think of a single place I wanted to be more than with her.

My good mood held until we stepped off her elevator and found her front door wide open.

Setting the supplies down, I cursed myself for not having my piece. Holding a finger up to my lips, I pushed her clear out of the path of the open door, then held my hand up and whispered, "Wait."

Her eyes went wide with trepidation.

Hating the fear that lingered just under the surface for her, I moved quietly into her place. With no weapon, I felt naked, but I knew a hundred ways to incapacitate a man.

Turned out I didn't have to.

"Brian," I clipped.

Standing in the living room, his back to me, the fucker spun around and sized me up. "Where's Evie? What happened to our place? Was she robbed?"

Ignoring him, I went back in the hall and purposely took her hand. "All clear."

"Who's...." She trailed off as I led her inside, her body going completely rigid. "What are you doing here, Brian?"

Holding a rolled-up piece of paper, he threw his arms up and looked at her like she was out of her mind. "What the hell happened to our place?"

"It's my place," she corrected the prick. "The cops needed to get inside, and they didn't ring the doorbell."

The prick glanced at our joined hands. "My name's still on the lease."

She didn't give him an inch. "Good for you. What do you want?"

Looking between us, he frowned. "Where's all your stuff?"

"Gone." She didn't elaborate.

His voice quieted with a concern he didn't have when his wife was lying in a hospital bed. "You were robbed?"

My free hand fisted as my other squeezed hers. I stepped in. "She's fine." Not that he gave a shit.

She pulled her hand out of my grasp. "You can leave, Brian."

Sighing, his fake expression of concern slipped. "I need to speak with you in private."

"Then you should've called."

"I did," the prick whined. "You didn't answer your phone."

"I had nothing to say to you."

"Really, Genevieve?" Still holding the paper, his hands went to his hips. "We're both adults here. I'm sure we can have a conversa—"

"That's it." Fuck this asshole. "You're done. Leave."

He glared at me. "I'll leave after I've spoken to my *wife*."

"Now she's your wife? When you need something? What about when she was in the hospital?" The fucking prick was lucky he was still standing. "She signed your papers. Get out before I throw you out." I took a menacing step toward him.

He backed away from me, but looked at Genevieve. "You didn't sign the part about relinquishing my last name. You need to do that. You know what I asked for. It's only fair."

Un-fucking-believable. "Her last name is her business name. She'll keep it if she wants." Even though it killed me to have her tied to this prick in any way, it was still her business. She got to choose.

"*Business*." The asshole snorted. "She sends out invitations and orders cakes. It's not like she's well-known or even a brand. She knows what she has to do, what the *right thing* to do is. And *my* papers?" he asked, incredulous. "Is that what she told you? That I asked for this divorce?" The prick shook his head at her. "Nice, Genevieve, lying to make yourself look better."

"*Out*," I barked.

The asshole held his hands up. "Don't shoot." He sneered at me. "I'm going." Moving toward the door, he eyed Genevieve. "Answer your phone next time I call." He threw the papers he was holding on her kitchen counter and walked out.

Not sure what to think, I looked at Genevieve.

Her gaze on him as he left, her shoulders defeated, she crossed her arms but didn't say shit.

I waited.

When she continued with her silence, I caved. "You divorced him?"

"He filed the papers."

Goddamn it. "Not what I asked." I didn't give a shit who filed.

She glanced at the couch. "It's complicated."

I'll bet. "It always is." Needing to pound something, I went back to the hall and grabbed the shit to fix her door because I said I would, but all I wanted to do was fucking pound her ex's face in, or leave.

It was the second time she'd lied, and I'd be a fucking fool if I gave her the opportunity for a third.

I hauled the material in as she dropped to the couch and turned the TV on. I spent the next forty-five minutes stripping the damaged casing and jamb, replacing them and putting in a new, more secure lock. I broke the damaged pieces of frame I'd pulled off over my knee so they'd be small enough to dump in her trash and went to the ground floor to the dumpster I'd seen earlier. Pulling the gate open, I tossed the wood in the overflowing dumpster, and my gaze landed on white trash bags at my feet. Barely tied off, there were five of them and they all had colorful clothing and material coming out of them. A box next to them was full of knickknack shit women put on bookshelves. I didn't have to riffle through them to know they were hers.

"Jesus," I muttered.

Making a split-second decision, I grabbed the bags and took them to my Range Rover. I returned for the box, loaded it in my SUV, then went back upstairs.

Still lying on the couch, curled in a ball, she stared at the TV.

"Door's fixed."

"Thanks." She didn't look up.

I told myself to walk away. I didn't need anyone in my life who lied, especially not a woman. Not to mention her moods flipped like a fucking switch. I didn't know what caused her change for the better on the way to the store, but I'd felt it. Now I was looking at the woman who'd ignored me for a week, the same woman who lied to me about being married.

I knew what I had to do, for my own sanity.

"The key for the new lock is on the counter. Goodbye, Genevieve."

She waited until I had the door open. "We had an argument."

My hand on the handle, like a fucking fool, I paused.

"He wanted us to get pregnant."

My blood boiled at the thought of her having a child with that asshole.

"I wanted to foster. Foster to adopt, actually," she clarified, taking a heavy breath before her voice went quiet as hell. "He said he wasn't going to raise someone else's problem."

Jesus.

"I was never his wife," she continued. "I was always his problem. I was his problem when I told him I didn't want to be married anymore, and when I refused to talk about it. I was his problem when I wouldn't see his side of it. I was his problem when he got frustrated and filed the divorce papers. I was his problem when I wouldn't sign papers that made me someone's mistake… again." Her voice got even quieter. "I was always someone's *problem*."

Jesus fucking Christ.

"Those papers made me feel like the failure my existence was had come full circle," she continued. "They made me relive every moment of being put in foster care. It was emotional and stupid not to sign. My rational side knew it. I had no hold on him, not that I wanted one after what he'd let slip about his true feelings. Besides, he has a new girlfriend and she's pregnant. He wants to marry her and make the perfect family." She pushed herself up into a sitting position. "Now he can." She stood. "You should probably go."

I didn't leave. I took three strides and cupped her face. "It isn't your fault he's an asshole, or that you wound up in foster care."

"No, it wasn't, but it felt like it was. I was a six-year-old kid with attention span issues who failed kindergarten, and my birth mom couldn't handle being a single mom with a problem kid. Just like it wasn't my fault that those carjackers joined a gang and decided to steal." She looked up at me with resignation. "None of it was my fault, but it all still happened, and it's all still my life."

She'd had everything in her life taken from her or broken by some asshole. Her trust, her stability, her spirit, her heart, but still, *still,* she'd looked up at me the first time she saw me and she'd given me a smile so pure of heart, it shone from her pretty eyes to her full lips.

I'd seen her as a lost doe, but she'd been waging her own battles since before I'd so much as thought about the Marines. She'd waged and won. Still standing, no training, no military support at her back, no family, no money, she'd navigated her own war zone and come out alive.

She wasn't a doe.

She wasn't even weak.

She was a fucking warrior.

I stroked her soft cheek. "You are not a problem, you hear me?" I tightened my hold. "Do not let anyone ever tell you differently."

Her eyes welled and a tear slid down her cheek.

I lost all restraint.

My mouth crashed over hers.

CHAPTER THIRTY-NINE

Genevieve

H IS MOUTH SLAMMED OVER MINE AND THE SEESAWING, EXHAUSTING emotions that had been plaguing me all week, driving me insane, they all evaporated the second his lips touched mine.

But he didn't stop there.

Pushing my back to the wall, tossing off his baseball cap, he plundered my mouth as his hands gripped two handfuls of my hair. All at once, he consumed me. Growling into my mouth, curving his body around mine, he tasted me and he kissed me.

And he tormented me.

His mouth, his hands, his sheer size—he was a dangerous game. Nothing else mattered when I was in his vortex and he was stealing my breath, making my body ache for the drug he was offering.

But I couldn't do this. Not like this. Not to him.

I pressed my hands to his chest and pushed at him hard.

Our mouths parted, and the sound of our broken kiss filled the space between my head and my heart.

His chest heaving, his eyes hooded, he watched me, but he didn't move more than a few inches away.

Trapped, in his gaze, in the cage between his body and the wall, I had no choice. I ducked and stepped away from him.

"Fuck." His hand on the wall, his head dropped.

"Genevieve," he said with quiet resignation. "I'm sorry."

"Just… wait." I went to the junk drawer in my kitchen and riffled, coming away with what I needed.

"What are you doing?" he asked, his voice tired.

"Taking control."

I was done with my past.

I was done being no one.

I was done feeling responsible for everything out of my control.

No more stressing about every single detail of everyone else's parties, immersing myself in lives that weren't mine, trying to be good enough for a life I didn't want.

No more.

I signed the papers giving Brian his last name back. I was no longer Genevieve Jenkins. I was Genevieve James, daughter of a woman who didn't want me. But I wasn't going to be owned by a last name anymore. I didn't need to be. I wasn't a name. I was me. A mess of red curls, chaotic thoughts and the hope of a dream.

A dream I wanted to chase.

I looked up at that dream.

Expression guarded, shoulders proud, Sawyer watched me like he'd done since I'd first met him—with an intensity that made me feel special.

"Do you want me?" I bravely asked.

His voice firm, he didn't hesitate. "Yes."

"More than once?"

His penetrating gaze took me in before he gave me a measured response. "I've already had you once."

"Because you felt guilty for what happened?"

"No."

"Then tell me why," I ordered, making my own demands.

"You're everything I'm not," he answered, no intonation in his voice.

Not expecting that answer, I wasn't sure if it was a compliment. "I could say the same about you."

"Your smile," he added, his body perfectly still.

I frowned. "A smile isn't a reason."

"It is when it's yours."

So very guarded, no emotion in his response, his words still made my stomach flutter, but I couldn't ignore the obvious. "We don't make sense."

"No, we don't."

It was as if a blade sliced through my stomach. "Then you should leav—"

He cut me off. "You smile and you mean it. You retain an innocence despite growing up in shit circumstances, and you breathe kindness." Taking a step toward me, his voice took on an edge. "But you also have a temper. When it comes out, it makes me want to bend you over my knee. And when you flutter around me with your nervous energy, it makes me want to tie you down and show you how to submit." He stopped in front of me and fingered a strand of my hair. "I want to wrap your hair around my fist as I sink inside you." His determined gaze cut into my very soul. "And I want to wake up to this look every damn day."

Oh God, I wanted that.

He dragged his finger from the corner of my eye, down my cheek and to my bottom lip. "These innocent doe eyes only seeing me, these lips wet from my kiss." He leaned down to my ear. "Yes, I want you." His open mouth landed on the flesh under my ear, and he sucked before whispering, "Over and over."

My entire body shook with restraint, but I wasn't finished. "I don't want casual."

"Good, because I don't share." His lips traveled down my neck.

I had to warn him. "I'm not the girl you met two weeks ago who dropped her tablet."

He pulled back just enough to look at me. "I know."

"I may never be her again."

"I apologize for my part in that."

Knowing what I was going to say next, heat flamed my cheeks. "I apologize for the shower at your friend's house. If I had known how you felt, I never would've asked for what I did."

His thumb brushed across my blush. "Violence makes people want to reaffirm life. I don't hold you responsible for anything that happened that day."

"You've seen a lot of death." It wasn't a question, it was an assumption, but he nodded once anyway. It made me brave enough to ask my next question. "Does it get easier?"

"Which part?"

"This feeling like there's a blanket over everything and I'm struggling to get out from under it."

"How honest do you want me to be?"

That nervous energy he'd mentioned about me, it was like a slow drip. Until it wasn't. Then it was a rushing stream, and some days I couldn't dam it up to save my life. But last week that nervous energy had taken a back seat to this heavy fog of guilt I was under, and I'd forgotten how debilitating the nervous energy was until this very moment.

One question about honesty, and I was back to the insecure girl who wanted to please everyone, but in the process of trying too hard, I was failing at the one thing that mattered most.

I wasn't being honest with myself.

So I took a breath and nodded. "I want you to be all the way honest."

"You were under the blanket before I met you."

I didn't want to take offense, because he was right, but his words hurt just the same. "Then why did you ask me to dinner?"

"We all have our demons."

"Meaning?" I knew what he meant. He was saying he had his demons, but I wanted to hear that from him and how it related to him making the first decision to take me out to eat. I didn't know why it mattered so much to me, but it did.

He searched my face as his thumb slowly caressed my cheek again. "You were brave enough to let yours show. You made no apologies for it."

"Maybe you just made me nervous."

"Maybe you've always tried to please everyone."

I didn't like where this was heading. The balance between us had never felt anything close to equal, but this felt like I was sinking. "Pleasing people was my job."

"Was?"

I hadn't told him. I hadn't told anyone. Inhaling, I braced myself for a wave of self-doubt, then I gave him the truth. "I quit my clients."

"All of them?" he asked without hesitation and without any change in his facial expression.

"Yes."

"Do you feel better?"

"I...." Wow. "That wasn't the reaction I was expecting."

"That wasn't an answer to my question."

"It's complicated."

"I have time."

I sucked in a deep breath. Then I let it out. All of it. "I'd never met anyone like you. So steadfast in your seriousness and intensity. Nothing about you wavered, not even when you were angry. I was immediately drawn to you for it. But what I'd failed to comprehend until I'd spent five straight days in your company was the profound impact you would have on me.

"I'd never been around someone so still, so sure of himself. And like a moth to a flame, I wanted to soak in everything about you, but getting that close came at a price. I no longer wanted to be myself. I didn't want to be the barely contained chaos that managed a hundred thousand details by the skin of her teeth. I wanted to be the calm, cool, collected Marine who caught someone else's fall."

"I didn't catch you," he reminded me, his fingers gently tracing the back of my head just above my neck. "You have a scar to prove that."

Oh, he'd caught me all right, and he'd changed me. "I don't care about the scar, but I need a fresh start."

This time, his expression did change. His eyebrows drew together in a stern frown.

I clarified. "In my next career." Whatever I decided to do.

"Which is?"

"My last client offered me a job working in her art gallery." She'd mentioned it in passing at the end of the party I'd organized for her, but then I'd gotten sidetracked with the caterer and I'd never told her no thank you.

Which was fate staring me down.

Fate and a six-foot-three ex-Marine who was heir to a real estate fortune.

He tipped his chin once, then quietly asked, "Are you done talking?"

Nervous energy bled out. "Your family will never approve of me."

"I'm not my family, and they're never going to stand between us. I would never allow that." He leaned closer and enunciated each of his next three words. "Are you done?"

"Yes." No.

His voice dropped. "Turn around, Genevieve."

CHAPTER FORTY

Sawyer

WAS DONE TALKING. SHE DIDN'T NEED TO HEAR MY WORDS. SHE needed my control.

"Turn around, Genevieve," I quietly ordered.

Her chest rose with a sharp inhale, but she turned.

"Good." My cock stiffened. "Walk into your bedroom."

For two seconds, she didn't move.

Then she graced me with the soft sway of her hips and did exactly as I'd instructed.

Taking my keys and phone out of my pocket, I followed her to where she stopped in front of her bed, her back still to me. Tossing my shit on her nightstand, I issued another command. "Take your shirt off."

Hesitating, she glanced at my stuff.

I gave her fair warning. "I like control, Genevieve."

Her red hair cascaded down her back in soft waves. "Always?"

"Yes."

"Why?"

Because we all had our demons. Because I never had control until I turned eighteen. Because the Marines taught me to be a man, but I spent eight years taking orders. "Because I can."

"So, in the shower…" She inhaled a steadying breath. "That wasn't just… just rough because of circumstances?"

"No." That's how I fucked. Rough and in control.

"Oh," she breathed, exhaling.

I dragged a finger down the side of her neck and watched her shiver as chill bumps raced across her skin. Then I gave her an ultimatum. "You need to decide." I knew myself. There was only one way this would work, but I wasn't going to make the decision to not choose me easy on her. Shamelessly, ruthlessly, I kissed the top of her shoulder, then brought my mouth to the sensitive flesh right below her ear. "Tell me to leave," I whispered, kissing her soft skin once. "Or take off your shirt."

"*Sawyer,*" she whispered, angling her head to give me more of her sweet-smelling neck.

"Decide." My dick was pulsing, and my mouth was watering to taste her. If she decided to draw this out much longer, I wouldn't be the dominating control I was promising her. I would only be rough.

"H-have you done this before?"

I knew what she was asking. "I don't sleep around." I could count the number of women I'd had on two hands, but most of those were when I was younger and navigating my preferences.

"I've never experienced anything like when we…. Like in that shower."

"I know." I drew a finger down the center of her back. "Now make a decision before I decide for you."

"I'm scared," she barely whispered.

"I won't hurt you," I promised.

Stepping away, she turned to face me. Then she gave me her decision. She took off her shirt.

The rush of victory going straight to my dick, I clipped out another order. "Pants."

Slow, deliberate, she pushed her leggings over the swell of

her hips and toed out of them. Standing back up, the errant curl I wanted to wrap around my finger fell over her eye as her face and chest flushed with excitement and nerves. She bit her bottom lip.

Fuck, she was stunning. "Bra."

Reaching behind herself, she unhooked the black lace and pushed the straps off. Her bra dropped to the floor and her heavy breasts fell free.

Fighting not to touch her hard nipples, hell, to touch her anywhere yet, I issued another command. "Turn around."

Submissive, beautiful, she turned.

Pulling my T-shirt over my head, I stepped out of my boots. "Get on the bed on all fours." I unbuckled my belt. "Keep your knees on the edge of the mattress." Hard as fuck, I kicked off my jeans.

She crawled on the bed, her sweet ass to me, then she dropped to all fours.

Fuck. *Fuck.*

Her cunt wet, her ass begging to be taken, she didn't just drop to all fours, she rested on her forearms and looked over her shoulder at me.

Holding her gaze, I stroked myself.

Her lips parted, and her tongue darted out.

She was fucking perfect.

Stepping behind her, careful of her still healing wound, I wrapped my hand around the back of her neck. "Head down." I gently pushed.

Still looking at me, her cheek went to the mattress.

"Good," I murmured, stroking her hair.

"Touch me," she whispered.

I stepped back.

Worry shot across her face, and she started to push herself up. "I didn't mean—"

"Head down." I traced an invisible line over her ass and down the back of one thigh. "Ass up."

Watching me with uncertainty, she rested her head against the mattress again.

I stroked myself hard. "I said, ass up." Just looking at her in this position made me want to come.

Dropping her lower back, she angled her hips up.

"That's it." Goddamn, she was fucking perfect. "Good girl." Her cunt was so wet, I could've shoved into her in one thrust. But I wasn't going to.

Taking in every inch of her submissive little body, I dragged my hand down her back and over her hip, then I gave her fair warning. "I'm not going to wear a condom."

Her back tensed. "I'm not on anything."

Squeezing the part of her hips that I wanted to hold on to as I pounded into her, I stroked myself harder. "I won't come inside you. Not tonight." But fuck, I wanted to. Leaning over her back, I nipped her shoulder and made a promise. "I will soon though."

A sweet moan escaped her lips, and her eyes fluttered shut. "Okay."

I dropped to one knee, and without hesitation, I licked from her clit to her ass.

Her back arched and her arms shot out as she fisted two handfuls of bedding.

She tasted like mind-numbing obsession. Groaning, I licked her again and again. Then I sank two fingers into her and stroked her G-spot.

"Ahhh!" Her elbows locked and her back went rigid.

Drowning in her desire and her scent, I grasped the back of one of her thighs and shoved her leg up as I latched on to her clit. Stroking her, sucking her, I took her clit between my teeth and bit.

She screamed, then her pussy was clenching.

I didn't hesitate. I stood and shoved my cock into her wet cunt.

Her scream turned into a groan that filled her small bedroom, and my eyes rolled back in my head.

Goddamn, she was tight.

And still fucking coming.

Pulling back halfway, I grabbed her hip with one hand, then I thrust deep. My finger still soaked from her cunt, I pressed into her ass.

She jerked and her elbows locked as panic laced her voice. "What are you doing?"

Easing my fingers and my cock out of her, I dropped my hands to my sides and waited.

When I didn't verbally respond, she looked over her shoulder at me.

I stroked myself. "Did I hurt you?"

Heat colored her cheeks, and her gaze shot to my cock before she looked back at me. "N-no."

"Did I make you a promise?" I asked, no intonation.

"Yes."

"What was it?" I demanded.

"That you wouldn't hurt me."

I lowered my voice. "Head down, Genevieve."

Hesitant, but so fucking beautiful for it, she kept her gaze on me and lowered herself back down.

Rewarding her for her submission, I entered her slowly.

Her eyes fluttered shut.

I pulled out and stroked the head of my cock against her clit. When she moaned, I pressed my finger against her ass, barely breaching her.

She tensed, but this time she didn't jerk away.

I rubbed against her clit harder and gave her the raw truth. "This doesn't work if you don't trust me."

"I trust you," she whispered.

"Do you?" I hadn't earned it. I knew that. And I was a prick for asking, but I wasn't going fuck her into submission missionary-style any more than she was going to enjoy a man who didn't take control. She was drowning in decisions she couldn't manage when I met her. The need to strip her bare in every sense of the word had been pounding through my veins since the second I'd laid eyes on her.

"Yes," she breathed. "I trust you."

"Good." Using my own spit, I circled the tight opening of her ass. "Does this hurt?"

She shook her head.

"Words," I clipped.

"No," she instantly replied, her voice tight. "It doesn't hurt."

I eased my finger an inch inside her as I steadily rubbed her clit. "Giving yourself to me means I'm going to touch every part of your body." I sank my finger in another inch.

She sucked in a sharp breath. "Am I?" A shiver went up her spine as uncertainty bled out of her mouth. "Giving myself to you?"

"You already did." I sank my finger all the way into her ass and drove my cock into her cunt.

A cry of pleasure ripped from her lungs, her pussy clenched

around my dick, and a new surge of her desire soaked my cock. "*Sawyer.*"

I lost my fucking mind.

Grabbing her hip, finger fucking her ass, pounding into her so hard my cock bottomed out on every thrust, I fucked her.

And she fucked my heart, crippling my control.

CHAPTER FORTY-ONE

Genevieve

IS FINGER SANK INTO ME WHERE NO MAN HAD EVER TOUCHED AS HIS giant cock slammed into my core, hitting the very end of me, and blinding me to all reason. Pain bled into pleasure in a thick swirl of confusion my body didn't know how to process.

I screamed. I moaned. I felt my inner muscles tightening again far too soon.

"No, no, *no*," I cried out, gripping handfuls of sheets in an attempt to hold on to my sanity.

The wet smacking sound of two bodies in heat instantly stopped. His cock roughly jerked out of my core, his finger slid out of my ass, and the abrupt loss of his touch almost destroyed me.

His heavy breathing filling the sudden silence, he spoke. "Are you telling me to stop?"

Oh God, oh God, oh God.

His tone, the hint of barely detectable anger, the gravelly intensity to his voice—the last thing I wanted was for him to stop, but something was happening that I didn't understand. Words vomited out of my mouth before I could stop them. "I want to please you."

His voice turned deadly quiet. "Did I hurt you?"

So fucking much. "No," I lied.

For three whole heartbeats, nothing moved except the drip of my own desire down my inner thigh.

Then he broke me.

"Get dressed," he ordered.

"*What?*" I was off the bed before I knew what I was doing. "That's it?"

His back to me, he picked his pants up. "Yes," he said without an ounce of intonation.

"What's wrong with you?" Confused, hurt, embarrassed, sexual frustrated like I'd never experienced—I didn't ask the question, I yelled it.

He spun, and a fury I didn't think he was capable of contorted his entire face. "*You lied.*" The two words spit out of his mouth like accusation, judgment and conviction.

"No I didn't!" I yelled back.

"*I hurt you,*" he roared.

I couldn't help it, I burst into tears. There was more emotion, more feeling, more *everything* in a single thrust of his body inside mine than anything I'd ever experienced, and I didn't know how to handle it.

So I just told the truth.

"Yes," I cried. "You did hurt me. You hurt my pride, you hurt my feelings and you hurt my body. Every *second* around you is a precipice I don't know how to navigate. I only know if I fall, it'll hurt worse than anything I've ever felt, because for once in my life, I dared for a second, *just for a second*, to hope for the promise you were dangling. That fairy tale of finding your soul mate. So yes, you hurt me. Your body inside mine hurt. It hurt my core, it hurt my heart and it hurt my pride. But none of that hurt more than the impotent feeling of wanting to please you and not being able to because I didn't know how to do… how to do…" I waved toward the bed and sucked in a breath. "I didn't know how to do *that*."

I didn't wait for a response.

I grabbed my clothes off the floor and fled to the bathroom. Slamming the door shut and locking it, I turned the shower on and sank to the floor.

Then the tears came.

Every emotion I'd been holding back for a week, every emotion that didn't come out when he'd stepped me under the cold spray of the water like a barbarian, every guilty feeling I was still struggling with, it all came out.

I hated a mother I could barely remember who abandoned me.

I hated Brian and his bullshit.

I hated planning other people's parties and never having one myself.

I hated that I wasn't good enough for a man like Sawyer Savatier.

And I hated all the tears because I wasn't sad. I was mad.

But my emotions didn't follow the rule book, so I cried. I cried so hard I didn't hear the door open or notice two bare feet in front of me until it was too late.

Huge hands snaked under my arms, and I was lifted all the way up and onto the counter. My ass hit the cold surface, and he grasped the backs of my thighs, angling my legs around his waist.

Then he did the very last thing I was expecting.

He fisted himself and unerringly eased inside me.

My breath caught, and his hand cupped my face. His stark blue gaze landed on me, making me feel as if I were the sole focus of his entire being.

"You do please me," he said, his deep voice calm and quiet again.

Oh God, the feel of him inside me. I forced myself to concentrate. "I'm sorry I yelled at you. That wasn't me." I wasn't a yeller.

His giant cock pulsed inside me, but he didn't pull back or thrust, he just held still. "You have to be truthful with me."

"I…." Oh my God. "I didn't know what you meant or how to answer your question." I needed him to move.

"Answer it now," he quietly demanded. "With honesty."

"It felt dirty," I blurted.

He didn't take offense or even flinch. "Did it feel good?"

How did I answer that? "I'm not experienced."

"I don't need experienced." His thumb swept over my check. "Answer the question."

I ducked my head. "Yes."

He tipped my chin. "And did I physically hurt you?"

"I-I don't know. I've never felt anything like that. It felt… deep." And life-altering and heartbreaking, and I didn't want to think of Brian, because there was no comparison, but Sawyer, he was just so much bigger, in every way, that I didn't have any ground to hold on to when it came to him.

Pushing my legs up, he thrust in deeper, hitting the very edge of my womb. "I'm as deep as I was before. Does this hurt?"

I bit my lip to keep from moaning. "Not now, but it's…."

"It's what?" he asked, grinding his hips.

He hit something profound inside me, and all at once my toes were curling, my nipples were achingly hard, and I was as desperate for more as much as I wanted to push him away. "It's not comfortable," I admitted.

Leaning toward me, he nipped my ear as his thumb found

my clit. "I'm not trying to make you comfortable."

"*Oh God.*" My fingers dug into his rock-hard biceps. "What are you doing to me?"

He ground his hips again. "I'm hitting your cervix and stroking your G-spot. Your body is small, your cunt is tight and my cock is large. I'm bottoming out in you."

Only a man like Sawyer Savatier could simultaneously make those words sound like sin personified and make me feel so, *so* sexy that it was me he was saying them to.

Suddenly panting, I had to concentrate to form words. "It hurts and it feels good all at once." Desire leaked out of me and slid down the crack of my ass.

He ground against me again. "Is the pleasure more than the pain?"

Shit. "Yes." *Definitely yes.* A thousand times yes.

"The more I'm inside you, the more you'll get used to the intrusion." Easing back as he spoke, he began to slowly thrust in and out of me.

"*Oh God*, I like the sound of that. Wait, no," I panted. "I love the sound of that, but what if—" I grunted as he bottomed out again. "What if I don't want to get used to it?" Holding on to his arms for dear life, feeling like I was going to come again, I looked up at him. "What if I want it to feel like this every time?"

Without warning, his hands gripped my ass and he lifted me off the counter.

Squealing in surprise, my arms went around his neck, and then he was thrusting.

Hard.

Holding my weight, holding my ass, controlling my body, he gripped me and he fucked me.

Every single dominating thrust, he slammed into my

cervix and stoked my G-spot.

My body slapped against his, and the pain I'd feared before bled into pleasure as the controlled expression he carried every second of every day turned into a fierce, hooded gaze, intense with lust and dominance.

"Come," he demanded, not even out of breath.

"I...." *Oh my fucking God.* "I can't." I didn't want to, not yet.

He slammed into me deep and gripped my ass so tight that when he ground against my mound, my clit wept with joy.

The orgasm exploded, touching every nerve in my body.

My mouth opened, a wail crawled out of my throat, and my pussy spasmed as my nails dug into his flesh.

"*Sawyer,*" I cried.

A growl, part groan, all roar, vibrated his chest, and his pulsing cock left my spent pussy a split second before his hot come shot all over my stomach.

Then he abruptly dropped me to my feet as his hand swept through his release on my stomach. "Turn around." He barked out the order.

I spun.

"Chest on the counter, legs spread."

His short, clipped, dominant demands throwing me off guard after his orgasm and mine, I did what he said without question.

My breasts landed on the counter that had been warmed by my ass, and I spread my legs.

His fingers, wet and thick, slid down the crack of my ass.

I sucked in a surprised, nervous gasp.

He shoved a finger into my ass at the same time as he pinched my clit.

I gripped the edge of the counter and went on tiptoe as my

body clenched against the invasion. "Oh my God."

"Exhale," he demanded, stilling his hand.

Holy shit, holy shit, holy shit. I tried to breath out deep, but I couldn't. I was being filled in a way I'd never imagined, and the sensation of his fingers in my ass and simultaneously on my clit had me reeling. I didn't know if I was coming again, or if I'd ever stopped, but the painful need to release was there again, and it was making me so edgy, I wanted to do something, but I didn't know what.

"I said, *exhale,*" he ordered, working my body.

Sucking in a deep breath so I would be forced to let it out, I did as he said.

I exhaled.

His finger, hot and wet with his release, slid deeper inside my ass, and he circled my clit with tantalizing pressure.

Stepping close behind me with his cock still hard, he rubbed against the back of my thigh as he brought his lips to my ear. "My come belongs inside you."

Oh my fucking God.

CHAPTER FORTY-TWO

Sawyer

I WAS GOING TO MAKE HER MINE, EVERY GODDAMN INCH OF HER gorgeous body.

Biting the edge of her ear, grasping her jaw, I brought her face up so she could see us in the mirror.

Her cheeks flushed, her hair everywhere, her breasts pushed into the counter—she sucked in a sharp breath when she saw our reflection.

I tightened my grip on her jaw. "You're mine." I stroked my finger once in her ass, pushing my release further inside her, then I eased out.

"I need to get on the pill," she blurted, giving away her thoughts as she trembled under my control.

"I don't want you on the pill," I admitted.

Her body stilled under me. "But, that means—"

"I know what it means." Holding her gaze and my fucking breath, I kissed the soft flesh of her neck.

Her hands gripping the edge of the counter, she tried to push up. "But I, but you, you can't mean…."

I held my body over hers, not giving her an opportunity to escape me or this conversation. "I mean exactly what I said." Every word.

She stopped fighting to get up. "But, why?"

Unwavering, I held her gaze. "I want to give you a family."

I wanted her to be my family.

She didn't blush. She didn't even blink. She went dead white. "Oh my God," she breathed. "Are you asking—"

"I'm telling you my intent." If I was asking her to marry me, she would know it.

She pulled out of my grasp and her head dropped. "*Shit.*"

Forcing myself not to react, keeping my movements controlled, I stood and brought her up with me. Turning her, I grasped her chin, but she kept her eyes closed. "Look at me," I demanded.

She opened her eyes, but distress tainted every inch of her face.

Damn it.

Manning the fuck up, I said what I should say instead of what I wanted to say. "If you don't want me, tell me now. I'll leave."

Grasping my wrist, she pulled my hand away and her head fell to my chest. "You don't get it," she whispered.

"Then explain," I clipped.

She looked up at me with every emotion written in raw vulnerability across her face. "I can't bring a child into this world when so many are out there who desperately need a home." She swallowed. "I want to foster and adopt."

I fell more in love with her. "Then we'll adopt."

She blinked. Her mouth opened, then closed, then opened again. "But you said you belong inside me and that you want to give me a family."

"Do you not want to have my children?" Would I be willing to give up seeing her body swell with my child?

She bit her lip, and her gaze drifted. Her voice dropped to barely a whisper. "Sawyer, please."

"We can't do both?"

Inhaling, she looked up at me. "Are we really having this conversation?"

"I'm not playing games with you." I was too old for that shit.

She shook her head. "I'm not either. I just thought... I don't know." She drew her lips in, then exhaled. "This isn't too soon to be talking about this?"

"No." I wanted my hands in her hair. I wanted back inside her body. I wanted to kiss her. Fuck, I just wanted to hold her, but I didn't do any of it. "I know what I want."

Slow, she nodded. "You want me."

Without a doubt. "Yes."

Something close to determination flashed across her features. "And you're okay with adopting?"

"Yes." I'd never thought about it before meeting her, but now I had zero reservations.

"Foster to adopt?"

Whatever she wanted. "Yes."

Tiny lines appeared between her eyes as she frowned. "But you also want your own children?"

I laid it all out. "I do."

"Both?" she whispered, unconsciously leaning into me.

The corner of my mouth tipped up. "Yes, both."

The hint of a shy smile spread across her lips. "Sawyer Savatier, are you saying you want a life with me full of children, some we have and some we take in?"

"Yes." I grabbed her ass and picked her up.

Squealing, laughing, she wrapped her legs and her arms around me. "Sawyer!"

I fucking loved it when she said my name. "Say it again," I

demanded, walking her into her bedroom.

"Sawyer, Sawyer, Sawyer," she chanted, giggling.

I dropped her to her bed and crawled over her.

"Sawyer," she whispered, wrapping her arms around my neck.

I cupped her face. "Be mine."

"Okay," she breathed, spreading her legs under me, and rubbing her wet cunt against my hard cock. "But only if you'll be mine."

Fuck. "I already am." I slid inside her.

EPILOGUE

USED THE CURLING IRON ONE LAST TIME, BUT IT DIDN'T MATTER. THE second I pulled the heat away from my hair, it mocked my attempt at big, loose curls. A spiral returned and fell over my face.

Blowing if off my forehead, digging in my drawer for a pretty clip, I cursed. "Shit."

His low chuckle filled the bathroom.

I looked up in the mirror.

His hands in his pockets, his suit light gray, his shirt a crisp white, he leaned against the doorframe as half his mouth tipped up in a smirk.

"It's not funny." Pouting, I picked up a tiny barrette and clipped the curl back.

His hands still in his pockets, he stepped up behind me. His body heat covered my back as he leaned over and kissed my bare shoulder. "Take the clip out," he quietly demanded.

I took it out, but I protested. "That curl's going to fall over my face all night."

Unguarded, he smiled. "I know." Watching me in the mirror, he nipped my ear and whispered, "I love that curl."

Heat covered my face. "I love you," I breathed, saying the new words.

His expression turned deadly serious, then he gave me

more. "I love everything about you." He always gave me more. "Not everything." I dipped my head, still shy under his scrutiny and intensity. "I'm not perfect." The couple weeks we'd been living together, I'd left my fair share of clothes lying around, dishes in the sink, shoes abandoned in the living room. He never said anything, he just silently eyed everything.

"There is no love in perfection." He kissed my cheek and stepped back. Then his voice took on an edge that made my stomach flutter. "Lift your dress."

I looked at him in the mirror. "We're already late." And I was already nervous enough about meeting his sister, let alone at her office. But Sawyer had been summoned to sign some paperwork a few weeks ago that he'd put off, so now we were stopping by before going to dinner so he could finally handle it.

"I'm not going to take you again. Not yet," he reassured.

I couldn't help it, I was disappointed. It'd only been an hour since he'd been inside me, but he'd turned me into a wanton mess of needy desire. Just being near him made me wet and achy. But it was an ache I couldn't ease on my own. Believe me, I'd tried. The few times he been working late and I was left by myself in his huge penthouse, I'd tried, but nothing had worked.

He'd turned me into his own personal harlot.

My body only responded to him.

And oh my God, did it respond.

The thought of doing exactly what he told me to do already had me wet, but I was on my second pair of underwear for the evening. "I'm not lifting my dress."

His voice turned even quieter. "Yes, you are."

My heart sped up, my stomach fluttered, and chills raced across my skin. I never had a chance at disobedience. I turned to face him and lifted my dress.

His huge, magical, glorious hands still in his pockets, denying me his touch, he stepped up to me.

Still inches shorter than him in my high heels, I looked up at my billionaire bodyguard. "As you wish, Mr. Savatier," I whispered.

"Keep holding that dress up," he ordered.

It was all the warning I got.

He dropped to one knee and slid my underwear down in one fluid movement. Then his tongue was on me.

"Oh God," I moaned, my knees bending.

Sucking my clit swiftly and surely between his teeth, he drove two fingers into me.

"*Ahhhh.*" Need, sharp and painful, consumed me as I fell back into the bathroom counter. "Oh God." I didn't care about being late anymore. I didn't even care about meeting his sister. I just wanted to feel what he could do to my body—what he did do to it every day.

His fingers stroked in and out of me, working me like only he could.

"Don't stop," I panted, rocking into him. "So close."

As swiftly as he'd dropped and put his mouth on me, he stood and barked an order. "Turn around, on the counter."

By now, I understood his clipped demands. And I didn't question them.

Turning and stepping out of my heels, I bent. My chest, my breasts, they pressed into the counter as I spread my legs and gave him my ass.

His fingers, wet from my desire and the orgasm he'd released inside me before I'd gotten dressed, coasted over my ass, then he pressed one finger in.

Going up on tiptoe, I gasped.

His other hand found my clit and circled.

"Sawyer," I pleaded, barely still holding my dress up.

He sank his second finger inside my ass and dragged his nail over my clit. "Come."

His rough command was all it took.

Bent over the bathroom counter, my cocktail dress in my arms, his fingers in my ass and on my clit, I came.

And I shook.

Because no matter how many times he made me come, he was wrong. My body never got more accustomed to him. It only became more insatiable.

As if reading my wayward thoughts, his back covered mine and his mouth found my ear as his fingers drove deep. "Get ready for me, baby, because I'm going to come here later tonight, filling you *everywhere*." Drawing out the last word like a warning instead of promise, he bit my neck. "Give me the rest of that orgasm," he roughly whispered, pinching my clit as the last of my release wrecked me.

"Oh God," I practically wept. "*Sawyer*."

His mouth found mine as he eased his fingers out of me, kissing me slow and languid until I stopped shaking. Then he stood to his full height and brought me up with him.

Staring at me in the mirror, he touched his lips to my temple. "Straighten up. The car's downstairs."

"Car?" I asked, still trying to catch my breath. He usually drove his SUV whenever we went anywhere.

"Yes." He winked at me. "Hurry." He walked out of the bathroom.

I gripped the edge of the counter and exhaled. Holy shit, that man. I didn't know what I'd done to deserve him, but I didn't question it. Not anymore. I straightened the deep olive silk dress he'd bought me, and I slipped on the gold bangle bracelet he'd given me after I'd moved in. Stepping back into my heels that matched my dress, I looked in the mirror.

I looked freshly fucked, and it looked good on me.

Sawyer looked good on me.

A smile spread across my face at my ridiculousness, and I walked out of the bathroom. It wasn't until I was in the entry, taking his outstretched hand, that I realized what he'd done.

"You did that on purpose," I accused.

"Did what?" He led us to the elevator.

"Gave me an orgasm to calm my nerves."

Flashing me a hint of a smile in his sideways glance as we stepped into the elevator, he winked. "You have no reason to be nervous. My sister's relatively harmless."

I scoffed. "Right. A woman who runs a multibillion-dollar company for your father is *harmless*."

"I said relatively. I wouldn't cross her in the boardroom."

Terrific.

He squeezed my hand. "I heard that."

"I didn't say anything."

His thumb stroked across the top of my hand as the elevator opened to the lobby. "Relax."

I didn't have a chance to respond.

Preston was standing there waiting in a Luna and Associates uniform. Looking everywhere but at us, he barely made eye contact with Sawyer and completely ignored me. "All set?"

Sawyer tipped his chin and rattled off an address downtown.

"Copy." Preston walked ahead and held first the door out of the lobby for us, then the back door to one of the Luna and Associates Escalades.

I got in first and Sawyer followed.

Before Preston got behind the wheel, I looked at Sawyer. "What's this all about? You never use the guys at work to ferry us around. You only have one of them pick me up on occasion when you can't get me from work." Sawyer had taken to driving me and picking me up every day at the art gallery at my new job.

I admit, at first, I was taken aback by his steadfastness at making sure I got to work safely, as he put it, but now I enjoyed the extra time I got to spend with him. And I looked forward to seeing him when he picked me up.

He leaned over and kissed my temple. "Maybe I want to have a drink with you at dinner."

Sawyer didn't drink.

Neither did I.

I studied him as Preston got behind the wheel. "You're up to something."

"Which entrance do you want?" Preston asked as he eased into early evening traffic. "Garage or lobby?"

"Lobby," Sawyer answered.

"Copy," Preston responded.

I stared at Sawyer. "You still haven't answered."

Chuckling, he leaned back in his seat.

"Okay, that's it." Sawyer never chuckled, and he definitely never sat casually, or even relaxed, let alone leaned back. "Tell me."

His hand landed on my thigh, and his eyes got a look I knew well before he dropped his voice. "Watch it," he warned, inching his hand under the hem of my dress.

I closed my mouth and my legs.

He squeezed my knee, and we rode in silence the rest of

the way to downtown Miami. Preston pulled up in front a giant, modern steel and glass high-rise with the words *Savatier Holdings* emblazoned at the top.

My heart rate kicked up and my nerves itched at my skin as Preston opened the door and Sawyer helped me out of the SUV.

"We won't be long," Sawyer told Preston.

"Ten-four." Preston nodded before getting back behind the wheel.

Sawyer led me through the automatic doors of the impressive granite-tiled lobby and to an isolated elevator at the far end of the room. A security guard greeted Sawyer by name, and a few people nodded at him, but otherwise, the people leaving work for the day swept past us.

Sawyer placed his thumb on a fingerprint scanner beside the elevator. The doors immediately slid open, and once we were inside, he pressed the button for the top floor.

I tried to exhale through my nerves as the elevator ascended. Despite Sawyer saying we would be in and out, that it was only routine paperwork he needed to sign, I felt like something was off.

Squeezing my hand, Sawyer slid his thumb across my knuckles. "It's going to be fine. Stop worrying."

"What if she hates me?" I had found out that Sawyer barely had any relationship with his father, occasionally tolerated his sister, and texted his mother once a week. He'd also sent his mother a picture of us. I'd thought it was cute, but now I was just praying she wouldn't be here.

"She won't hate you," Sawyer reassured. "She reserves that honor for me."

"That's not funny," I scolded as the elevator stopped and

the door slid open to a lavishly appointed reception area with an even more elegant young blonde behind the reception desk.

The blonde got up and walked toward us, holding her hand out to Sawyer. "Mr. Savatier," she cooed in some kind of fake-sounding accent. "Such a pleasure to see you."

Sawyer briefly shook her hand. "Raquel."

Raquel barely glanced at me. "And who do we have here?"

"Miss James, Raquel. Raquel, Miss James," he clipped. "Is Savina in her office?"

"Yes, of course." Raquel smiled only at Sawyer. "Can I show you the way?"

"No." Dismissing her, keeping his hand on the small of my back, Sawyer led me down a long hallway of mostly dark offices now that it was almost six p.m.

"I kinda hate Raquel," I admitted in a hushed whisper.

Sawyer took my hand and squeezed it once. "Me too. Always have."

That made me smile as he took a right turn and led us to a corner office.

Pausing to kiss my forehead, Sawyer smiled down at me. "Don't be nervous. It'll be fine, we'll be in and out." He knocked once on the door.

"Come in," a female voice called from inside.

Sawyer pushed the door open and, one stride inside, he froze. "What the fuck, Savina?"

Sullivan Savatier, his wife, and a tall, thin blonde woman who could have been Sawyer's twin all stood in front of an ornate desk that overlooked the Miami skyline.

"Do not speak to your sister like that," Sullivan Savatier boomed, his angry expression matching his son's.

Oh God.

"I'll speak to her any damn way I want when she ambushes me with a family reunion," Sawyer barked.

"Oh, shut up, both of you." Sawyer's sister pushed past both men like it was nothing and walked right at me. Her smile practiced, her poise professional, she held out her hand. "I'm Savina. You must Genevieve. Ignore these two." She nodded at her father and brother.

Swallowing past the sudden dryness in my throat, I shook her hand. "Nice to meet you." She wasn't just beautiful, she was stunning.

Sawyer wrapped his arm around me. "Introduction's over, we're leaving. Courier the damn paperwork."

"Sawyer, please." His mother spoke up. "Don't go."

Sawyer didn't relent. "I'll talk to you next week, Mom. Savina, you're on my shit list." He turned us toward the door.

"You walk out that door, you lose everything," his father boomed.

Sawyer's entire body stiffened. Slow, with a deadly calm, he turned to face his father. "Are you threatening me?"

"You think we don't know what's going on here?" Without taking his lethal glare off Sawyer, Sullivan Savatier tipped his chin at me. "You think we don't know you're shacked up in my penthouse with her? A nobody, an *orphan*," he spit out. "The writing's on the wall, son, grow up."

Sawyer's nostrils flared. "What did you just call me?"

"Like it or not, you are, and will always be, *my son*," Sullivan snapped, pointing his finger at Sawyer.

Sawyer growled with rage. "You stopped being a father the minute you—"

"Enough!" Mrs. Savatier stepped between them. "Both of you, cut this out!" She turned to her son. "Sawyer, we just want to reason with you. We know you like this young woman." She paused to smile warily at me. "And she's so very lovely." She looked back at her son. "But we want you to just… play it safe." She grasped his shoulder.

Ignoring his mother, Sawyer glared at his sister. "You did this."

I wanted to sink into the thick carpet.

"Oh come on, Sawyer." Savina threw her hands up. "She's living with you, and she hasn't even signed an NDA."

A nondisclosure agreement? *Holy fucking shit.* I stepped out of Sawyer's grasp. "I think it's best if I wait outside." I forced a smile for Sawyer. "I'll wait with Preston." I turned toward the door.

"No," Sawyer barked.

My back stiffened.

"Is that what the Marines taught you?" Sullivan's deep voice, not unlike his son's, boomed. "To yell at women?"

"At least I don't cheat on them," Sawyer threw back.

"*Sawyer!*" Both Mrs. Sullivan and Savina yelled.

"All of you can go to hell." Sawyer grabbed my hand.

"She needs to sign an NDA and a prenup," Savina warned.

"I haven't asked her to marry me yet!" Sawyer roared.

Oh my fucking God. *Marry?*

"If you marry her without a prenup, you lose everything," Sullivan threatened.

"Don't fucking threaten me unless you have the balls to back it up. The penthouse is in my name, and you can't touch the trust or my seat on the board," Sawyer threw back.

Savina sighed. "Yes, he can."

Sawyer's chest heaving, he was clearly taken off guard, because he didn't immediately retort.

"Got your attention now, boy?" Sullivan almost gloated. "You watch who you're talking to, *son.*" He pointed an ugly finger at me, but kept his glare on Sawyer. "You marry this orphan without her signing an ironclad prenup, you get *nothing.* Read the terms of your trust." He pushed past him, but paused at the door. "How's that for balls?" Walking out, he slammed the door behind him.

"We just want to protect you, Sawyer," his mother quietly added.

Sawyer's glare cut to his mother. "You should've left him twenty years ago." Turning on his sister, he spit more anger out. "Keep the trust. I don't give a shit about my seat on my board." Yanking the door open, then grabbing my hand, Sawyer led me out of the office.

Stunned speechless, I let Sawyer lead me back to the elevator. The receptionist gone, the private elevator thankfully still waiting for us, I thought I would be able to breathe again in a few seconds once we got back outside, but Sawyer pressed the button for the floor below the one we were on instead of the lobby.

I took my hand back and crossed my arms. "What are you doing?" My voice shook.

The elevator opened to the floor below. Almost an exact replica of the floor above, but slightly less lavish, the space thankfully didn't have a receptionist behind the desk, but I didn't care. I didn't want to be here. I needed to get out of this building.

Without a word, Sawyer took my hand and pulled me down another long hall as he fished keys out of his pocket. When we got to the corner of the building, he slid the key into a closed office door and threw it open, dragging me inside.

"Where are we?" I asked nervously.

"My office," he clipped, shutting the door and pushing me against it.

I barely had time to take in the perfectly placed desk and furniture that looked like it'd never been used. "You have an office here?"

"Yes." Taking both of my wrists and pinning them over my head, Sawyer leaned into me. "What did I promise you?" he asked roughly.

Oh God. "Don't you dare," I warned. "Not here." I knew that voice.

His nostrils flared, but his voice turned even quieter. "What did I promise you, Genevieve?"

My eyes welled. "Please don't do this."

"I'm not taking your clothes off." His jaw ticked. "*What* did I promise you?"

"That you wouldn't hurt me." I wanted to cry. But not for me. For him. His family was awful. No wonder he'd hid me away from them for the weeks we'd been together.

His shoulders relaxed marginally, and he inhaled. Then he threw me. "What have I told you about you taking birth control?"

"That you don't want me on it," I answered, remembering our conversation that night weeks ago.

"Why?" he demanded.

Heat flamed my cheeks. "Because you said you want children…" I was barely able to swallow past the lump in my throat. "With me," I whispered.

"What does that tell you?" he demanded.

"That you love me." Because he'd also told me later that night that he would be honored to adopt or foster children with me, but that he also very much wanted to see my body swell with his child. I'd smiled with joy and half joked that we could have three and adopt three. He'd very seriously agreed, and I'd fallen asleep in his arms.

"That's correct."

"Sawyer—"

"I want you, Genevieve James, not all of this bullshit." He brought my arms down and wrapped them around his neck. "I don't give a fuck about my father's company, my seat on the board, my trust—none of that. The penthouse is in my name, I have my own money, and no matter what, I will always take care of you." He leaned closer, and his hard length pressed into me. "I will *always* be there for you."

"I-I don't understand. Why are you saying all of this now?" Especially after what had just happened.

"Because I made a mistake."

My stomach dropped. "A mistake?"

He cupped my face. "I told my mother I was ring shopping."

Every muscle in my body went perfectly still.

Reaching into his pocket, Sawyer Savatier dropped to one knee.

My heart stopped.

Taking my hand, he held a giant diamond in front of my ring finger. "This was not how I planned this. I was going to take you out. Dinner, drinks, a long speech about how perfect you are and how imperfect I am. Instead, the fucking mess that's my family happened. I don't give a damn about my father's company or making him more money, I never have. It's why we argue, but through every ugly, dysfunctional word upstairs, I knew one thing to be true." Unwavering, he held my gaze. "I love you, Genevieve James. We've weathered a hell of a lot worse than a few angry words, and I know without a doubt, we'll weather anything else that comes our way. I want to wake up every day to your smile, and I want to spend my life making you happy. Will you do me the honor of becoming my wife?"

Tears dripped down my face. I knew what I wanted to say, but instead I said what I should say. "I won't marry you without a prenup."

His chest rose and fell twice rapidly as if he were waging a war. "I am not asking, nor will I ever ask, you to sign one."

"I'm not letting you walk away from what's rightfully yours." And I wasn't going to let him walk away from his family for me either. I didn't know how I would do it, but I'd try my damndest to bring them together. Or least have them not want to kill each other when they were in the same room. They were a family, and that was precious.

"I want you more than all of this bullshit," he protested.

"You can have both."

"I only want one."

"We're a package deal," I whispered.

His eyes closed and he inhaled.

Then he slid the ring on my finger, stood and brought his lips to mine. "Done."

"Sawyer." I choked on a sob that was part shock and all joy.

His mouth slammed over mine.

And he kissed me.

God, did he kiss me.

His hands in my hair, his dominant control possessing my mouth, he stroked through my heat and he claimed what was already his.

A groan, his, mine, ours—oh God, *ours*.

I abruptly pulled back, not believing this fairy tale. "Sawyer

Savatier." I grasped each side of his face. "You asked me to marry you."

His lips wet from our kiss, his expression deadly serious, he pressed his hips into mine. "And you said yes…" Leaning down to my ear, he ground his hard length against me. "*Wife.*"

I shivered. "Husband," I whispered, as I took in the biggest, most gorgeous princess-cut diamond ring I'd ever seen. Even in the ambient light through the windows, it shone like a thousand lifetimes of happiness.

His mouth found the sensitive spot right below my ear as his hips left mine. "Do you like it?"

"I love it and you. Especially you." More than anything, I loved this man.

"Do you know what I'm going to do you right now?" The sound of first his buckle quietly clanking, then his zipper going down filled the darkened office.

"Oh God." My inner muscles contracted in exquisitely torturous anticipation and I momentarily forgot about the heavy, new ring on my finger. "We can't. Your family will find us."

"You're my family." His hand slid up my thigh and he bit my neck.

"Sawyer," I admonished. "We can't."

His hand breached the nothing wisp of my thong and pushed the silky material aside. "We can." His thick fingers found my clit, then dragged through my wet heat. "And we will." He sank a single finger inside me.

My eyes fluttered shut, and for a moment, I breathed it all in. Him, a part of his body inside me, the love I felt—it was more than I'd ever dreamed of. "You were wrong," I admitted.

Lifting my leg to his waist with his free hand, he sunk a second finger inside me. "About what?"

"No matter what part of your body it is, I don't ever get used to the intrusion of you inside me." I opened my eyes and focused on him. The lights from the cityscape at night filtered across the sharp angles of his face. "And I don't want to. I want it to always feel this way."

"It won't." He slid his fingers out of me only to replace his touch with the swollen head of his cock. "It'll feel better." Rough but controlled, he thrust into me hard.

I half gasped, half moaned.

He grabbed my other leg, lifted it around his waist, then shoved into me even deeper.

Bottoming out, hitting a place inside me only he could reach, he slammed me against the door and crushed me with his chest. A roar of satisfaction and pure dominance erupted from his chest as his mouth found my ear, and he did what he did best. He gave me more. "I fucking love you, Genevieve James Savatier."

THANK YOU!

Thank you so much for reading RUTHLESS! If you are interested in leaving a review on any retail site, I would be so appreciative. Reviews mean the world to authors, and they are helpful beyond compare!

And make sure to check out the other books in the Alpha
Bodyguard Series!
SCANDALOUS
MERCILESS
RECKLESS
FEARLESS

Have you read the sexy Alpha Escort Series?
THRUST
ROUGH
GRIND

Have you read the Uncompromising Series?
TALON
NEIL
ANDRÉ
BENNETT
CALLAN

Turn the page for a preview of SCANDALOUS, MERCILESS,
RECKLESS and FEARLESS,
the other exciting books in the Alpha Bodyguard Series!

SCANDALOUS

THE ALPHA BODYGUARD SERIES

Bodyguard.

Babysitter.

Chauffeur.

Not what the hell I thought I'd be doing with my life.

Especially not for a spoiled Hollywood actress on location in Miami Beach. But triple pay and carrying a gun had its advantages. I'd shove away paparazzi and screaming fans for a lot less. The Marines trained me to be Force Recon—intimidation and crowd control was child's play compared to four tours. This assignment should've been easy money.

But the doe-eyed starlet with the perfect ass dragged me down her rabbit hole. Living for the spotlight, she leaked the perfect scandal. I warned her making headlines wasn't in my job description, but she kept smiling for the cameras.

Now she was going to find out just how scandalous a bodyguard could be.

MERCILESS
THE ALPHA BODYGUARD SERIES

Bodyguard.

Mercenary.

Gun for hire.

I didn't care what you called it, the end result was always the same.

You paid me for a job, you got results. The Marines trained me to shoot, but life taught me to aim. Working for the best personal security firm in the business was a stepping stone. Put in my time, build the résumé, then move on. I didn't do attachments on any level.

Until a smoking-hot former one-night stand crossed the street in front of me, holding hands with a kid who was my spitting image. She tried to play it off, deny he was mine. She said she didn't remember me, right before she picked her kid up and ran. She thought she'd made a clean escape.

But she was about to find out how merciless a bodyguard could be.

RECKLESS

THE ALPHA BODYGUARD SERIES

Bodyguard.

Escort.

Bad boy.

I didn't come from the wrong side of the tracks. I was the wrong side. Every cliché you could think of, my family embraced. The only advantage I had was being the best-looking out of all my brothers. Except when I joined the Marines, looks didn't count for shit downrange.

I wasn't active duty anymore, and working for the best personal security firm in the business, my looks were getting me in more trouble than they were worth. I just didn't realize how much trouble until a princess from a country I'd never heard of asked for me by name. Her request was simple—me, my gun, and an art opening. But she recklessly failed to mention one crucial part of the assignment… pretend to be her new fiancé.

Now she was about to find out how reckless a bodyguard could be.

FEARLESS

THE ALPHA BODYGUARD SERIES

Bodyguard.

Sniper.

Morally corrupt.

I didn't care who I aimed at. You paid me, I pulled the trigger. I sold my skills to the highest bidder, and trust me, I had skills. The Marines trained me to aim a sniper rifle, but life taught me to get the job done—at any expense.

Except hostage recovery wasn't on my short list. I didn't give a shit the personal security firm that'd hired me was paying double to get some rich businessman's daughter back without casualties. I didn't negotiate with terrorists. Ever. I had my own plan. Take out anyone in my sights, recover the hostage, and get out. But then I laid eyes on the half-naked, bleeding brunette, and I changed my mind. I was gonna do a hell of a lot more than simply pull the trigger.

Now they were gonna find out how fearless a bodyguard could be.

ACKNOWLEDGMENTS

My dad asked me once why I became an author. I launched into a long diatribe about stories I'd written since I was young, an idea for a book I'd had since I was even younger, the creativity of making a world all your own, and characters who demand your attention until you put them on paper.

My dad, ever patient, listened to my whole, too long explanation, then he simply said, "I thought maybe I would've inspired you to be an author."

I felt like an ass. No, scratch that, I was one.

My dad's an author.

He's been writing since before I could walk. My earliest memories are of lying on the rug in his study in front of his bookshelves. I'd pull book after book out and look at them before I was old enough to read, and I'd make a mess until my arms were too tired to hold up another book. Then I'd fall asleep. All the while, my dad would be at his desk typing.

He never, not once, scolded me for making a mess in his study. He let me look at all the pictures in his Encyclopedia Britannica collection, and as the years flew by and I learned to read, he answered any questions I had. I took pride in seeing his name on books, journals and papers, even though I didn't understand the subject matter. All I knew was that my dad was a professor and an author. And I thought that was pretty damn cool.

So Dad, I was wrong that day. And if I could redo that conversation, I would in a heartbeat. I'd erase everything I said, and I'd say the one thing that mattered: Thank you, Dad. Thank you so much for inspiring me to become an author.

XOXO
Sybil

ABOUT THE AUTHOR

Sybil grew up in northern California with her head in a book and her feet in the sand. She used to dream of becoming a painter but the heady scent of libraries with their shelves full of books drew her into the world of storytelling.

Sybil now resides in southern Florida, and while she doesn't get to read as much as she likes, she still buries her toes in the sand. If she's not writing or fighting to contain the banana plantation in her backyard, you can find her spending time with her family, and a mischievous miniature boxer.

But seriously?

Here are ten things you really want to know about Sybil.

She grew up a faculty brat. She can swear like a sailor. She loves men in uniform. She hates being told what to do. She can do your taxes (but don't ask). The Bird Market in Hong Kong freaked her out. Her favorite word is desperate, or dirty, or both, she can't choose. She has a thing for muscle cars. But never rely on her for driving directions, ever. And she has a new book boyfriend every week.

To find out more about Sybil Bartel or her books, please visit her at:

Website: sybilbartel.com

Facebook page
www.facebook.com/sybilbartelauthor

Book Boyfriend Heroes
www.facebook.com/groups/1065006266850790

Twitter
twitter.com/SybilBartel

BookBub
www.bookbub.com/authors/sybil-bartel

Newsletter
eepurl.com/bRSE2T

Made in the USA
Columbia, SC
27 July 2024